A PLACE TO HIDE

ACKNOWLEDGEMENTS

"Evening Song" was first published by *Fiddlehead Magazine* (Canada). Thanks to Colin Channer for his good eyes and masterly "mixing" on this dub track. Thanks to Bill Bauer who first told me to make something of these stories so many years ago in the middle of a very frigid Fredericton winter. To Jeremy Poynting and Hannah Bannister for their good eyes and their faith in this work. Thanks to Mama (Sophia Dawes), my mother, for her wonderful art work for the book design.

OTHER WORKS BY KWAME DAWES

POETRY
New & Selected Poems
Progeny of Air
Prophets
Requiem
Jacko Jacobus
Shook Foil
Back of Mount Peace

FICTION
Bivouac

ANTHOLOGIES
Wheel and Come Again: An Anthology of Reggae Poems

NONFICTION
Natural Mysticism: Towards a New Reggae Aesthetic
Talk Yuh Talk: Interviews with Anglophone Caribbean Poets
Bob Marley: Lyrical Genius

To be read to the music of Beres Hammond, with the bass full and mellow in the mix

A PLACE TO HIDE

KWAME DAWES

PEEPAL TREE

First published in Great Britain in 2003, reprinted 2011
Peepal Tree Press Ltd
17 King's Avenue
Leeds LS6 1QS
England

ISBN 9781900715485

Supported by
ARTS COUNCIL
ENGLAND

CONTENTS

A Place to Hide   7

At the Lighthouse   27

Vershan I: Burdens   55

Tending Rosebuds   67

Foreplay   99

Evening Song   107

Vershan II: Let Me Go   131

Flight   139

Sinatra   159

In the Gully   171

Vershan III: Chokota   199

The Poet   205

The Clearing   229

Vershan IV: Burnt Offering   239

Marley's Ghost   249

Vershan V: Scratch Madness   301

For
Lorna,
Sena, Kekeli, Akua
Also for
Gwyneth, Kojo, Aba, Adjoa, Kojovi
And for
Mama The Great

A PLACE TO HIDE

On rainy nights like these she would imagine her house the way he had seen it the first time from the terrace of a house on the hills above Kingston. She had gone there one evening after playing squash with him at the Liguanea Club, playing politics as the other junior managers at office would call it, or playing with fire in the words of her sisters in the church, each and every one of them, like her, a fallen angel. When she pointed to her house in Mona Heights, his response was simple: "Neat." One of the Americanisms he had picked up at college in Miami.

But what did he mean by neat? She thought now as she tugged her skirt and sat down on the toilet seat. Perhaps it was the tic-tac-toe predictability of the streets, rows of concrete houses, each one like the next, the regimented hedges, the squareness of the civil servants. She knew what he had meant by "neat" but it was hard for her to say it. Neat was everything that she was not; her desk, her blue Ford Escort, her apartment in what used to be the maid's quarters. She was careless and untidy, or as he used to call her before their separation: "A nasty slob."

Standing before the mirror in her brassiere, her blouse and skirt heaped in a pile, she traced the dark lines that curved on her cheeks.

She wiped away what was left of her make-up with cool cream and tissue. Her nose, she observed, grew darker the older she got. Thirty now. In ten years it would be a deep mahogany. It was the size. An African stamp. Maroon blood. Sometimes she was proud, sometimes she needed someone else to affirm it. He never did. When he called her "big nose" or "nosifus" they were terms of endearment, he once explained, and she had wondered how he would have felt if she

9

had called him "red skin" or "short ass". But then, he wouldn't care – he was blessed with that masculine ability to blame a woman for her perceptions of his shortcomings. He wouldn't care because she was with him, and that was evidence enough that she was only trying to hurt him. Anyway, she did not have the distance of anger, then. Not like now.

Turning from the mirror she pulled off the brassiere, her breasts resting snugly on her rib cage. He had asked her if there was no way to get rid of the yellow stretch marks that lined her breasts. Before that she had never felt awkward about the marks. Now she was very conscious of them. She rarely looked at her body in a full-length mirror. She threw the damp bra on the pile in the corner and stepped into the shower.

As the water beat her muscles, she allowed herself to think about the day. It had started already, the short-temperedness, the moodiness, and the day-dreaming fantasies that never failed to disturb her. Even on the bus, with her legs held tightly together to prevent the pressure of water in her, at each bump of a pot-hole she sensed a tingling warmth flowing through her body in response to the images that swirled through her mind. It annoyed her that these thoughts were of him. It was during these days that she had most wanted him around, and they had wonderful times when he did come. But he was not going to come. She tried to convince her body that discipline was necessary.

She filled her mouth with warm water and then let it hang open, so the water tumbled out in a smooth flow down her chin. The bathroom grew misty in the heat. Reaching out of the shower curtain, she groped for her panties, feeling the water pound on her back. She was going to wash them with the shampoo that gave them the sweet smell he liked, but then decided to leave them there, sweat-soaked with the day's tensions.

She stepped out of the shower, careless of the huge puddles she allowed to form on the tiles. She flushed the toilet and watched the pink paper spin in the yellow water as it foamed and then turned transparent. The gurgle of water forcing its way through the tight neck of the bowl changed to a long whining sound. That was her cue to flick the lever until there was another change of gear, this time a high pitched whistling that faded slowly to silence. Then she cleaned her teeth, wiping a clear patch in the thin film of steam that blurred the mirror, catching sight of a mouth full of bubbly foam beneath what now seemed like something gross, a grotesquery of flesh.

She switched off the bathroom lights and moved into the bedroom, which was dark. In bed, small goose-bumps formed on her body. She had left the window open and now looked through the louvres at the dark green mango leaves shaking on black branches. For a moment the dark clouds cleared a patch so she could see the thin pale line of the moon.

The black-green leaves glistened under the amber streetlight when she opened her eyes. The drizzle had waned but had begun again. It was soft on the asphalt and concrete outside and, mixed with the cool breeze from the hills, it was sweet to the nose. She breathed deeply. The smell of rain. She was never able to decide why the rain had that smell. It was like the sweet taste of water in a thirsty mouth.

She was slowly forgetting the hot day, the oily oxtail and rice that still weighed heavy in her stomach. She would not eat now for fear of heartburn that would torment her for the entire night. She was too tired, anyway, to try and make another interesting meal of corned-beef and green peas. She had no more fresh meat in her refrigerator. She wasn't particularly inclined to buy more meat since he was the one who had to eat fresh meat. He had stopped coming by so she could now return to the ulcer and pain of her old ways of eating and drinking.

A gust of wind swirled around the room, making the curtains flap. A bizarre shadow moved across the walls. She felt droplets of rain blowing onto her skin. She brushed a breast to wipe a drop off. Her hand remained there, her fingers lightly following the tiny bumps. She stretched her legs, curled her toes, her thighs tensing and then relaxing. Then she turned onto her stomach lying on her hand to keep the warmth inside. As she faded into sleep she mumbled to God that he must understand.

She was drifting to sleep when the harsh clanging of a rock on the grill startled her.

She rolled over, looking towards the door, listening. She was not expecting anyone and it was late. She decided it must have been for the old couple in the front house. But she had not heard them come in, which at first made her nervous. Violence was lurking everywhere. But what did she have to fear? She was not mixed up in anything. And although her conscience wasn't clear, for she had sinned with her body, she could sleep at night, although at times she did not think that she deserved it.

As her body relaxed, the clanging started again.

"Fred open the door, nuh." The old lady's voice trembled from inside the house.

"Is by the flat," her husband's gravelly voice replied impatiently.

Sitting up, she listened again. She heard swishing of the leaves just outside the windows. She rose quickly, pulling the sheet over her body. She knew somebody was out there. She would hide in the bathroom, she had her robe in there.

"Sarah…" She recognized the voice. Her shoulders tensed. "Sarah! You in there? Open the grill, nuh. Is me. Jacob."

"Suppose the police see you out there and shoot you? What you doing by my window like a thief?"

"Open the grill, nuh Sarah. Is rain out here yuh know. I'm wet. I'm wet. I'm soaking wet."

"I'm waiting for you to move. I want to dress."

"Dress for what? Look, I getting wet, just open the blasted door!"

Jacob Lawson, insurance agent, lapsed Seventh Day Adventist – the man she was secretly seeing for almost a year until a month ago (when he confessed what she had already known but had chosen to ignore: that he was seeing another woman, called Jane Tipman, a brown-skinned physiotherapist he had met on the North Coast, that he was sleeping with this bitch regularly while still making his twice a week visits for sex with her); the man who had arrived when she needed to fall into sin, to blackslide; the man who became her vehicle of rebellion, a tangible man, just the kind of person she had been avoiding for years, keeping herself pure; the man whom she never thought to love but allowed to see her in a way that no other person had – muttered impatiently and moved from the window.

These days, every time he appeared, she found herself rehearsing the year with him, and the transformation it had represented after the five years of holy living. February a year ago marked the five years since her baptism in the overflowing Hope River, some six miles up into the Blue Mountains that loomed over her home. Salvation had come as a New Year's resolution.

Her father's first heart attack had shattered the family during the Christmas vacation. She remembered the hours in the hospital, the talks with doctors, the comforting of her mother, the procession of family from abroad to see him as if to pay their final respects, the sick feeling she had eating Christmas dinner with him in the yellow-walled ward of Andrew's Memorial, the amount she drank and threw up on Boxing Day when she went to a friend's party to try and forget everything, and the realization that she really loved her father, feared him dying and wanted to find a way to prolong their time together. She prayed a lot during that time.

She convinced her father to go with her to church on New Year's Eve. Her intention was to have him saved just in case. Things did not quite work out that way. That night she went forward. Her father laughed at her for being silly. She never told him that she was making a deal with God – a simple deal to prolong his life. She never told him that when it was clear that he was not going up, she realized that she would have to go up as a kind of proxy for him.

A month later, she was wading into the river to be baptized. Her father's grey Austin Minor was parked a mile down the road, tucked into the gravelled soft-shoulder of the winding road. He was in a bar – the kind of dark but reliable watering hole that served, along with the ubiquitous churches, as milestones on Jamaican country roads. He was back to drinking again. Death was not a fear for him. Her salvation was amusing to him.

He was on her mind as she gripped the pebbled river bottom with her feet, desperate to make it to the elder. The tongue-speaking elder, with his gleaming bald pate, his thick and curly beard, and his shimmering skin the colour of olive oil, waited as she moved through the river. It was a bright, blue, cloudless morning, but the river was thick brown, rough and foaming near the rocks – a storm had passed through overnight and the river was still convulsing and shivering long after the rain had dumped its load and passed out to other rivers, other seas. She trembled, afraid of being caught in the undertow, but more afraid of what she was doing – she was giving everything up – that is how she had prayed – giving up her right to choose for herself.

What she was thinking was slightly different – she was making a compact with God. She would give him everything properly, thoroughly, not in the half-hearted way she had done when she was thirteen and then when she was eighteen – all those years when she counted on the accident of her persistent virginity to secure her place in heaven. Now she would give him everything as an investment. She wanted in return some peace of mind, the total healing of her father, his guarantee of a life beyond the grave – a selfish desire on her part, but one that had to be at least half-noble – and, she had to admit, a man for herself.

For five years she was sure that it was her holiness that was keeping her father alive. Then he died. Without warning his heart gave way. He died in the garage, his firm, veined hands covered with the sweet-smelling grass clippings that spurted up from the manual mower he used to keep the lawn neatly level. She found him lying there. She realized something was wrong only when she saw how his right leg was folded under his left thigh.

"Sometimes we can make some bad deals, bwai," she said to herself as she imagined Jacob walking, stiff-backed and without the slightest bop, around the house.

Jacob was a poor return for those five years invested. Maybe, in retrospect, Jacob was not God's idea, since, after all, Jacob was what she chose as her own reward after God had let her down. If God had given her the man she had wanted – the good Christian man she had wanted, then Jacob would not have been an issue. If God had saved her father's life, or at least given her a hope that he was not dying a rum-drinking reprobate, then maybe there would have been no Jacob and none of this sickening feeling of desire and revulsion that she felt at his coming back with his confident sense of entitlement.

Retrieving her thin silk dressing gown from the bathroom, she moved barefooted to the grilled-off porch area, her feet touching the cool water that had formed on the tiles.

As soon as she opened the grill he brushed straight past her, sucked his teeth and headed inside.

Sarah stayed looking out through the grill. She would ignore him so that he would realize that he was wasting his time and disappear. Did anyone hear him knocking? If so, they would be looking now, and with the light behind her she would look like she was naked – ready and waiting. Opening the grill for a man on a rainy night, only one thing could happen – some slackness. Why did he have to come?

Since their big fight a month ago he had not shown his face, phoned or even sent a message. Now he walked in as if he had been there the night before.

In her living room, his clothes plastered to his body, he undid his tie and threw them on her coffee table, unconcerned about her magazines. The thwack of silk on paper startled her and she put on the light. His white shirt was like something draped to dry on a river stone. The regiment of Bics in his Mutual Life Society pocket-holder looked bizarre, like soldiers standing fast for no reason. Even soaking wet, he had that tidy orderliness about him. He stood still, like an impatient teller using a glare to bully and belittle an old lady who had forgotten to sign her cheque.

Finally, he spoke: "I need a towel."

She caught the scent of sweat and Rightguard as she passed him, tossing off an answer: "You know where they are."

15

She sat on her bed and listened as he flicked on the lights and she went outside and turned them off, reasserting her control.

"They're all dirty," came his voice from the darkness.

She wanted to respond, but she was ashamed. If she had known he was coming she would have washed. And that was not good. That she still belonged to him embarrassed her.

"I like them dirty," she declared, a little too late, she thought, to have real impact. She lowered her face in her hands.

She wanted him to go. But why had he come? Something crossed her mind, something about testing and faith and God, but she did not want to hear these things, for they would bring her to a place where she would have to face her choices and she did not want to do this. God is absolute. Her father would have told her to tell him to go to hell. But he always believed there was a way out. He always believed that something better was coming. Her father believed in heaven, but he never planned for it. He just believed that after death, better would come. After the funeral she was angry. And he spoke to her in that ironic manner of his, his white moustache jumping on his dark lips: "What a waste of all that good sweetness and juice in your body, eh? So you still gwine deprive yourself? Girl, live!" He would never talk to her about sex, but what she heard that afternoon as she sat on a rock overlooking the same baptismal river, was his voice, his way of looking at life. She jettisoned absolutes. She embraced her anger and her father's relativisms. "Sin is a matter of circumstance, babylove. Remember that."

The month apart had been painful but she was getting there. She had come to some harsh conclusions. She had been depressed for a year and a half. She understood this now. It was as if in that year she was feeling what she had felt under the thick brown water of the river – the moment of panic and anticipation, of helplessness and dependency. She was trusting the elder to bring her back up, but she was quite ready to be dragged down the hill, swallowing water all the way.

The year and a half since her father died, she was buried in that helplessness, and she had been waiting for Jacob to pull her up. God was no longer so reliable.

Once she had decided on God's fallibility, she discovered a self-assurance that she did not know she had. So when they first met at her office, their banter was playful – she wore the happy air well, a kind of nonchalance about everything, a giddy, confident brightness. She wanted him to trust it and allow what she knew to be his attraction to her to pull him in. She had long decided that she was going to sleep with him. The thought did not excite her – not in that arousing kind of way – but it left her feeling giddy, powerful and lightheaded.

He had been the latest insurance salesman to come through their offices. These guys developed their lists from contacts in churches and from the university. She had gotten on his list and he was working hard to get her to switch policies and go with Mutual Life.

When she teased him about his sexy voice he did not trust her.

"I don't really deal with backsliders, you know?" he said.

"Who said I'm a backslider?"

"Well, you sounding like one. Not messing with no Christian woman, either," he smiled. "When it come to the real business, you people don't know your mind."

"Oh, I know my mind, baby," she said and crossed her legs, allowing her skirt to slide up her thighs. To guide his eyes there, she ran her hand along her thigh. She saw his leer turn into a sheepish smile. It was too easy. He was too easy.

For the first few weeks she was convinced that she had won him – that she had controlled it all. For the first time in a long time she was proud of her body, her allure and she even failed to hear the edge behind his teasing. He must have made jokes about her nose from the beginning, but gradually, the jokes began to reach her. No, not gradually. It happened on one of those tender days before her cycle began, when she had spent the entire day feeling sorry for herself and reassuring herself that he would hold her that evening and make her feel good about the day. He came in laughing a lot. Asked why she was so miserable. Who trouble you, eh? Who trouble you? She told him she was "pre" as casually as she could; and he grinned back at her, his hand pressed down on top of her head, twisting it so that she faced him – he did it firmly, her neck hurt. Then he laughed into her face, "Jesum, I should a know. Your nose grow like twice the size when you seeing your period, you know?" Then his smile stiffened, grew cold with just the edge of disgust. He turned from her. "Why you never call me and tell me?" She should have told him to go to hell, told him that all she wanted was for him to hold her and comfort her, told him that in that moment he made her feel like a piece of dirt and he had no right to do that. But she didn't. She feared that he would walk away, leave her alone. She did not want to be alone that night. "I said 'PMS'. I am not seeing my period, I am just feeling…"

That night she observed him watching her with uncanny interest as he laboured on her. She could not help thinking that he was staring at her nose, or that he wanted to observe every single reaction he forced from her. He was not enjoying what her body was doing to his, he was testing her, watching for each response, amused at each groan she made, the way her mouth opened. She hated herself for moving and sounding the way she did, but she was trying hard to stop his smug smiling. She moved hard against him, doing everything she could to make him crumble before she did, but she only hastened her orgasm. Each convulsion angered her – the strange pain of not being in control. He watched her, studied her. As she looked away, panting and trembling more than she wanted, he dragged himself through her now over-sensitive flesh, grunting every time she shuddered. "Yuh hurting me," she lied. Her body was not hers. He stabbed sharply into her, grunted, and chuckled softly. "Man, yuh wild tonight, Christian." He did not fall onto her. He kept himself aloft, propped by his rigid right arm, and he then climbed off her body, taking care, it seemed, not to let their sweat mingle. He sat on the edge of the bed. "Get me a rag, nuh." As she walked to the bathroom pulling her robe around her, she knew that this was not going to last.

Had he seduced her just to see what her nose would look like in the throes of passion? Would it swell? Would it quiver?

Would her nostrils clamp shut? In the bathroom, with the damp rag in her hand, she stared at her face in the mirror and imagined what he had seen in her face. She was disgusted with herself. She was nothing but a freak, a freak of the worst kind, not the kind that makes a man compliant but the kind that makes him strong, not a sex freak, a circus freak, a fucking ugly bitch. Now what kind of man was that?

So had he come back on this rainy night to remind himself of the sweetness he could muster from seeing her ugly face? He was moving in the place like he lived there, like nothing had happened. She was annoyed, yet not enough to throw him out. The sensation was familiar. It was the sensation of weakness.

"So you don't have any clean ones, big nose?"

"Jacob, just leave me alone. Just go back to where you coming from and leave me alone. Just leave me. Just leave me. I can't deal with it tonight."

"This what?"

"You."

"So I'm an it, now?"

She heard him move toward the bathroom, grunting as he sniffed at discarded towels. Something in the grunt evoked the animal way he always took her, the way he used her up like food, the way he pinned her down with his hands, keeping his body at a distance, and how, even in her anger and disgust, she still was left with a pathetic sense of worth in being a source of strength and vigour. Even now, right now, despite her annoyance with him, she wanted to be prone again, to throw her head to the side and fight with him as his saliva splashed against her neck, her legs interlocked until he overpowered her and took full advantage and she surrendered her soft pink meat to him.

She was thinking these things when he entered the room.

He threw his shirt on the bed, sighing as if her smell was the most disgusting thing in the world.

"You not tired of living like this?" he asked. "Look at the place. Why you can't like neat?"

Neat. That is what he had said when she had shown him her house that first time. Neat.

She began to anticipate what he would do after they made love; she had accepted that this would happen. He would shower and wash his underwear and replace them with the ones in his leather satchel, making her feel so dirty, making her feel that he was right for sleeping as far away from her on the bed.

"You were sleeping?" he asked as he slid beneath the sheets. He tugged them and she stood up until he had gathered them around himself. "You coming?"

He raised the sheets.

She slid in beside him, wondering if she should have showered, if that would change anything.

"You very cold tonight," he whispered as he touched her shoulder. She twitched somewhere deep inside herself. "Yuh still vex with me."

"Please... look... I don't feel up to anything. I don't want to see you." It was her anticipation of the post-coitus depression she was fighting. She wanted the indulgence, the satisfaction of being touched, but she knew that tonight, the way she was feeling, she would fall into a hopeless depression if she let him touch her, let him do what he wanted with her. What kind of person would that make her? What would it say about her ability to manage her own life? She did not love him, but she needed him. Until now she had felt some hope because she could count the days of not trying to call him, not having to admit that she needed him – those were days of triumph. Now, here he was, back, slipping into the bed with her, and her body was responding as if he owned it. In her head, the lyric of an old song was taunting her:

Make me laugh when I don't want to,

Are you so strong or is all the weakness in me?

"Why you bother to come here?" she asked him.

"Because..." he said palming her thigh and gently putting pressure on it so that she would open for him.

"Well, I really don't need this," she said. Did she sound like she was pleading? She must not sound like she was pleading.

His hand was on her stomach now, pinching, accentuating the rim of fat below her navel, the one he liked to tug when he took her from behind.

"You know, Sarah, I should be the one who is vex with you. After what you did? And look at me, now. Making peace when rain falling. Leaving sure for unsure."

His fingers were inside her underwear, tickling her wiry hairs. How could she let him do this when she knew how it would make her feel when they were done? Like a carcass.

"Are you made of stone?" she asked.

He put her hands between his legs. This was his reply.

"Feel like rock to me."

He realized that she had not been breathing when she gasped: "And then as soon as you come, it come in like dust, just like your feelings. And then I can't sleep and you gone to sleep and I have to listen to you snoring. That nuh right, Jacob. That no right."

"So what you want me to do? Leave?"

"Yes," she said, but in a sudden intake of breath. There was nothing convincing about it.

He had begun to move against her now.

"I really don't want to see you, okay," she tried again.

"Answer the question."

He slipped his thumb inside her and trailed her wetness up between her breasts into her mouth. She turned her face away and tried to bite him. She missed but he replaced the thumb and let her bite him, then he slipped the throbbing thumb into her vulva, and watched her raise her hips so he could ease himself further down into her.

"Suppose you had teeth down there. Is so you woulda bite me?"

"I'm so angry with you, Jacob. You just wouldn't understand."

"And I was angry with you but I forgive you."

"What goes on in your head? Eh? Can you tell me?" She drew one of her knees up to her ear. He removed the thumb and stretched her open with two fingers. "You forgive me? So

I am the dog who caused all this, nuh? Jesus, man... I think... You know I could hate you? You make it so damn easy, you realize that? Who... who... ?"

She began to laugh in disbelief. The more she thought about it, the angrier she became. The flood of anger poured out in a torrent with as she felt her body softening into water.

"You come in here, walk in like nothing happened. For a whole month you don't say dog to me. Well, I don't mind, because it is finished; you called me a stinking bitch, a money grabber and announce the end. And then you walk in here like you live here... like... like you own the place, coming to tell me how you forgive me. You know what? Just leave, please... leave. Remember that is you throw dirt at me... Just leave, you hear, because I don't want to see you, and I don't want Mrs. Jenny to have to come out here..."

She stopped abruptly. She was trembling. The pain came like a force of tears pressing against her throat.

"Are you finished?" he asked.

"I done say what I have to say."

He sat up and shifted away from her and pressed his back against the wall, muttering to himself, "End of story. Period."

And she began to cry, drawn into the recollection of what until now had been their final argument, a month ago. The room had been a mess, sheets all over the floor, evidence of the true slob that she was. They had been arguing about the woman, the physiotherapist, Jane, the one she had always known about, the one he was really mad about, the one he would play squash with, the browning with the pointed nose and straight hair.

He had begun to pull at her body and she had told him she was seeing her period.

"Lie that."

"I don't practice to lie."

"That is why you don't do it perfect. You nasty, stinking bitch."

She reached inside her pants behind her sanitary pad and brought out a hand smeared with blood and showed it to him.

"Yuh satisfy?"

He spat at her. She slapped him. He grabbed his face and tried his best to stand up steadily, blinking away the tears. He did not expect it. He did not know how to respond. He stood stiffly, staring at her, the redness smeared across his cheek, the tears streaming down her face and her blood mixing with his sweat on his cheek.

Then, with a silence and calm that she had never imagined he possessed, he walked to the bathroom and she listened through the door to the water and closed her eyes as he walked out of the room without saying a word.

How could I have done that? Sarah thought as Jacob leaned back slowly and drew his foot away from her and tucked it underneath himself, pressing his shoulders into the wall as if he too was remembering the shock of that moment, the smell of piss and sour blood.

Now Sarah wanted to hold him, to reassure him, to say that she was sorry, sorry for being so ugly and gross. She did not ever touch her own blood, not this blood, but she had been provoked and he was good at provoking her, pushing her. He did things like that, like that night soon after they had started sleeping with each other when he had held her head down on him, trying to force her to swallow. That night, she had stood in the bathroom and watched the mixture of her spit and the thick off-white streaks swirl in the water and disappear while he fell asleep in the bedroom, comfortable, assured, as if nothing had happened. She had stayed there after rinsing out her mouth, her whole body seething with the insult, trembling with the relief of being able to breathe. It had been like drowning and he did not understand.

They were always arguing about sex. He wanted it, she wanted something else, something that would make sex end with a pleasure, a sense of peace. He never believed her reasons for not giving him what he wanted. She could not explain anything to him. She had spoiled him, made him convinced that her resistance was merely the annoyance of a woman who was a slut but not willing to admit that she was a slut. And every time he managed to get her to change her mind, every time she came after saying no to him, he was more assured of her whorishness. And when she crawled into herself afterwards, ashamed, angry, he read it as his cue to comfort her, to assure her that he accepted her for what she was. And she knew what he was thinking but accepted the tenderness as something else – as regret, as understanding.

"I am sorry," Jacob said softly. "I should not have come here tonight."

She turned away.

"Did you tell her you were coming here?"

"Who?"

He reached out and caressed her with his foot, passing his instep along her thigh, teasingly.

"You take me for such a fool."

"That is finished, man." He uncoiled himself and lay beside her and rested his hand on her side, his thumb resting in a sweaty roll of flesh, his forehead wrinkled by the burrs of unprocessed hair along the nape of her neck. "That was nothing. Just sports."

"Look, you better leave," she said. Lying together simply like this unnerved her. She was accustomed to resistance. She did not know what it was like to lie with him in comfort, in safety. There was something dangerous in this kind of bliss, she was realizing now. Instead of resting, her body wanted to open itself, to yield up its sweetness.

"I should leave?" he asked, quietly daring her.

"Yes. I want to sleep."

"And if I am here then we won't sleep."

"No."

"We'll talk. Yes, we will stay up talking all night. There is so much to talk about."

And he continued to talk about talking, his tone light but sober, careful not to get too close, not to pressure her as he felt her body deflating then expanding now into his space, languidly, a thing of beauty, the slowness awe-inspiring and at times frustrating, but ultimately satisfying like witnessing the transformation from a rolled bud into a flower.

After he left, Sarah lay down on the bed, staring into the darkness. She listened to the clank of the gate. He had not showered, but the corners of her lips were aching and there was a taste like salt and soap in the back of her mouth. Her stomach hurt with the dull, hollow cramp of loss.

At four in the morning, it was still dark outside. She gathered some things and stepped out into the cool, heavy air and drove up into the hills. Not the hills where he lived, but the hills behind those hills, where it was still possible to sense the presence of God in the shadows of the ferns and cedar branches that shifted in the mist.

From a ridge she gazed down into the river where she had been baptized, raised her chin and saw the reservoir, cool and blue, and the white buildings of the university, her neighbourhood of neatness chopped from view by the angle of the slope.

The path down to the bottom was muddy and slippery, some of the topsoil beaten away by the rain. A mist hung over the valley in the early morning chill and the bushes that glided against her shins and thighs were wet with rainwater and dew.

She pulled a branch from her path and a shower of water fell gently on her face. She slid down the slopes, mud sticking between her fingers. She wiped them on her jeans.

As she neared the river, she quickened her pace. Its sound, bearing the rain waters from the hills, thundered in the valley, yet she could hear the urgent calls of birds amongst the trees.

The water was brown and busy. She watched leaves and twigs race downstream, colliding against the rocks, straining to break free and then hurrying on, till they were pulled down a fall of water over rocks.

She braced herself against the cold and picked her way upstream in search of the pool where she had been reborn. It was just below where the river became a lively waterfall and it rippled in spreading circles where the water crashed. Then it rushed over rocks, heading down river till it disappeared round a bend.

Standing on the bank, she looked upwards again and the hills loomed over her, protecting this green seclusion. She looked around to see if anyone was nearby. Assured that she was alone she took the long white smock from her bag and pulled it over her body. She then pulled off her trousers and underwear, stepping out of both of them at the same time and carelessly throwing them to one side where they landed in the mud.

Under the smock, she pulled the T-shirt off her body, throwing it onto the pants. Then slowly, allowing the hymn that had filled her head in the car all the way up the hills to break forth on her lips, she walked towards the pool.

When the water covered her stomach, she stood still, legs apart and her toes bracing her body against the current in the pebbles and sand at her feet. Looking up, she saw a haze of sunlight glare behind the clouds. The trees dizzied above and a flock of birds darted through the patch of sky, a pool of grey lined by green hills. Still looking up, she shouted above the roar of the water.

She bent her knees. The water closed above her head. The swirl of water on her chest and face was sudden. With her eyes shut tight, dizzying flashes of colour raced through her mind. She stayed under, leaning against the current that battered her body.

On the bank again, she leaned against a tree and watched the river disappear around a corner, taking a part of her. Drenched, she lay on a patch of grass beneath a boulder and felt the earth receive her and began to sing a song of praise. She was alone and yet accepted. She curled her thighs into her breast, keeping her warmth, keeping her warmth. Holding on.

AT THE LIGHTHOUSE

AT THE LIGHTHOUSE

1

"Ready?" Joan said, turning around to face Sonia. Her breasts were now fully exposed as the robe parted, drooping with the weight of a woman slightly older than her twenty-two years, the nipples spread broad and dark. She looked sleepy, as if lulled by the music and the breeze.

"Yes, yes… One second," Sonia said, hurrying behind the easel after a too long pause staring into Joan's eyes. "You mind if I smoke? I know you don't…"

"Enough breeze here to blow it away. Go ahead."

Reggae throbbed from the speakers behind the bar. The clouds climbed in clumps above each other, moved lazily across the jagged outline of the green hills.

Joan let the robe fall to her thighs.

"You a nervous smoker?"

The question was casual, but Sonia felt the weight of it in her own nervousness. She tried to laugh.

"You could say," she said, dragging on the cigarette and then quickly tossing it to the floor.

"Uhuh." Joan said, smiling. "So, you sure this is alright with… what's her name?"

"Sandra." Sonia said. "She is on Flora Isle today. Taking the day off."

"Nice life, eh? I suppose now she don't have to worry about making money…"

"She said it would be alright until about seven-thirty. She

does it every Wednesday. She lets me work here, you know. I've done a few landscapes from here."

"Any like… like this?"

A cool sea wind tickled the raffia curtains that lined the eaves. When the last sugar company went bankrupt, the port went dead, and the lighthouse, after years of disuse, was reinvented as a bar by Claude, a Bostonian who had married Sandra, a local bartender. The marriage had lasted fifteen years, and then Claude got ill. His family – his ex-wife, really – convinced him that he needed to be in Boston near the doctors. He died six months later. The ex-wife was happy enough. In those six months she became his care-giver and Claude was a kind man. He made sure she was looked after. Sandra was left with his beach cottage on the island and the lighthouse. He left her two hundred thousand dollars. It was enough for her and she was still young. Her Wednesday holidays were spent with a young Charlotte banker who had bought a getaway on Flora Isle. Sonia envied Sandra's gumption and confidence. It was the same thing she saw in Joan. But Joan was far more intimidating because Sonia liked Joan – really liked her.

Joan sat in the corner absently staring out, her bathrobe loosely open, revealing her breasts and slightly pouting stomach, her fingers tapping a tattoo on a pair of conga drums, her eyes following the path of a gull dipping low over the sea.

Will she see me like Sandra saw Claude? Is that what it was about? It had not gotten anywhere near that, but Sonia had imagined it. With Joan it was impossible to tell. Joan was looking out at her island. Sonia followed her gaze knowing that where Joan saw home, Sonia saw quaint, a refuge, difference.

The sea wall was strewn with bottles, coconut husks, old tyres and large metal barrels dumped there by cruise-liners. The quaint capital she always spoke of was really a squalid unkempt village – an old decaying colonial outpost. The roads were narrow; all the houses were covered with rusted zinc roofs that glowed red and silver in the brilliant sunlight.

Sonia pulled at the strap of the loose muslin dress she was wearing. It was impractical for the work she was about to do, but it was flattering to her stomach and allowed her to not wear a bra and still look alluringly modest.

She busied herself with the easel, her sheets of paper, pencils and sticks of charcoal, not taking her eye off Joan – almost as if she expected this girl she had met one day on the beach to suddenly open her arms and pitch her body out of the glassless lighthouse windows and fly.

She kept rubbing the leathery, over-tanned patch of skin on her elbow, a nervous affectation she had developed in her ten years in the tropics. To her friends at home in Chicago, she had changed. She had abandoned her hair to the elements. Wispy and bleached to a pale dirty brown by the sun, it lacked the virginal grooming of her high school prom night. Now she gathered it in bundles under a green and gold tam, and bobbed around in leather sandals, living loose.

As she worked, she kept glancing up at Joan whose eyes had glazed over, enjoying the sensation of being repeatedly struck by the perfect roundness of her face, her tender nose, her pouting lips, cheeks that caught the light when she smiled, the way this solid roundness was given flight by her eyelashes, which curled upwards.

Her casual way with the robe, the way she undressed and slipped it on, neither ashamed nor brazen, suggested a neutrality that could be given direction, that could be steered.

Sonia had first seen Joan three months ago sitting in her two-piece on the beach, rubbing at some tar that had stained her calf. Sonia always came to this beach and she had never before seen Joan. On this island strangers were noticeable, especially black strangers. Sonia had been living and working on the island long enough to have gotten over the peculiar foreigners' affliction of not being able to distinguish one local from another. She noticed Joan at once. It might have been her neck, its erect assurance – or the oddness of a black woman sitting in the sun as an act of leisure. The long-limbed, dark brown-skinned woman was rubbing vigorously, her body speckled with sand, her breasts gathered together and swelling between her upper arms, shaking slightly; her softly muscular back rising and falling at her aggressive ministrations.

In that moment Sonia felt the vulnerability of this girl-woman, her mouth twisted in concentration, her brows curled with a hint of impatience at the defiance of the stain. This first time was as close as she had come to seeing Joan naked. They had talked that day, and as they spoke, Joan put on garment after garment until she was fully clothed and ready to leave. They became friends, but the clothes stayed on. Sonia spent many late nights sketching that body – the fluent back rippling in the sun.

As she considered this now, the music from the speakers suddenly sounding monotonous and loud, she tried to articulate the meaning of this friendship based on nothing. There were no secrets. No interests. No past. Nothing. Nothing. What was Joan? Who was Joan? Her old lover Helen had asked this on the phone late one night and she had answered: "The most exciting thing that had happened to me in years."

"Since me," Helen said.

"Yes, since you," Sonia smiled. But she was lying. Joan was more exciting than Helen ever was. Helen was predictable. They met in a bar. Sonia had gone to a bar to meet someone. She met Helen. With Helen, it was all about lies of accommodation. Helen still believed that she was Sonia's first lover. Helen was like Sonia – a convent school trained, Mid-Western woman of Swedish heritage, a feminist failed artist, a closet activist lesbian divorced mother of two. Joan was as different from Sonia as one woman could be from another. It was more than race. When Helen had asked, Sonia was caressing Joan's lower back with her pencil. She had answered without thinking: "The best thing that has happened to me…"

Today she would say something different: Joan made her want to discover another person's privacy. Joan revived her curiosity about another soul. Now, for example, she wanted to know how her navel really looked. Jutting or coiled tight in the roll of her stomach? How did she cook? How did she cut her vegetables? What spices did she toss into her pot and how did she stir it? How did she boil her rice?

And how did she sleep? Curled into a fist, on her back, on her side, her long arms clutching the pillow, her mouth half-open with a tender snore?

"You drawing or you posing?"

Sonia looked up.

"What?"

"I feel like I wasting me time."

Joan glanced out the window and Sonia followed her glance. Joan was looking at the spire of Pastor Mavis's church. She watched as Joan looked away and folded her arms over her chest. Sonia looked back at the steeple, its severe symbolism staring back like an accusation.

"Nudes aren't easy," she said quickly. "The body has so many curves. It's not like doing buildings." Nudes aren't easy when nudes look like you, she thought to herself and smiled.

She was not going to let anything spoil this moment. She never expected this to happen, never expected Joan to pose naked for her, but she anticipated it like a teenager about to get the kiss she had always dreamt about. She anticipated it with the terrible nervousness and strange certainty that something was going to spoil it, take it away from her. She had a strong, inexplicable urge to laugh.

Joan squinted.

"Finish off the cigarette and come back then, nuh."

Sonia stubbed the Rothmans.

"If we going to do this, let's do this."

Sonia made a fuss about the music and went behind the bar and found some Nina Simone, but she began to wonder how the change would affect Joan's mood, so she put on more reggae. When she returned Joan was naked, the robe rumpled at her feet. Her thighs were spread on the chair, taut. Her pubic hairs were thick curls compactly veed with thin spills on the inside of her thighs. Sonia could not help staring. Her armpits stung.

"What happen, now, Sonia? Put it on back?"

"No. Stay. No lie down. Yes. Lie down on the floor. Spread out. That might be a good idea."

"So, how you want me?"

"Relaxed... Just a touch of... of vulnerability... You know."

"I don't know what the hell you're talking about, girl!" Joan laughed.

"Well, do what you want. This will be a ten minute pose."

"Ten minutes..."

"It will pass quickly."

"Ten minutes," she said again, this time almost to herself. Then she turned towards the town again. "I can look this way?"

"You can. That's fine."

Joan straddled the chair and hugged its back, then using her feet, she rotated it until all she gave Sonia was a quarter-face.

Joan pouted her lips and used them to point to the steeple. She chuckled. "I wonder whose business Pastor Mavis broadcasting now? Whose nastiness? What lies she telling, eh? They so bad-minded in this rass place. They like to tell people what to do. Flesh is a very slippery thing. Is easy to backslide."

"I need to see more," Sonia interrupted. "I prefer if you faced me."

"I not too comfortable, you know." She pointed at the steeple. "You ever notice how high that thing is?"

"What thing?"

"The steeple. Miss Mavis steeple. That thing must be the highest thing in Road Town. That way when the spirit is passing over it can be drawn down, like lightning..."

Sonia muttered, "I need you to turn round."

"Sometimes is like lightning, yes. The way that fire come down and burn you right in there..." She placed her hand on her lower abdomen. "Right in there, till all you can do is shout out."

"Uhuh," Sonia said.

"You don't like when I talk so, eh?" Joan laughed, her hand still on her stomach, her fingers pointing downwards.

"I want to get this thing started. Can you turn around, then

I can listen better and work at the same time." She picked out
another cigarette.

"Beg you, don't smoke. The breeze die down."

"Okay. Well, let's get going."

"You getting impatient." Joan turned the chair around. She
remained straddled. "Better?"

"Can you sit properly, please?"

The flash of pink against the brown was distracting.

"You want to see everything?" Joan said, standing to her full
height. She stretched her arms as if to demonstrate that she
could show everything. Her armpits were dark with week old
infant hairs. "If Sister Mavis could see me now she would kill
you."

"She is just crazy."

2

But Joan understood it to be more than that.

There was so much that Sonia did not know about Mavis,
about Joan.

Joan had left the island a certified virgin when she was
seventeen, returning five years later with an MFA, one suit-
case, a purse full of antidepressant pills, a leather satchel full of
loose-leaves with neatly etched poems – maybe five hundred
of them, none longer than ten lines – and a slim chapbook of
poems titled *Sands* that she published with a small independ-
ent press in the US.

But Sister Mavis, it was clear to Joan, knew that she had
returned with something else, something Mavis could not
articulate, could not put her finger on, though she tried. So she
concluded, wrongly, that Joan was no longer a virgin.

The truth was that Joan had returned to the island as pure
as she had been before she left. The truth was harder for Mavis
to accept because the truth was that she had played a part in the
spoiling of Joan. Joan had abandoned her virginity with the
help of Mavis's ex-husband who ran a small hotel and wharf

on Flora Isle. Mavis had sent Joan there regularly to collect his tithe, which Mavis had demanded in lieu of alimony. Mavis's holiness was thorough. From the evening of the first visit, Joan was certain that something would happen with this well-kept, breezily dressed man, who could laugh with the kind of abandon that Joan had never seen in Mavis. It was clear to Joan that his laissez-faire manner was more than a personality trait, it was an expression of liberation – the unbelieving joy of a man released from prison. It was contagious, perhaps, because Joan sensed that he could recognize himself in her, and without saying it, that they shared the common language of Mavis's oppressive presence. Sex for them was an exorcism. Yet Joan felt guilty. After she left Flora Isle and watched the steeple of Mavis's church coming closer as the ferry bounced on the sea, the giddy freedom was replaced by a heavy shame. When she went to Mavis, confessed and asked for healing, her sin became the text of a sermon.

Mavis's intent was to destroy her, to shame her. But this rash act, captured in the stuttering vitriol that spilled all over the congregation that morning, showed Joan Mavis's terrible weakness, her petty humanity. People whispered and stared, but Joan was outwardly unmoved. She understood that each Sunday she sat in the congregation staring back at Mavis would be an act of triumph. Joan went to church every Sunday, refusing to be ridiculed. She became, instead, a spectacle, something to be admired, preferably at close range, a woman on a small island, who would not be shamed. How did she do it? How could she go to carnival and jump-up and laugh with the pan-men? How could she slap Sister Mavis on her full and firm backside and scream "Fire in me wire? Girl, you wasting all that wonderful backside, you know? People will pay for a firm shapely bam-bam like yours!" And she could tell from the sliver of a smile and the half laugh coming from Mavis that she found it hard to be really upset with Joan – that Mavis was stirred in some disturbing way by her daring. She noted the way Mavis's hand rested just so long on the side of her backside she had slapped. Joan enjoyed the power of that.

Where was her fear of God? Had it left her that morning? She still felt something like guilt when Mavis rose to speak, but this time, that strong woman, that sharp-faced black woman, seemed tenderly small, a wounded creature. She felt guilt because for the first time she knew she could hurt Mavis.

3

Pastor Mavis took the pulpit and gazed across at the congregation with a complex mix of proprietorship and a shepherd's care. Tall black woman whose ancestors, she knew, were all purebred Africans, so black that the few whites who lived on the island did not even think about tasting their flesh. Now she understood the emotion of the slave master.

She cared for the congregation, she took time to pray for them, to heal them, to feed them, to guide them in the right things; but she expected loyalty from them, she expected respect, and she expected obedience. For the most part, this colourful congregation, gleaming each Sunday and Monday and Wednesday and Thursday in their pastel greens, reds, oranges, yellows and powder blues, would obey her.

Her pulpit was the place where the law was offered. When she spoke, her head always tied in a brilliant white bandanna and her smooth black face gleaming with the certainty of her proclamation, they heard her and obeyed.

The Deacon was moving his hand in sharp angles, trying to whip the congregation into true worship. They did not seem willing to respond.

Pastor Mavis, sat in her red velvet chair, her face a mask of deep lines and hollows. What had that little man been doing? What wrongs? What else but giving her sap to the devil so he could dry it out. Two weeks off this island and everything crash. Listen how they singing like they hungry? Nobody was feeding her sheep. Nobody looking after them. And if you don't look after them they will go astray.

The anger rose up inside her, and in mid-song she stood up

and walked to the pulpit, causing the deacon to step back as if repelled by a force.

"I don't understand this," she declared. "I have been away for just two weeks and you mean you telling me that in two weeks you let the devil steal your joy? Brother Larkin, what you was doing all this time with my sheep? Eh? Tell me. Look at that one face. Screwing up your face like that. Look here, I been telling people in Antigua that I have a firehouse for a church and I come back to a people cold like flame. Who the Spirit has set free is… FREE INDEED! Free indeed. He made my feet to skip upon the what? MOUNTAINS! Hallelujah! Where the Spirit of God dwells there is? There is? LIBERTY! LIBERTY!

"Let me hear you good, because all you when you ready to go an' watch that basketball game suddenly yuh get voice; you could shout and cuss and tell people them is heroes. Telling human beings them is stars, but you all can't find a voice for the Lord? Say Amen! Amen. Look at that one too, eh? You going to sit down all your life? You think it's your right to sit on you fat behind in the house of the Lord because you come to church lazy one day? And don't come and tell me that you meditating. I ask you to do dat in the quiet of your home. Now is the time to worship the Lord.

"Dance! Dance! The Lord give you feet to dance. And I will tell you something, and it might get some of you upset, but I will say it anyway because it is true. We is not a people that lacking in energy. We is a people that God give rhythm. It is natural. When I was in darkness, I used to party, eh? I used to go to the Carnival and I could move. Move my little body like i's nobody business – all for the sake of lust and pleasure – all for the devil. It was a natural rhythm. But the things I used to do, I no longer do them. Amen! Now, I must dance for the Lord. I must move this body like i's the Lord is my partner. Yes. And when time I am dancing, when I am moving my feet and stepping. Oh Glory! What you think is happening? Trampling down the head of the serpent, that is what. Crushing the head of the serpent in the name of Jesus! In the name of Jesus!

Are you hearing me, church? Are you hearing me church?

"Because I can see what is happening in your hearts. I don't have to look far. I can see who start to run out of service early on to use the bathroom five six times. And who is to tell me that I won' see something big growing in front of she in a few months? Stand steady, church! You know yourself. I talking the word here. Eh? Eh?

"Some of you laugh. Some of you laugh, eh? It start like that, you know, sit in church and can't praise the Lord. Sit down and hold down your head and pray and read Bible for the whole service. Yes. And then they stop pray out loud, eh? Yes. No loud praying any more. Then you notice how they quietly refuse the body of Christ! Refuse the blood of Christ. Look here, nuh, I am preaching hard today, but i's a new time now. A new time."

From the hill she could see the heads of Joan and Sonia in the lighthouse, sharply etched against the gleaming sea. Her stomach clenched and she felt a terrible urge to piss.

Pastor Mavis tried to push away the thought of the two women. She could feel the pressure of her bladder and she knew that unless she looked away, unless she focused on what she needed to say to the church this morning, she would not be able to hold back her more personal indignation. She faced the church again. Stared hard into the faces of the congregation who, she could see, were hungry for her attention, her abuse, her tender forgiveness.

Now she had them, she had them in that familiar place of power. Sometimes she would become so angry with them, with the easy way in which they fell into line, the way they became followers and would do whatever she asked them to do. But now she relished the power, the control. She needed the surge to reassure her that it was not all slipping out of her control. She continued to speak, sweeping her arms over the congregation.

"People been talking things 'bout this congregation and nowadays i's a new era. Better they stay out than come in and tarnish the church. I am sorry, but that is the way it going to go from now. Put them from your midst. Eh? Then they start to sit at the back of the church. Linger-linger like they don't belong. Then you don't see them. You can't see them. And you hear they living with some woman. Living in the sickness of abomination. My God! Book learning rot them brain. Sweet Father knows I did get my degrees. I have a Masters, brethren, and I ain't boasting, for what does it profit a man to gain the world but lose his soul? I had to unlearn all that worldly knowledge and replace it with heavenly truth. Hallelujah! Canker, disease. Uh!

"People say them is poet and writers, and all they could do is write about sex and fornication… and you people can't say yuh never notice it. Eh? Yuh all sitting in the Education Auditorium and clapping hands and saying how nice it is that they could publish her. Eh? You think I wasn't invited, eh? But I ain't no hypocrite. I see the writing, I know sinfulness when I read it, yes. All you must learn to stand up, even before man, an' mek your voices heard. Call it what it is, Jesus!

"And they start to speak evil about God's anointed! They start to spread the rumour when they living in the abomination of sin. They shall burn with lust for one another. Woman and woman, man and man. You remember what happen to that boy, Brutus? You remember how the Lord strike him down. He know it was wrong, but Satan eat out his soul with lust and the boy is rotting in the Caribbean Sea. They couldn't even find his body. Saviour! Saviour! But the Lord see.

"Church, I know some of you been spreading them stories, eh? Because it is in the high school it start. Yes, I know. And then in Social Development, too. Black people, why? Why? The Lord will vindicate, because I shall be his instrument of intervention. Come. Church… I warning you all. The Lord see every deed. Every deed. So you all better come and confess.

"The one with the child she carrying now, it don't make sense you try to hide it. You come forward and confess. Come and talk to me, because the Lord know and if you want me to call you name, stay there in that seat and I will call your name. Stay there. And you brother, you who say you travelling on

Government business in St. Thomas. You think you could hide from the eyes of the Lord? You think the Lord can't look into them movie house there with all that filth and evil and don't see what you carrying on with while your wife waiting quiet at home? And you dare come to service and clap hand like spirit inside you! Come up. I ain't calling no names. I ain't naming no names. Not yet. Not unless you don't plan to respond to the Lord. The Lord is watching... Hallelujah. Hallelujah!"

Raising her body to its full length, she opened her arms wide and brought them together in a loud clap. Then a rapid syncopation of claps erupted from her. At first it seemed erratic, without any clear pattern, but soon a rhythm emerged that caught her and the congregation and made them begin to move in an old poly-rhythmic fashion that called back centuries of dance and song, something distant and yet so constantly present. Her flat deep voice led the congregation in song.

He paid a debt he did not owe
I owed a debt I could not pay
I needed someone to wash my sins away
And now I sing a brand new song
Amazing Grace
for Jesus Christ paid the debt I could not pay.

4

"What you think she would say, eh?" Joan asked, scratching a path at the root of one of the four large loose plaits that sat untidily on her head. "Damn hair needs washing," she muttered, clicking her nails as she flicked dandruff into the wind.

"Would you just keep still?" Sonia said. "I *have* started."

"You want me to lie on my back? I mean pose, you know? Nice and thexy." She said the word with a lisp, opening her mouth widely to laugh.

"Oh!" Sonia said, violently erasing.

"Oooh… Sorry, sorry, sorry. It spoil?" She assumed her babyish voice.

"It's just a damned picture… a sketch. It won't even look like you." Sonia started to sketch again. The lines flowed easily, long and elaborately experimental, trying to find the right curve, the right turn of the face.

"I know." Joan stared at the back of the easel. Her silence made Sonia look quickly at her eyes. Joan smiled, but stayed silent and still. The sound of the waves started to insinuate themselves as the music faded out. When the tape stopped, the wind joined the soundscape, and then the faint murmur of cars and trucks forty feet below where the coastal road wound through Road Town.

Sonia drew quickly, with an almost carefree abandon. Occasionally she would catch the correct slant of a body part and linger around it, shading it carefully, a small detail in the mess of undecided lines.

"Look. You ask me a favour. You not paying me."

Sonia looked away and tried to find a way to make this easy – for Joan and for herself. There was nothing wrong in paying if one was not receiving pleasure. Payment made things clear and truth came with clarity.

"I don't want you to take it the wrong way, like this is a money thing," Joan explained. She seemed to realize that she was sounding heavy and with effort changed her tone. "It's not easy to keep from scratching your ass, you know. Just chill."

At first Sonia smiled and then she laughed.

"You ever pay for it?" Joan asked. "Ever worked with a professional?"

Sonia tried to concentrate on the slight muscles of Joan's throat. Achieving the strength without distorting the delicate smoothness and flow of the skin would be difficult. She quickly decided against definition and shade; she would stick with lines. Her shading would be only of the hands and the soft of the breasts.

"You should try," Joan was saying. "Not necessarily with me. But I would like to observe you. To see what you would

42

be like with a person who just knows what you want and how to do it the way you like it. Not like me who need discipline and direction." She paused, breathed and then when she spoke again she spoke with greater ease, as if the slow creeping of the late sun across the tiled floor brought a relief of tension. The air was cooler now. "It woulda feel better. For you, of course. Maybe for me. Jees, I woulda do anything. I mean not because of the money, but when people paying, well, you kinda feel that they have a right to expect you to do anything. I would do anything, yes." She paused as if reconsidering the assertion.

"I am sure you would," Sonia said, for something to say.

"I woulda give you all some of them compromising poses, eh? You know, casual-like? Jus' walk in here soh, an' drop the robe and pose. Then I woulda say, 'Five minutes smoke break, darling.' You know the way." Her head jerked back with laughter.

Sonia winced. The hand she was working on had flown in a blur into the air in a mock gesture of cool-pose.

"And I wouldn' even look on the work – not interested, man. Why? My job is to flex out and twis' up the body how you want it. How you desire it, darling. Like a vase of flowers. And if somebody ask me, I say, 'Hey, the pay good, what more you could want? After all is just a body. She looking but not touching. Take my pay, and gone'." She calmed down with a slight chuckle. Then she added, shaking her head, "Can't do that now, though. Nobody paying, so I want to see the damn picture when you done."

"Joan. There is something I want to ask you."

5

Pastor Mavis was in full flight. Somehow the passion of her vision of the abject sinfulness of her town had driven back the pressure of the sight of the two women in the lighthouse from her mind. Miraculously, the pressure in her bladder had eased, and she was now able to stride across the platform, holding tightly to the microphone that she had wrested forcibly from its stand. She stared over their heads, her eyes focused on the blank wall at the back of the church – a screen of images of deprivation seemed to play out themselves.

"For when he come, it won't be what Mavis say. I's what him say. What him say. As those Jamaicans like to say, it will be hell and powder house for many. Don't be caught napping. You hearing me? Yuh hearing me? You think it's a joke, eh? You remember Mr. Henry? All you remember him well? You think is one time I talk to that man? You think is one time I climb up that hill to his yard and witness Jesus to him? The morning before the Lord show him mean business, I go by the man house. I say to the man, 'You hear the word of the Lord, you know your sin, you know that your heart want to turn to the Lord, you know that the Lord see and know everything what going on inside your heart. You know. You know that the Lord calling you, Mr. Henry.'

"And him say to me, 'Yes. Yes.' So I say to him, 'Mr. Henry, you must be born again.' What I tell him? 'You must be born again.' You all hearing me? You must be cleansed by the washing away of your sins. So that you might stand up naked and holy before the Lord, so that he might clothe you in robes of white. And it won't be like when you pick up a lickle pickney from the mire, an' you don't even bother to wash him off, and you give him white garments, and when people see him they think him clean, but make him take off the clothes, nuh. You will see the dirt. Dirt. Hallelujah. Not like that. No, you shall be whiter than snow.

"And same time, people, a sweet breeze pick up on that hill, and the sky start to dark with cloud and I know that God showing me, and showing that man that him was talking through me. But hear what that man tell me. 'I gwine have to give up the girl?' Hear him to me, people, in midst of the elements showing forth the glory of God, right there when thunder start to roll, and my voice full of the Holy Ghost. Hear what the man ask me. 'If I gwine have to give up the girl?' Which girl, I ask him. 'Which girl?' Not him wife. Not the woman who been minding him, caring for him, coming to church daily and praying for him all these years, the woman who carry his pickney, not that one. No. But the lickle whore from Dominican Republic. That lickle whore with her long hair and sweet eye. Saviour. That man dare to ask me, 'But I gwine to have to give her up?' And I tell him, 'Yes. YES! Of course, yes. Give up all of that nastiness. Yes…'

"He stop and look on me. I see the living eye water in his eyes, and I know. I know what was happening. Spiritual warfare in high and low places!

"It is not a easy thing. No, no. He shake his head, brethren, and he say, 'No.' He say, 'Cyaan do it, Sister Mavis. Cyaan do it.' Like that. Oh, my heart was rent asunder. And witness brethren, for it is not a lie I am telling you. That very same evening, that very said same stormy night right here on this island, while that man was with that woman in her burning bed – let me not mince my words for it is the truth – Amen! Amen! That very night, while the man was riding the woman, that same Santo Domingo woman, riding out his little life, wallowing in the ugliness of sin, of adultery, of fornication, of perversion – while he was thinking to himself, how sweet it feel, how nice it feel, how lovely it feel to be here in this stormy weather with this woman flesh under him – you know how you men does think – head full of weed and rum, enjoying his joy ride, you know what happen? Right in the middle of that joy ride, the man come. The man come in his long black coat, eyes shining, carrying his bag of stinking souls. And he say to Mr. Henry, 'Your time now, Mr. Henry. Your time now.' Henry heart give out. Before the man could even relief himself he fall dead on her ungodly bosom!

"And all of you sitting here today, you think you ready? You think you can flaunt God's mercy like that. I come to you and tell you to be born again, to get your life right, to stop the nastiness, and you think you can ignore that and just walk away. You have no idea how much I see when I pray for you at night time. You have no idea the filthiness that some of you sitting here go on with. I know. I see it. I see it and I have to pray for the Lord to protect me from what I see. I see it. So don't think the Lord don't see. You waiting for the man in the long robe to come? You waiting? GET UP! GET UP!"

And as she expected, the entire congregation rose. And then in a wave of passion, men and women began to run towards the altar. Pastor Mavis watched them come forth, her chest heaving from her exertions. As they fell before her, she closed her eyes and turned her face towards the sea. It was already afternoon. The sun was no longer at its height. The lighthouse was caught in tender light. She could see the heads. Her bladder grew heavy again. Her stomach unfurled in loops.

6

They listened to the evening drawing in. A boy howled at another as they ran zig-zag lines along the waterfront and vanished into a bush of hibiscus near the lobster restaurant perched where the broad-walk ended. Sonia decided to stay with the same sketch. It was evolving nicely. She was afraid to rip it off and start again. Joan would want to see the aborted effort.

The moment she had said the words, "There is something I want to ask you," she regretted it. She felt relief when Joan did not respond, when she did not even look up. It would not have been hard for her to imagine that she had not spoken the words out loud. Joan started to sing a familiar chorus that Sonia had heard in Mavis' church.

And now I sing a brand new song
Amazing grace

Then her voice turned into a hum before she fell silent, her head still nodding, her eyes far away. Sonia decided that Joan had not heard and this was good. She was too afraid to say it, anyway. She continued to sketch.

"Which part of me you drawing now?" Joan asked.

"Your arm…"

"Which one?"

"The left… I mean the right. Your right."

"Tell me."

"What?" Sonia looked up at the woman, now divided in shades of light and dark by the shadows.

"Tell me… What you doing. Where the pencil is…"

"I'm trying to concentrate." Sonia felt her hands tremble slightly. This was the gem – the tiny bright moment to replay.

"It will help me relax," Joan said. She spoke with the flatness of one declaring an ancient fact, long tested, one that needed no explanation.

"You seem relaxed." Sonia offered feebly.

"You think?" Joan's voice was distant now. She fell silent. Then Sonia, sensing the ebbing of the moment, started to speak, her voice shaking slightly. She spoke in a dry mono-tone.

"Your thumb. Your right thumb. I'm trying to get the curve. The way the finger curves. It's hard; your nails are so tiny, not normal, and almost transparently thin. They are very thin. So, light, really light strokes, there… Now, the rest of the fingers. The little folds in the skin, the lines of deep brown; and the way the finger bends… bends… bends. There. It's like shaping, shaping. That is… right. Now your shoulder. I have to get the feel of the roundness, but you have these muscles, a hardness barely there beneath the soft roundness. It has to do with the way the light lands on it and makes these shadows. Round and smooth, round and smooth, then light, light strokes, round and smooth. I have to caress it softly, make the lead pliant to the texture… Round and smooth, then long strokes to the breasts, without breaks, without destroying the wholeness. I have missed the bone – the collarbone. I need to leave it like a line of untouched light to bring out the delicate in it… softly shading the shadows all around it, all around it, but not touching it."

"Touch it, damn it! Touch the damn thing. Touch it!" Joan shouted from deep in her throat, a long-drawn loose laugh rushing from her stomach. Her body fell forward with exag-gerated desperation. "Lord, touch it. It is driving me craaazy!"

She said the last word with a guttural roll in her throat.

"Oh stop it!" Sonia smiled.

"Sister Mavis should see me now," Joan said, fiercely rubbing her collar bone. "The damn thing is actually itching me. You better watch out when we get to other parts." Then she laughed loudly again. "Oh God, I am so rude. Sister Mavis woulda dead."

"She is not exactly omniscient, eh? Not quite the Holy Ghost," Sonia said with a noticeable edge of impatience. "Anyway, it was your idea to do this. You're a big woman; at least that's what everybody seems to think."

"Everybody like who?" Joan had given up on maintaining the pose. "Like who? You mean that bunch of hurry-come-up illiterate them in that kiss-ass school? You mean them? That wutliss set who going around declaring themself American, and spending how much dollar to born them pickney in St. Thomas, like it is a promise land? You mean that set? Well, you shoulda know better than to follow that set, Sonia. I told you I don't like people talking me behind my back. Not my friends, anyway."

"Did I say I was talking to anybody?" Sonia did not want to back down, but it seemed that the evening was slowly crumbling into something that would leave unease – an absence of closure. "Look, can we forget it? Just stop with this Sister Mavis stuff, alright. I hear enough about her take on the universe in the week. I just don't need it now."

"From the natives, nuh? The poor superstitious natives." Joan's eyes stared back with bold mischief. She was playing, but it was not the kind of game that assured good-naturedness.

"You mean your illiterates? You called them that, not me."

"Well, forgive me. Forgive me, darling." She turned the chair to face the ocean. Her back was to Sonia now. For her the silence was dreadful.

Joan stayed there, her lithe back moving slightly with her breathing. Sonia was not sure how to continue.

"I just hate when you play that game… Like teasing," she said lamely.

"Please continue." Joan's tone was brittle.

"That was not the pose…" The words came out with more impatience than she had wanted.

"Well fling weh the old one. Ten minutes gone long time, anyway. I'm watching the clock." She kept looking out to the sea.

"Look, I'm sorry…" Sonia started, and then stopped. The silence brought back that old fear to Sonia. She was not going to get the kiss. It was all going to fall apart. Her life was like that. She always came close to it, then something went wrong. Joan spoke with her back to Sonia.

"What you was going to ask me?" she asked.

"What?" Sonia said, trying to stall. When she had said it, she was not sure what it was she was going to ask. Will you let me kiss me? Does sitting like this turn you on? Do you know how I feel about you? Are we sinning? Do you care if Mavis can see us? Do you want Mavis to see us? Do you know that I touch women? Will you be my friend? She was afraid of all of the questions.

"You said you was going ask me something," Joan said.

When Sonia had said it, Joan had gotten silent. Then she had began to sing a song. Soon the question seemed to have faded away. Sonia was relieved. Now Joan wanted to hear. She tried.

"Do you want me to pay you? I will pay you, if that is what this is all about. If it will make you feel better."

"Shit!" It was hard to tell whether she was laughing or terribly angry. The word just hissed out.

"Well, what the hell is it?" Sonia pulled a cigarette out and lit it. The long intake of smoke calmed her somewhat.

"You take me for a idiot? Sonia, I look like a fool?" Joan still spoke to the dull sun.

"What do you…?"

"You don't think that maybe I wanted to come and do this? That wasn't clear? Payment is for whores, *puta*, you know…" She seemed about to continue but didn't.

"Maybe you felt sorry for me. Is this a pity thing?" Sonia

wanted the answers now. It was coming to a head quickly and she decided that it would be better to know now, to be clear where they stood so that she could, if needed, abandon her tiny dreams, that bubble of expectation she carried around.

"Why you love complicate the hell out of everything, eh?" Joan said, turning around. Her arms were open. Her breasts jutted. Sonia looked away.

"Maybe life is just complicated. I mean, I do feel awkward about all this. You're not blind. You know where I'm going with this. You do. And then you keep bringing up the sin of the whole thing. I really don't give a fuck about Mavis, you know that. It's you I am thinking about. I mean, well this would just screw things up some more, and maybe what you need is Mavis and her precise rules…"

"I know what I need," Joan said.

"You were at the altar last Sunday. Folks say you gave your heart to the Lord. Today you're naked on this lighthouse bar with me."

"He give me you," Joan said smiling.

"You mean you weren't serious about going up there." This was almost a hope for Sonia. It would make things less complicated.

"Of course I was serious. Never feel nothing like that before. Frighten, happy, hurt-up inside, vex, confused, blue so till I couldn't stop weep, and giddy till I woulda laugh and laugh and laugh – everything ball up into one. And the sweat just a flow off my body, my heart racing like a drum – blood in my head and suddenly I seeing a million visions. Visions so till I couldn' stop turning and turning to catch everyone of them. In me face, all kinda spirit. Like I could touch death and life all at one time. Never feel nothing like that. Nothing never wear me out like that." She was leaning forward staring intensely at Sonia. Her breath came in laboured pants, as if she was bringing herself down from the spinning of her in-filling.

Sonia could see this woman, turning and turning on the thrashing floor, flaying her limbs, her head flung back. The image was disturbingly erotic in the crudest way. In her vision, the wild acolyte Joan was as naked as she was sitting there on the chair in front of her.

"I am tempting you away from all that," Sonia said, really to herself and she hoped Joan. She knew that what she meant was that she had tempted herself away from purity and was now longing to take Joan with her. But she also knew that Joan was the one who was in charge of everything that happened. She was responsible and yet could never be fairly accused of being the sinner, the culprit, the temptress. That was Joan's genius.

"That is foolishness. You can't do that. That will stay wid me forever. Some things stay forever. Sometimes a small thing, like the way you was talking about the collarbone. Who gwine tek that? Nobody. That is mine, forever." She spoke with the cadence of a diviner – deliberate and authoritative.

Sonia felt puzzled by her feeling of peace. It bothered her that Joan was able to dispel her real and practical fears with this tone, this confidence. It bothered her more that she so quickly allowed Joan to succeed at it. But it worked. She was slightly flustered.

"I don't understand you sometimes, you know. I really don't. You…" She stopped short of saying something that would sound like complete nonsense. She allowed the relief to spread into a smile.

"Look here nuh, I been holding my backside on this tough piece a board for so long now, I think the shape gwine mash up." Joan rubbed her bottom. "I getting weary, so if you plan to catch something good this evening – a nice artistic piece, you know – a piece of heaven, you better tell me now, quick, or I will just fling on back the robe and take a sweet exit."

"Just don't move, crazy broad," Sonia laughed, moving back behind the easel. "Let me finish. Stay like that. Like that."

"Talk to me." Joan smiled boldly at Sonia.

"It's… kind of…" She broke off.

"Kinky?" Joan's smile lingered.

"Yeah."

"Yeah." Joan laughed.

The silence of the space between them became filled with

the lull of the waves. Trees rustled in a stronger turn of breeze. Joan waved at a buzz around her head.

"Keep still," Sonia said, her pencil curving lines on the sheet.

"Promise me seh you won' fling this one out."

"This will be the masterpiece… I can feel it," Sonia said jokingly, yet wanted to believe it.

"I know what you feeling and is not no master's piece," Joan grinned.

"Good Christ, you can be crude."

"You corrupting me," she said. Then after a pause: "Promise."

"I promise," Sonia said, and kissed her across the space.

"You won't try lock me up in the painting and then sell me to some touris' from America, right?"

"This will be our piece," Sonia said. She felt the bubble returning and multiplying itself around her.

"Alright, alright then… So, talk to me. Talk to me," Joan said in almost a whisper.

Sonia spoke softly into the gathering dusk. Her lines caressed the mute outline of Joan's dark shape. A gull called far away. The waves lapped. A mento band kicked into sound for the tourists in the distance.

7

At dusk, the church was empty. The sounds of night were gathering around Pastor Mavis as she sat on the stump of a mango tree outside the church. She had been sitting there staring down to the lighthouse after the last member had walked down the slope to the main street. Against the mellow red of the sunset she could see the silhouettes of the two women, their bodies crossing each other, then touching in shadow, then falling away. It was a slow dance. All the fire that she had carried in her was gone now. She had burnt so gloriously that day, and every bit of indignation, anger and sickness that had filled her was gone, and what she felt in this moment was the helplessness of a woman alone. Joan was gone. After she came forward on Thursday, after she fell at the altar, Mavis had felt a rush of power, a sense that she had won back what had been lost. When she reached down and lifted Joan, she embraced her and was frightened at her inability to let her go, release her. Joan was weeping, then Mavis was weeping and saying "Sorry, sorry." Mavis could feel Joan's sweat mingling with hers, their tears touching. Then Joan pulled away, gently, but firmly.

"I need to pray, I need to pray," Joan said.

What Mavis saw in the face that looked back was not what she had imagined she would see. Mavis realized suddenly that what she expected to see in Joan's eyes was something tender, something like love, something carnal. In that moment she realized her own hunger, the terrible sensuality of it and she felt ashamed, for Joan was caught up, not in the flesh, but in something beyond her, something outside the heat of the church, something holy. She let one of the deacons pray for Joan as she stepped back to the chair on the altar. Joan jumped, shuddered, wept, laughed, danced, her breasts moving, her hands waving, and then she settled into rest. Mavis watched and hated Joan for doing this to her. Then Joan walked away from the altar, calmly nodding to Mavis as she walked towards the door of the church, her backside swinging casually, defiantly. Mavis knew where she was going, and she knew that something had broken at the altar.

She saw the two silhouettes come together in the lighthouse. Soon they were one shadow and they stayed that way until she looked away. Her face was wet. There was nothing she could do. She would have prayed in the silence but she had no words. Instead, she listened. She could hear the sound of reggae riding up the hill like a mist. At first in snippets and then slowly in melodies and moods that she could sense before she could hear. The trees seemed to grow thick around her. She sat there in the dark humming the tune in the air.

Vershan I

BURDENS

BURDENS

He was thirteen when he first had sex with a woman. It was a blur of sweating bodies, limbs crashing clumsily into each other and the feeling of being consumed by mud. The backroom of the laundry behind the garage smelt of rat droppings and the stopped-up stench of the moss-green drainpipe at the back of the house. It was where the cows came to drop their dung and lick on the dripping water from the rusted pipes that twisted and curled against the raw cement wall. In this room he had made love to Mary's daughter – a sixteen year old who felt sorry for him more than she felt love for him. He still had the tightly folded note in his hand when he left the room, that and a fist full of tissue and the slippery remains of a used condom.

As he walked back through the garage, his brief sense of elation was replaced by an overwhelming feeling of dread and aloneness. He was afraid of what had happened, afraid of this thing he had waited so long for. In that moment, standing in the half-light of a sliver of moon, he felt again his aloneness, felt the weight of not having a father or a mother to run to. He wanted to run to his aunt, to knock on her door, to wake her and tell her what an terrible thing he had done, to let her tell him, as he knew she would, that it was time to open a bottle of wine and toast him; to let her wake Umberto, her husband, and tell him to congratulate the little stud for his good work. But he knew that what he really wanted was to crawl back into something like a womb and feel, at least for a moment, like a child again. He wanted someone to remind him that he was not yet a man and that he did not have to be a man. Josephine had treated him like a man, for as long as he knew. She did not have the tender womb of a mother, the quiet calm that he

57

dreamed of. Umberto could never be a father – he was a friend. At best he was a quirky uncle, the kind who came to the family Christmas party every year, got drunk, would vomit on the floor, and everyone would raise their eyes and smile at him, at his good ways and at the tragedy of his weaknesses. Umberto would just say, "Son, sometimes a man must do dem tings, for a man is a man." That was not what he needed to hear.

So he was alone, standing there with the weight of this thing he had done paining in his groin, in his heart. It was the finality of it all. Now he was not the same. Now he was not waiting for this thing to happen. Now he was something else and he could not understand it.

He went to his room and cried.

It was on nights like this he conjured up a myth of family – a myth so thorough that he spoke of his father and mother in such concrete detail that many people remembered and still asked after them years later. He wrote songs about his father's heroic acts, a man who held strong political beliefs, a Marxist who traveled to Angola to take up arms in the struggle for independence; a man who traveled to Rhodesia and was there among the rebels, with their dreadlocks and their sweat-stained voices, singing the sweet folk hymns of resistance, calling Zimbabwe into being. His father was there in Zimbabwe when Marley took the stage and sang

Dread it up inna Zimbabwe
African a liberate, Zimbabwe
Everyman got a right to decide his own destiny

He borrowed from everywhere for stories about his father. When he knew that he could make of his father anything he wanted, he felt a sudden rush of freedom. He was sixteen when he came to that truth. For years he'd felt guilty about lying. But then something pragmatic took root in him and he understood the comfort and pleasure of making one's own myths to cope with one's own tragedies. So he found himself remaking his family. Stories, family stories. His father who would never set foot in America or any country that had ties to America. His father standing on the Great Wall of China with Mao. His father at the Kremlin learning about the truth of Marxism, his father arrested in North Africa for the red visas he had in his passport, his father writing poems about Che Guevera – whom he had met at a conference in Mexico a few years before the revolutionary fighter was killed. His father was a tall black man with a history of revolutions under his belt, with prison in his system and torture in his limbs.

The one who told him all these things was his mother – the woman who was not with him because she was with his father, looking after him, waiting for him in a small village in Ghana, staying up late at night for him to arrive through the bushes with his gun and his tales of adventure. And they always remembered their son. It was for him that they were fighting, so that he could have a better life, so that he could live in a world that was free of all the woes and abuses of capitalism.

He dreamed these myths so hard that they became as real as any actual memory he had of his parents. They were truer than anything he could recall about them. When he came to write his songs, he would write about his mother, not as the woman who was somewhere in New York, dying or dead, nor about the supply officer turned civil servant in Accra whom he heard was still alive. No, his songs were about revolutionaries – a man and a woman who would invite him into a small tent in the dry bush of Northern Ghana, under the speckled light of sunshine filtering through a yoyi tree, to teach him things, things he had never heard of before. These were the worlds he had lost. He imagined how, when he had a child of his own, this child would know about these heroes. This child would know of nothing but these heroes.

One night, in a dream, the revolutionary warrior's help-meet spoke to him a lyric that he woke up with in his head. He wrote it down. Then he hurried to the studio down town where he found Pedro smoking a spliff and complaining about the wickedness of Babylon. He said to Pedro, "I have a choon." And Pedro said, "Play it nuh." And he played the tune. And while he was playing the tune and singing, Pedro started to stir, and he joined him and they played it together. And in three hours, the rest of the session musicians were in the room playing the tune. And a man with a head of unruly hair – not locks – and a strange gaunt look on his face and a stare of absolute insanity, sat at the control boards and began to tweak and turn knobs and slip and slide levers, and talk to himself and occasionally rise and do his skank – a sharp-edged skank – the angles clean and efficient, his fists always tight. This man had a lean muscularity and he skanked away barefoot. When he spoke it was in rhyming couplets – a metaphysical hymn that was a mysterious marriage of cocks, roosters, Jesus Christ and the blood of menstruating women – that seemed to make no sense at all. All the while he made this music smell of poor people's dinners, made it stink like something that bubbled from underground, smelling of some faraway place. He made the bass so fat it took over the pulse of your heart, and in the spaces that he made with the high tinkling sounds of guitars and keyboards, the body longed to be soothed with the rumbling bass again.

Into that well-made bed of sound the youth sang the song his mother had told him in a dream, told his story to those who were gathered there in the studio. The man at the boards kept speaking softly into the intercom:

You have arrived in the ark of arks, my bredda
You have come into the ark of arks
Neither flesh nor blood did reveal that unto the I

It was the last time he would tell the story, the story as he told it then, the story of his father who was a griot, who was called by a shaman to bring truth to the heathen, who was called to be a warrior, who was washed in the Volta river and transformed into a warrior. It was the last time he told the story of his mother who was born in Maroon Town in the hills of St. Ann, who had her head anointed with the blood of a white rooster and white rum and told that she would travel the world and bring freedom to the suffering.

It was the last time he would tell the story of his miraculous birth in the old slave factories of Elmina – born there because his mother was in such deep labour and sorrow at the memory of the millions who had died on that Middle Passage that she had to birth him there and then, on the floor of the dungeon to the sound of the lapping Atlantic, eating away at the black sand of the coast. It was the last time he told that story.

Behind the high voice of the youth was the most simple of bass-lines riding a one-chord minor riff that grounded everything. Then the horns, two saxophones, two trumpets and a sorrowful trombone took up the anthem of journeying, like elephants blasting their truths across a sea of bones and unmoored spirits.

> *Your father, dear son, has gone away*
> *Gone away to a land of pain*
> *Land of pain where black seed won't grow*
> *A land where the guns spill blood in the snow*
>
> *Cause he carries the burden to fight*
> *Vampire authority, they call him public enemy*
> *He's a burden, he's got so much fire in his mouth*
> *A heavy burden, ole nigger in the South*

As he sang this song, he saw his mother waiting there in the wilderness for him to come so she could explain what had happened to his father. This father who had never really been present for him, but who had been there in another strange way.

> *They've rotted the spear that's in his hut*
> *In his hut where there is a sharp knife*
> *A sharp knife to cut fresh meat*
> *The meat of the enemy we must eat*

And then the men in the studio – the singers and players of instruments – began to sing with that strange molasses-soaked harmony of Culture, of the Congos, of the Abyssinians, of

Burning Spear, of Israel Vibration, of the Gladiators – that reggae triple harmony so wet with lamentation and meaning, a clean sweet harmony that belied the knife blade beneath. And he rode them out, his words punctuating their voices until that final line when the whole band, including the strange man with the wildness in his eyes, shouted:

OLE NIGGAH IN THE SOUTH!!!

And the youth called into the bridge with the plea, "Give it to me." And the wizard, the strange man from the cockpit country, standing on the slopes of Switzerland with a skull in his hand, began to make a tapestry of abstractions and rhythms on his system. And the place was drunk with the sound of the bass and drum and the travelling horns, with the sweetness of a harmonica wailing something very Delta and Blue trying to be heard through the flame of this militancy.

He knew when to come in. He knew when he saw the faces of his parents standing there in Ghana, a man in army fatigues, his boots unlaced, his beret clean and sharply folded, his eyes calm, calm as a killer's eyes would be, standing beside a woman in such flowing white she seemed otherworldly. She stood there with her head bandannaed, her dress billowing out in the wind, her feet dusty in dark sandals, carrying a Kalishnikov, cradled in her arms like a baby. Behind them the desert swirled and the hut was a blur. The woman was pregnant. He could tell he was in her womb.

From generation to generation earth births living me
The burden bearer of my father and the load of history
He took his gun and shot the enemy
And now my old man is dead, gone away
And now they are looking for me
they want me stone cold dead

And every rude bwai in the place fired a shot, and every rastaman in the place shouted Jah, for in this simple lyric was caught every myth of the hero that these people knew, that he knew, that the country knew, and when it came at them like that, this passing on of blood and seed and violence and survival, a righteous gunshot salute filled the air. Now anything could happen. They smelt blood.

If a fire, mek it bun. Blood must run if it must. There was a community of history upon him. He felt, there in that studio, more real and more truthful than he had ever felt. For the first time, this middle-class boy, who kept coming downtown to find himself, felt that he had found his story, the one that would sustain him forever, the one that everyone around him could understand, could reach for and touch. For how many of them there in the studio, making music, hanging around and trying to get their own break or just a smalls from someone, how many of them knew who their father was, how many of them carried the history of their existence clearly in their heads? They caught his fire:

The meat of the enemy can be sweet
Can be sweet when the heart is full of pain
Oh, Mama, oh, Mama, I'm-a going away
I'm going away to bring guns to play the drums

Then the train sound of Pedro's chomping rhythm guitar, shaking up the room like the inexorable locomotion of Bo Diddley's guitar, began to make a march of the tune. The room was jumping. The mad man at the controls was standing and skanking, shaking and thumping, making this thing magical on the spot.

Coming from the South
Coming from the South
On the freedom train
Freedom train
On the underground railroad
On the underground railroad
On the freedom train
Freedom train
Crossing over the Jordan
Crossing over the Jordan
Jordan, Jordan River
Jordan, Jordan River

The silence that followed this prayer, this hallelujah of sound, was complete. No one spoke. Only the ticking of herb seeds popping in the flame as a dread took a sip, sighed and allowed the meditation to seep into his system.

He was sweating so that no one could see that he was crying too. He remembered that night standing in the blue light of a thin moon, that night when he so wanted to have his father or his mother to comfort him, the night when he became a man but felt simply like someone who had gone across a river to another country that he did not understand and where he was not sure he belonged. He remembered the way the girl had ground her waist into him, and pulled howls from him. He remembered her the next morning, standing there by the back door of her room in her yellow nightie, her dark breasts showing through, her red panties orange against the yellow. He remembered her smiling at him, at his fear. He remembered her saying to him, "I glad fe 'ave your pickney, Baby. African yout'." Mary must have found out. The girl went away and never came back. He fretted for years about what happened to his seed that night. He wanted to tell someone, but he had no one to tell. Instead he found stories to tell himself and others about his parents. And here in this studio, the stories had brought him home to a place of peace. He would never tell the stories again. Not after this. He would only sing this song. He did not need to tell the story again. It was, after all, completely true now. Completely true.

I'm a burden against Vampire authority
I'm a burden, you can call me public enemy
I'm a burden, I've got so much fire in my mouth
A heavy burden,
Oh, oh, oh, nigger, nigger, nigger, nigger, yeah!

The song was pressed on the B-side of a forty-five and "Burdens" was a strange success in Jamaica for months. It was something that no one really could explain. It was a haunting track. The man at the controls had taken the youth's thin eerie voice deep into the earth, so deep that when it came back out it carried with it every echo that had been collected there, arriving with the deep weightiness of prophecy and truth. But those were days when people believed in mystery.

TENDING ROSEBUDS

TENDING ROSEBUDS

The foetus was dead.

First there were the pains, like period cramps, then came the vomiting and diarrhoea.

The doctor explained that she had miscarried. She tried to be gentle about it. She spoke slowly as she assured Sandra that she belonged to the eighty percent of women who miscarry their first pregnancy. There would be some bleeding. With a little rest and some antibiotics, she would be good as new. Sandra considered the phrase. Nothing would be as good as new in her life; not any more. After the bleeding nothing really healed.

They made an appointment for later in the week. Not to worry, she could try again in a month or so.

Outside the clinic, the heat engulfed her; the traffic clamoured in her head; the sun made her eyes squint. She sweated cold, felt weak. She decided it was hunger – she had not eaten in a day and a half. She bought a lukewarm patty from a street vendor, ate half of it, rolled up the rest in the oily brown-paper bag and stuffed it in her bag. She knew that this erratic eating was not doing her any good. Her stomach burnt with too much acid and her clothes hung loosely on her now. Her limbs, normally long and lithe, seemed ever more gangly, her body turning from muscular gracefulness, developed from years of competitive swimming in high school, to something quite fragile and awkward.

But while her body grew thin, it was as if her hair conspired to suck every spare nutrient from her and grow in lush, thick black forests. It was growing at an alarming pace – and all over her body. For the first time in her life she let it grow in rich silky strands over her legs, under her armpits and over her upper thighs leaving a gleaming film of black over her sun and chlorine-smooth deep brown skin. She wondered whether this luxuriant abundance would now stop; whether the long plaits that dangled down her face like locks framing her oval face would return to the dry and brittle hair that she had before the pregnancy. Even the first hint of wrinkles around the edges of her full-lipped mouth, that had come up when she turned thirty, had somehow smoothed out. This too would go. She could feel her sap drying away. Her body felt, for the first time ever, completely used and discarded.

She caught a mini-van in Half-Way-Tree. Her car was still in the garage. Something to do with the alternator. The truth was the whole system was collapsing. The mechanic had not been very encouraging; it would cost her a lot of money to fix it. She did not argue, simply abandoned the car to him with the admonition: "Don't run it as taxi, you hear me? I swear, police will come look for you if me see my car on the road as taxi." He laughed as if to say that kind of thing never happened. He was lying. Everybody in Jamaica was hustling; it was as simple as that. Hustling. Two jobs, three if the hours could stretch. It was not that employment opportunities were great. They weren't. No one had two legitimate jobs. One was legitimate, the other was almost always a starter effort financed by some generous gift of US dollars from relatives abroad. No taxes, no registration; just the kind of operation that linked the Jamaican middle class to the modern world of computers, cellular phones and internet investment opportunities. The perfect job was her kind of job – a government supervisory job. That way you could work the schedule around your flexible hours. One provided a basic salary, in the other the risk was greater but the returns far more impressive.

She was one of this new breed of youthful entrepreneurs. They worked hard, saved and bought sub-standard government-built homes, square, unimpressive boxes neatly organised in large stretches of open land in Spanish Town and Edgewater: no-frills homes. A box: two bedrooms, a kitchen area, a bathroom and that was it. Cupboards, sinks and paint were all your responsibility. You bought one of these places, made additions – garages, more bedrooms, patios, and so on – then rented the place out to lower middle-income people and used the rent money for the mortgage. In the meantime you rented a place in Kingston proper, or if, like Sandra, you were lucky, you stayed in the home abandoned by parents during the flight of the seventies, until you could afford to move out.

The reality was that the government encouraged this kind of individual. They were well-trained people with marketable skills the country could not afford to lose. So the government happily allowed them to start their own businesses, regardless of whether they gave the government agencies competition, and often awarded small business contracts to them first.

Sandra made good money. She worked for it. She ran two farms in St. Mary that she visited twice a week. She also worked as a private consultant in land evaluation, investigating claims and providing useful real-estate information to larger organisations as well as her own government agency. It was a good arrangement, even if a bit untidy. The bottom-line, however, was always attractive. She ran the private business with two schoolmates she had met while studying in Britain: Alonzo and Leslie. Leslie would have been the father of her child. The arrangement typified the way they worked with each other. No strings, no commitments. It was just a little "accident" and she was quite able to handle it. Yet, on the bus, she kept feeling a strong need to talk to Leslie, to tell him what had happened.

"How's it going?" He was using his car phone, the signal was breaking up.

"Fine… Well you tell me, nuh?" She was at home at three in the afternoon, a dull, quiet time she rarely experienced. The neighbourhood seemed an alien place, inhabited by strangers: gardeners, day-helpers, postmen and noisy school children. She wore a thin light cotton shirt as she sat by the bedroom window that looked out onto the backyard.

71

She watched the gardener next door meticulously pile almond leaves beside the hedge to burn. Everything was dry. She wanted to warn him that the whole avenue could burn up.

"You saw Carlisle?"

"They might buy it, you know," he said. "Why we waiting for that bandooloo guy, Sandra? Carlisle will buy it now."

"I know, I know. But I promised." Already she was beginning to regret the call. She felt the cold sweat again. She wanted to tell him.

"We might just lose the whole damn thing, that's all I'm saying... Shit!"

"What?"

"Man, you mad? You mad!" He was shouting away from the phone. She could hear the horn blaring. "Them gwine kill me in this country you know? He couldn' blow, eh?" He was laughing. "Jesus!"

"Look, I will call you back."

"No, no. It's alright. What you was saying now?"

"Nothing. Just checking to see how things was going." She was not going to let him to know this way. It should just come out in conversation, casually. Everything between them had been casual, and this too had to be casual – it was the unspoken contract she had made with him.

"What happen to you today?"

"Nothing, why? Took a holiday." The gardener squatted over a pile of rubble, his bony knees almost touching his ears. He poured what must have been gasoline from a small juice box onto the pile of leaves and twigs.

"Oh, I see..." She could tell that he knew something was wrong but was afraid to press.

"I had an appointment," she said quickly.

"Oh?" He paused for a second. "Business?"

"No. Not really. Personal." She tried to say this in a tone that would discourage further questions.

The gardener was coaxing the fire, stoking it with a blackened stick. Black smoke clouded the air. The flames were licking at the hedge. The man walked behind the house leaving the fire to its own devices. He *was* going to burn down the neighbourhood.

"You alright, Sandra?" Leslie's voice was gentle.

"Look, I have to go. Somebody want to burn this place down... I need to talk to the yard man. Alright, then... Later..."

"Sandra..."

"See you. Call you later." She put down the phone and started to dial the number for her next-door neighbour. Then she changed her mind. She didn't really care. She was too tired.

The flames caught some of the dry bramble on the hedge. Flakes of burnt leaves spun in the gentle breeze. Everything was dry, bone dry.

The television was still on in the living room when she woke up. The heat was stifling. The bed was wet under her. She turned to the digital clock on the bedside table. It was just after eight. She had been sleeping since five. Her head was still groggy and clouded. She reached for the lamp. The light was jarring. Then she saw the blood. It was a good thing that she had remembered to put the plastic bags under the sheets. She was shocked nonetheless. She moved slowly to the side of the bed expecting to be stunned by a wave of nausea and abdominal cramps, but the pain in her groin was gone.

She sat on the edge of the bed for a few minutes trying to breathe, trying to clear her head. Then she stood up, again tentatively, as if expecting to feel pain. There was no more pain. She wrapped up the sheets without looking too closely at the mess. She took the bundle to the kitchen, stuffed it in a plastic shopping bag and left it leaning against the back door.

At nine-thirty, the phone started to ring for the third time. She counted the rings. At seven, she decided to answer it and then unplug it. It was Carl from the church.

"I woke you up?" Carl always seemed nervous talking to her. But he still called. He, like his fellow young "elders" from the Charismatic movement, believed in the weight of their responsibility. The doctrine was clear: as a shepherd, the fate of the sheep was in his hands; he would be held accountable at the judgement seat. At best, these young men were motherly in a somewhat overbearing kind of way, asking about the most private things – because they had the responsibility to know everything about their sheep's lives. At worst, they would hound, cajole, bully, insult, abuse – all with the righteous authority of the Word. For some, power was intoxicating and the pleasure of toying with the emotions and desires of the young, available women who made up a good proportion of the flock was an indulgence rarely spurned. Carl was somewhere in the middle. He liked Sandra and wanted to enjoy her needing him. But he still had the good grace and irony to wonder at the power he had with some of the congregation. Sandra, though, was a challenge and because he could not assume his power with her, he enjoyed her company. Perhaps enjoy was too strong a word, but he never left her company without feeling that he had been to another place, a different place where new things sprouted and blossomed.

And when she allowed him to feel as if she needed his attention, it felt like something clandestine and sinful. It is not that there was no sexual attraction for her – there was. But with Carl, sexual attraction to the thirty-odd year old single women in the church was inevitable. Their singleness and the fact that he knew that many were contending with the usefulness of their virginity or near virginity made them deeply sexual for him. He understood the value of affection, that the show of affection and care on his part served as a substitute for sexual desire for these women. His maleness was pampered by the intimacy, but morally, he allowed himself to feel pure: he had done nothing physical – at least not with Sandra. She was immune to his sense of power. He knew this. *She* chose when to talk to him. Somehow, this flattered him.

"Yes, you woke me up," she said flatly.

She did not want to talk to Carl, but she was slightly curious about what he would say. She had not been to church for a month. Not since the meeting when Carl had brought Alice

and herself together and made a feeble attempt to ease the
tension and malice between them. He had sat between them,
silently. Nobody spoke. Finally he suggested that they prayed.
Alice wanted to know if Sandra's heart would be in it. Sandra
had answered dryly, "No". They did not pray. She stopped
going to church. Alice kept going. Carl stayed in touch with
both of them, became a confidant who quietly encouraged
each to "share" her hurt with him.

"You remember what today is?" he asked, half-laughing.

"Tuesday, September twenty-fourth. Why?" Deadpan.

"Well, we were sitting here, you know, and wondering if
you needed a lift out." He was sounding more and more
uncertain of himself now.

"Oh, house group." She pretended to have just understood
his little joke. "No, I don't need a lift."

"Are you coming."

"I don't think so, Carl." She felt her impatience slowly
creeping into her voice. She did not want to insult him.

"Well, it is important, you know… You can't keep running…"

"I'm not running from anything, alright?" Her voice was
sharp.

"I didn't mean…"

"No, listen to me, Carl. I just need time to myself, alright?
Don't need no pressure…"

"We're not trying to pressure…"

"*We*? Who the hell is this *we*? Which *we* is this?" It was too
late now for politeness.

"You don't have to talk like that, Sandra." He was regretting
the phone call.

"Oh, so you want to tell me how I must damn well talk now,
right? Well, let me tell you what the hell I want. All I want is
to be left alone. I will work things out, me and the Lord will
work it out. Alright?"

"Well, I just wanted to say, we, I mean I, was looking
forward to seeing you…" He stopped as if expecting her to cut
in. She didn't. "Didn't mean to upset you, or anything. Just

want you to know we, I mean, I am… praying, and call me… You have my number, right?"

She was silent. Through the window, the cinders still glowed. The fire had caught on the hedge but it hadn't spread. Carl was still talking.

"…Fellowship is important. That is just the law of the Lord. So, you know, even where there are problems…" He trailed off. "Sandra?"

"Yes." She suddenly felt very tired and so far from everything.

"Look, Ellen and I are going to see a movie on Friday. We were wondering…"

"I gave up movies. Couldn't find anybody to go with."

"Oh?" He sounded shocked. "Well, Ellen thought that, maybe you would… because she saw you with… well with some guy the other evening…"

"Bye-bye, love. I don't want to use no indecent words on you and your sweet Ellen tonight. Pray for me, you hear. And yes, I did go and see a movie with an unsaved friend of mine. He is the one who slept with me and made me pregnant. Now you know. Feel better? By the way, I am feeling quite fine. I know you meant to ask. Say howdy to the posse for me. And, oh, if Alice is there, tell her howdy, too. A special one." She hung up. She was shaking. They were spying on her. Following her. What the hell did it have to do with them?

The phone rang again. She let it ring thirteen times, and then she lifted the receiver and listened. It was Ellen.

"Hello? Hello? Sandra. Sandra… She's not answering."

"Give it to me…"

"Sandra. Hello… I said she's not answering."

"I said give it to me." There was a rustling of the phone. Carl's voice cut in.

"Hello, Sandra. Look, answer me… Sandra."

From a distance she could hear Ellen. "I told you not to say anything about…" She put the phone back in its cradle and quickly unplugged it.

After the calls, as much as she wanted to return to the dull numbness and almost dreamlike blankness of her state, she kept thinking about the church, Ellen and her thin body playing holy wife of man of God, and Alice… Alice.

The problem with Alice was something of a cliché in the church – of women at thirty-something who are growing aware of the shrinking options in their love life. Alice had cut into Sandra's blossoming relationship with a young American graduate student who had started to come to the church, by creating enough suspicion around the union to cause it to flounder. Alice's thesis was basic: Sandra, a mature Christian, was a poor mate for a young Christian like Lewis. Lewis was five years younger than Sandra and had been saved no more than six months ago at a mass rally at the Urbana Mission Conference in Illinois. He was completing a doctorate in entomology at Brown University when he got the call to go to Jamaica to "tent-make" as a student missionary. He enrolled at the University of the West Indies in a special program on tropical diseases. He was happy. After the wasteland of an Ivy League college in the States where his chances of finding a really wonderful black woman were absurdly low, he liked Jamaica. He found Sandra's church easily enough; it was close to the university and frequented by many graduate students.

They met on his first day at church. She found him out in the courtyard during the service plucking bright yellow coolie plums that had ripened to a pungent sweetness on the trees that filled the courtyard. She asked him for a few. They shared the plums and told their respective stories. She liked him at once. He was smart, attractive – an unruly mass of hair like an Afro gone crazy, big hands, and eyes that were in a perpetually droopy squint.

But he was a "babe in the Lord". Translated: Sandra was robbing the cradle and since Lewis represented one of the few eligible bachelors in the church, this seemed unfair to younger single women like Alice. He was a catch and there was no question that somebody wanted to get him. Sandra, Alice's theory went, would dominate him and he would not feel free to exercise his authority as a man of God. Lewis, after all, was a quiet liberal with feminist sympathies. He had a great deal to work out.

Most people bought the argument, including Lewis, whose long interviews with Alice sparked a friendship between them that seemed to be more fitting to his age and status in the Lord. Alice was Lewis's age and was not yet interested in a relationship. This was something she made known to the congregation on a daily basis. She just wanted a friend, and Lewis needed a friend. Sandra wanted a relationship, she wanted a husband, she wanted to start thinking about children, she wanted to have sex, regular sex, she was looking for the man who would take her virginity, who would help make redundant her struggle with the morality of masturbation. She had said as much to Lewis. Sometimes he liked this – liked the promise of Sandra's directness, but Alice's skill was to seem totally sincere about only wanting to be a friend while working her way towards winning Lewis. And Lewis wanted to be taken in that manner. He was drawn into the absence of commitment in his relationship with Alice, and just when he felt most comfortable, just when he had ended things with Sandra, he realized that he was committed to Alice. Alice was speaking at least twice a week to his mother. Alice was in his life in ways that Sandra had never been. Within a year, the two were engaged and the church was too ashamed to admit that it had witnessed a remarkable piece of bitchery right before its very holy eyes.

Sandra appeared to have taken it all in her stride. She had. While she was angry with the church for supporting Alice's spurious arguments, she was angrier at herself for thinking that Lewis was worth the effort. He was a vacillator with no ability to make decisions for himself. She began to notice that he dressed too slickly for her tastes and his Southern accent was becoming rather annoying. Before long, he was denouncing feminism publicly.

So all would have been fine and forgotten had Alice not come to her, after a moving service in which people wept for their hidden sins of hatred and resentment, and declared that she was having a hard time sleeping at night knowing that Sandra's unforgiveness was damming up the flow of blessings that the Lord had for her (Alice). Alice understood the politics of manoeuvre in church and timed her approach with precision. Before the church, she confessed that she had hurt Sandra, and that what she had done was not entirely "in the Lord". But the Lord had worked "things together for good", and now that she and Lewis were preparing for marriage, it was important that they got her blessing and forgiveness.

Lewis sat looking at his feet. Sandra stared at him. He did not look up. Alice waited with the church for Sandra to forgive. They waited for the tears and the breaking down; for the embrace and the joyful segue into a praise song. But Sandra merely smiled at Alice, whose eyes were filling with tears and said: "I will think about it." The church was in shock. Nobody said a word and the moment of rejoicing was lost. That was the beginning of Sandra's troubles.

That night, Sandra concluded, God truly played hardball. It was the day she had decided to have her child; it was the day she had made up her mind to risk the wrath of public prophecy and denunciation and go ahead with the plan that been shaping in her mind for months. She had expected prophecy, expected one of the more reliable sisters in the Lord to rise up and declare to the congregation exactly what evil rebellious thoughts she was harbouring. She had not expected Alice's "prophecy". God really played hardball. Alice stuck by her prophecy and began a crusade to bring Sandra to her knees before the altar of God. Sandra simply withdrew and found refuge in her new business, and her plan to defy God and the church.

She had become pregnant easily enough. She and Leslie had sex only once. Sometimes she felt she had trapped him. It was after a long drive into the country on business. She timed the proposal perfectly.

They were in his car and it was raining. She was ovulating. She had come to know the sensation. Leslie was being careful on the narrow and uneven Junction Road. The bridge to Port Maria had been destroyed by the hurricane that had ripped through the island in August so they had to ride the long way around the island's coast to get back to Kingston. Sandra did not mind; this route was never too busy and the view reminded her of the possibility that one day the country might find peace. She pretended to sleep for most of the way until it started to rain. They were now climbing a rather steep incline and Leslie was blaring away at the horn to warn any truck hurtling down the other side of the road at break-neck pace. She stared into the hillside. The hills had a soft, velvet-like texture on this side of the island, where the vegetation was thick but not very woody. They passed two boys huddled under a roadside kiosk that was leaking like a sieve. They were trembling, soaked to the skin but still sheltering under a soggy piece of cardboard. Leslie stepped on the accelerator for this short stretch of flat straight road. There was nothing coming from the opposite side. He quickly shifted gear and muttered something as the van groaned. He did not avoid the puddles. Mud splashed on the windshield and left streaks of brown as the wipers rubbed rapidly and noisily against the glass. He had turned off the radio.

"You have a date tonight?" she asked. It was the first thing she had said in almost two hours. He smiled with feigned impatience. He did everything so well; everything came easy for him. Making her laugh was one of the things he did without effort. His body had the finished look of a good swimmer, not angular or knotted, but taut, muscular and still rounded at the edges. His face had a weightiness: firm jaws, a full nose with a thin bridge and a forehead neatly lined by his tight crop of low-cut hair. His skin was smooth and dark as a tamarind seed, with the soft sheen of someone who spent hours in some buttery substance. "Well do you?" she said, staring into the night.

"No." He reached over and turned up the radio. Reggae.

"Oh." She continued to look out.

"Barely doing sixty. You want me to slow." He geared down for a corner, blasting the horn, and then accelerated.

"No, no…"

He turned up the radio. "I like this song." He started tapping his fingers on the steering wheel and humming the tune badly.

She reached over and turned the radio off.

"What? I said I like the song."

"I want to talk." She leaned back in the seat. "Is that alright?"

"It couldn't wait to the end of the song?"

"I can turn it back on, you know..." She leaned forward.

"No, it's alright. Song soon done anyway." He stared ahead. "Go on."

She expected it to be difficult but, so far, she was having little trouble.

"I've decided to have a baby," she said, and waited.

"Takes two to tango."

"Bingo."

"You found a partner? You mean all this time I been trying a thing, you been dealing with somebody else," he laughed. "That's a good piece a news. I thought something was wrong with me. Who him is?"

"Hold on," she said. "There is nobody else."

"So who is the father?"

"There is no father... yet."

"But you decide to have the baby."

"Yes."

He laughed. She knew what was coming next. Leslie repeated himself a lot, especially his jokes. "I ever tell you about the doctor and the girl..."

"Yes. A million times." She touched his shoulder. He turned and looked at her. She looked directly into his heavily lashed eyes.

"What?" He looked back at the road. "Jesus! No."

"What?" She hoped he had understood, but she didn't think he had.

"You said you was telling me something. Tell me." He was taking no chances.

"I need a favour."

"A favour?"

"I like you. I trust you. You're a sensible kind of guy, and you understand me. Right?" She stopped. He was waiting for more.

"You do? Well, we get along fine. I don't mind travelling around with you, and we talk good. You like me, and maybe sometimes you really want things to happen with us, right?"

"Go on."

He was trying not to smile. She hit him.

"What?"

"This is serious," she said. "Now I not promising anything, and I will tell you straight, I just looking for a favour. I want this child..."

"And you want me to be the father." He was laughing now. "Wait, what you want me to do? Sperm bank? I never know them have that in JA. Or you mean that you want me and you to have sex? That's what you really saying, Sandra?" He turned to her. His eyes glinted.

"Yes." She was smiling.

"Why you doing this to me, Sandra?"

"What?"

"You working my brain, working my brain. I always come straight with you, alright, always. None a this dancing here and there, none a that. Not my style. You know what I want and you know seh you can't give me that, and I respect that, right? I respect it. So what is it, now? Somebody tell you something about me, about something I said? Who?"

"What are you talking about?" She realised that he did not believe her.

"Or is this one of those psychological tests? Suppose I said yes, will you just write me off as a piece of shit who just looking to get into your pants? But if I say no, then you will ask me if I am really your friend, right?" He faced towards her.

"It's not a test. I... Look forget it." She would have to wait until next month. "I am ovulating now and it seemed like a good time to ask you..."

He was laughing openly now. For a moment she was uncertain but then she started to laugh as well. They continued laughing for a few minutes and then slipped into silence. He turned up the radio slightly. She rolled down her window to clear the steam from the windshield. Raindrops pimpled on her arm. The sound of the engine drowned the radio. He turned it up some more. It was the news. Five more killed overnight. The dollar was still holding at forty-six to the US dollar. A government minister apologised for suggesting that black people could not make good Prime Ministers. Rain and more rain in the forecast.

She invited him in. They watched television. She offered him something to eat. They watched television. She sat close to him. He reacted as she had expected. He reached his arm around her and pulled her against him. She allowed him to do this. They kissed. She felt nothing. They held each other and watched television. Then he turned to her again. The kissing was tentative, as if he was waiting for her to say stop. She didn't. They had sex quietly on the living room floor. He kept his shirt and trousers on. He was gentle, tender, quietly encouraging her, but never exuberant. If he enjoyed it, it was not obvious. He acted as one eating a very good meal; with appreciation but with a realistic awareness of the unremarkable nature of a good meal. It was easy for her to relax, and even respond.

Somewhere in the middle of the sweating and grunting, she felt a sense of warmth towards him, a feeling of gratitude, and she held onto him as he collapsed in orgasm. They lay on their backs listening to the television. He was not sure what to do.

"You better go," she said. Not moving.

"Yes." He got up, straightened his clothes and buckled his belt.

"The bathroom is through there," she said, still lying on her back. She was watching the television. A rerun of *Cannon*. She had followed the episode throughout the encounter. She heard the bathroom door shut, the splash of water. He was gargling. Then the lavatory flushed. The door opened. She knew he was standing in the living room waiting for her to say something. She kept silent. She heard him near the dining room table fiddling with his keys.

"Breadfruit was nice." He was chewing.

"Yes." She raised her knees trying to keep the semen inside. "Make sure to pick me up in the morning, eh? My car is still at the office."

"Yeah. Yeah." He got up and moved over to her. "Look, I'm sorry."

"For what?"

"You alright, Sandra, I mean with all this?" His face betrayed deep distress. "It don't mean a thing, you know? I mean, I don't expect anything from you. It's not changed anything... I really mean that Danielle and I, we serious, you know... I am not expecting anything from this... Nothing has changed..."

"Question or statement?"

"Statement..." He started and then stopped. "And a question too. I don't know..."

"No, it changes nothing. Nothing happened. We're big people, Leslie. I won't tell Danielle, okay. Step out of here and put it behind you. It never happened. You have been faithful. You heart wasn't even in it. Which is good. You never force me. I wanted it. Remember, I *am* ovulating." She tried to laugh.

"Shit. Sorry." He was giggling. "Sorry."

She sensed his relief. It annoyed her. "You thought I was joking?" She smiled up at him.

"You're serious?" He was suddenly serious.

"Relax, Leslie. Relax. This is my body, okay? You see it, my body. I don't expect anything from you that way, alright." She realised that she was naked from the waist down. He was staring at her legs. "Stop lusting, boy."

"Sorry, sorry." He was genuinely embarrassed. Suddenly he looked deeply uncomfortable, as if he had walked in on her. "We'll talk, right. I better go now. Bingo must be starving."

"Yeah, go feed Bingo," she said distantly.

"I could stay if you want." He was already at the door.

"No, Bingo must be hungry," she smiled. "Call me before you come in the morning. Don't forget the papers on the Vaz property, eh?"

"Yeah." He opened the door. "Take care… I feel like I left something." He was patting his pockets. "I brought a briefcase in here?"

"I don't think so. It's in the van."

"Yeah… Alright…" He was still uncertain. It was still raining and there was a wind rustling the mango tree in the front yard. "I gone."

"Leslie…" she said softly.

"Uh?"

"Why I couldn't just settle for a dog or a cat like everybody else, eh?" She chuckled.

"Yeah." He was still at the door. She watched a spider crawling along the stained pine ceiling. Shots, sharp reverberating reports, came from the television, mixed in with the sound of squealing tires. "Tomorrow," she said, releasing him. "Tomorrow."

Leslie left, shutting the door gently behind him.

Sandra thought a lot about what she was doing to Leslie. She needed to commit this sin and in many ways she was placing him in jeopardy. God could, in an act of serious anger, exercise his vengeance and wrath on Leslie, who for all intents and purposes was an innocent victim in the scenario. She also knew that Leslie cared about her. He cared about his children as well. He had three: two for his ex-wife and one for Danielle, who had helped to break up the marriage.

Danielle was Sandra's friend and yet because she knew that Leslie had not been entirely faithful to Danielle, she always had the feeling that the engagement would not lead to marriage. It might have been more than that. Danielle had never liked Sandra working so closely with Leslie, and yet he had maintained their friendship over Danielle's objections. Sandra felt she had a right to him. He had chosen. She knew things about him that Danielle would never know. No, it was not the betrayal of Danielle that bothered her, but the fact that she was using him, taking advantage of his kindness. She was in a deep mess. Now the tyranny of her needs consumed everything she did. Danielle and Leslie looked after the children and he played the good father, supporting them, carrying pictures of them in his wallet. He was proud of being a father and he would want to be a father to Sandra's child. But this was not what she wanted. Her plan was to leave the island before the birth, to visit a girlfriend in St. John, New Brunswick. She would have the child there and start to make plans to move there to study. Leslie would be forgotten, out of the picture – a photograph the only icon for the child to connect with.

She knew that he was not in love with her. She hoped that he would not start constructing a paternal myth about their relationship. If he co-operated with her plan, if he was open-minded enough to understand why she must handle this alone, her only concern beyond that would be with God. God had been an important factor in her choice. Leslie was relatively safe because she was not in love with him. Emotional attachments in this situation would have played into God's hands. To punish her – which she was convinced he would do – he could use her guilt to destroy whatever love she felt for the father. In her moments of darkest dread she wondered whether God might not destroy the child, but mostly she convinced herself that the punishment would be hers alone. This she was prepared for.

She knew what she would say to Carl, Alice, Ellen, and all the other church folks: "I slipped but I am going to live with my mistakes and work it out with God." She would be lying. Many of the single women in the church would understand. They, like her, were bright, educated, professional, highly motivated women who were doing well economically and socially. But they were lonely and watched with some envy the parade of burgeoning families that clotted the church hall every week. It was they who often led Sunday school; it was they who looked after this overflow of children. They knew how to change diapers, feed and burp the little ones, they knew the schedule of vaccinations, the symptoms of baby illnesses, the three stages of labour, and anything else that had to do with giving birth and bringing up a child. In all this contact with children, they knew that they wanted to have children as well.

But the choice of male companions in the church was dismal. The single men of their age were generally the type who flitted from woman to woman, enjoying the pleasure of being desired, but fearing the responsibility of commitment. They were sufficiently fluid with their theories of celibacy to allow for the pleasures of the flesh without the ultimate act of sin, penetration. In their thirties now, they were comfortably single. It would take another ten years and the flattering adoration of some twenty-year-old to get them to the altar. They were waiting for younger, less assertive women to lead into the graces of God. For the women of Sandra's age, anyone who capitulated and married one of these men, did so with the full understanding that they would have to embark on a grand-scale miracle of transformation. Most did not have the energy or spiritual fortitude to do God this favour.

Some resigned themselves to a life of singleness. Others travelled down to Oxford Road to join the long lines of penitent and humbled Jamaicans seeking a visa to the United States or Canada. Nurses, in particular, did well at the embassy and many of them were already in the United States making money and becoming yoked with unbelievers. Those who stayed accepted that in this life it is impossible to find full happiness without a little sin, a little pain. Some regretted every moment of the liaisons with the unfaithful, testified vaguely about their failings and requested the brethren's prayers. Some formulated a theology of evangelism that made relationships with unbelievers an especially effective means of winning sinners to the Lord.

Sandra's plan was unusual because it was so blatant. She had even planned to continue to attend church until the day of her departure to Canada. She knew that it was going to be very difficult.

While she waited to see if she was pregnant, she realised that her chances of this happening after one encounter was quite small. She took a strange comfort in that. At times she used the odds of her conceiving as a sign of her relationship with God. If she got pregnant it would mean that God approved.

And so God spoke, and she swelled, grew nauseous and felt the heaviness in her breasts. Her periods stopped. She was pregnant.

When she was sure of her pregnancy, she called Carl and told him the news. There was a long silence after the announcement. He asked if she would come to his place to talk about it. She agreed and went. She admitted that it was intentional and that she did not regret it. They prayed for her. Carl was nonplussed. Ellen was angry. It was she who told Alice. Soon, the congregation was praying for Sandra. There was no need for prophecy. Everybody knew everything about everything. Sandra preferred it that way.

Sandra decided against going to work the next morning. She woke up at four thirty and turned on the radio. She sat up in bed and looked out over the city. From the hills where she lived Kingston glittered like a jewel. She heard Chickita open the back grill at about six o'clock. She heard pots and pans clanging as the helper washed them. She was singing an old hymn. Sandra was sitting on the edge of the bed in a dull state of limbo between moving and keeping still when Chickita knocked on the door and walked in.

"Morning, Miss P." She moved to the bathroom and pulled the plastic bag from the dustbin. "You up early, m'am."

"Yes…" Sandra kept staring out. The sky was now a lighter grey. Dogs were waking up with their relay of half-hearted yelps.

Chickita came back into the room and picked up a newspaper. "You finish with this m'am?"

"Yes."

"Uhuh. Stale news, yes." She stuffed it into the plastic bag and walked out of the room. Sandra smelt Chickita's heavy perfume mixed in with "Life Boy" soap. She watched as she crossed the front of the house with the huge plastic bag of garbage and placed it on the gatepost. It looked precarious, but the garbage men were generally early during the four months before Christmas. It was their way of improving their chances of the sizeable bonus they hoped would be stuffed in the yellow envelopes that they left under a stone on the concrete gate columns.

Chikita always walked with a high-bottomed assurance, her hips round with the children she had carried and dropped so casually. For her, Sandra thought, this whole business was so simple, so normal. Chickita would laugh at Sandra's emotional trauma. "Woman 'tronger dan dat," she would say.

Sandra could not move from her sitting position. Pain ran through her legs and wrapped around her abdomen tightly. If she kept still, she thought, the wave of nausea would go away. She sat still, staring out, her mind running fast, repeating the words: "Please, please, please..." The pain passed again. She needed to stay still.

Chickita called to the gardener next door who waved a machete back. He was bagging bramble and broken branches. Chickita leaned back holding her bottom and yawned. She walked back towards the house scratching her head underneath the yellow head tie that bobbed as her fingers rummaged through her uncombed hair. Chickita was about thirty years old. She looked forty. She had worked with Sandra's family for fifteen years. Sandra had grown up with Chickita; and, while they were the same age, their sisterly relationship lasted only until Sandra was fourteen. Chickita understood the change and assumed her position in the background when Sandra's friends came to visit. She stopped arguing with Sandra and suddenly became mature about everything. She became the dispassionate confidante; the one who came into the room after a boyfriend had gone, to comfort Sandra, to tell her what she needed to do. They were no longer friends; Chickita simply serviced Sandra's needs. One day Sandra realised that Chickita had a whole life away from her. At first she felt angry, and then she too acknowledged the nature of their arrangement. It had remained that way.

Still, as she watched Chickita moving around the house this particular morning, Sandra felt closer to her, felt a certain comfort in her presence. Sandra watched the gardener dragging bags of junk to the sidewalk outside the gate. Three dogs drifted by her gate. They looked at the bag and then continued on after circling for a few seconds. Not long after, they were back. One eyed the gardener while the other two started to leap at the garbage bag on the gatepost. The gardener wasn't watching. Sandra was amused. She wondered if the dogs would get to the bags. The bigger of the two finally nosed the bag and it fell into the yard. The dogs peered through the gate. The gardener heard the bag and shouted something at the dogs. They reluctantly slunk away.

Five minutes passed and Sandra noticed the dogs on the far side of the fence. One scrambled over it into her yard. She began to try to shoo it away, but lost interest. The others scrambled over. The dogs trotted to the garbage bag, looking cautiously towards the front door. They began to rip through the plastic with their teeth. They were dragging boxes and pieces of rotten vegetables all over the driveway. Then one of them pulled out a bloodied white sheet and began to nuzzle into the folds. Sandra felt exposed. As she stood up the gardener looked over and shouted to the dogs. They were fighting over the sheet, their muzzles stained with blood. Sandra ran out of her room and down the stairs to the front door her thin housecoat barely covering her body. The dogs heard the door open and scrambled over the fence. One fell on its back, then took a few paces back and jumped again.

Sandra stood among the garbage gathering the sheet together. The gardener was flinging stones at the dogs. Chickita came to the front door and found Sandra trying to fold up the sheet. The blood had stained her nightdress. Sandra was crying. She fell down and began to wipe the blood onto the sheet. Chickita came behind her and held her shoulder, lifting her.

"Come, Sandra, come… come girl, come… Mek we go inside." She tried to take the sheet from Sandra but she wouldn't let go. "Come, Miss Purvis…"

"I thought it was just the blood, you know. I never knew… I never saw it in there… I thought it was just the blood…" She was walking slowly and looking back at the lump of blood on the pavement. "I wouldn't just throw it out like that... I wouldn't."

It was growing dark. Traffic was still steady on the Nelson Mandela Boulevard. Sandra drove towards Three Miles, then swung right at the circle onto Spanish Town Road. A tall man loped slowly across the road forcing her to slow down. He looked at her and smiled. She nodded. He knew she couldn't touch him. The entire street of slowly moving citizens would devour her. Orange light filtered through the occasional trees. She pushed in a cassette of praise songs before she remembered that it had been chewed up by the recorder a few weeks ago. It began to warble after a few seconds. She punched it out and a long string of tape unreeled. She let it fall on the floor. She switched on the radio, low. A local drama serial. She barely listened.

A car horn blared behind her. She slowed to let it pass. It was a dual carriageway and there was a car in the outside lane just in front of her. There was no room for the car behind to overtake. She slowed as the car pulled alongside. It was a red sports car, tinted windows, sleek and clean in the low light. She slowed some more, but the driver made his move before she expected him to, before there was enough space, swinging in front of her. She thought they were going to collide. Then, shifting gear, he accelerated and pulled away, the tail-lights wobbling. Sandra was trembling as the car disappeared.

By the time she entered Spanish Town, it was dark. She drove through the narrow lanes avoiding people who strolled nonchalantly across the street. She turned unto an unpaved track that led into a large open field. In the distance was a line of house lights. The van bumped on the roadway behind a S90 Honda bike. The rider balanced a bundle of sugar cane on his head. He was too big for the bike but he handled it deftly, avoiding the rougher spots in the road with a casual sway of the bike. There was an acrid smell of garbage burning in the air. The dust from the road pricked her eyes.

The road became paved where the houses started. Most of these houses were hollow, unfinished buildings, new additions to the housing scheme. Sandra knew her house now. It was not like that the first time she had come out to look for it. All the houses in the development were identical at first. She had arranged with a worker from the office to come and put a fence around the house. Then she had rented it to a woman who worked in Montego Bay during the week, but visited her lover in Spanish Town at weekends. She was willing and able to pay rent to cover the weekdays. The man, who lived in Kingston, was married and she just needed a place of their own. Sandra was not sure who was paying the rent, but it was regular and she had given up trying to justify her tacit complicity in this sinful arrangement.

The house was on one of the vaguely defined corners where the houses had a little more land around them, though the price was the same. It was Wednesday and there would be nobody there. The place was in darkness. There had been no chance to do much else with the place. There was no porch, no garage, no awnings over the windows, or anything of the sort. Just the box.

She parked outside the fence and turned off her lights. Then she leaned back and looked at the house. In three months she would own it completely. She would own a piece of the island. After that, leaving would mean something completely different. A couple walked towards the van staring into the windshield. They drew abreast, walking in the middle of the road. The girl kept staring.

"Evening," the boy said.

"Evening," Sandra replied.

They continued to the end of the street where they joined a group of young people who were leaning on the cement fence of one of the more developed homes.

Sandra knew she would never live in this house. She knew this even when she was buying it, even when she was designing the additions and making plans for herself and her child with the house in mind. She did not belong to this area. It was far too dangerous, alien territory where she did not know the codes, how to walk, how to recognise danger. Once, she had seen her street's name in the paper. Somebody was shot on it. Rather than fear, she felt an odd sense of pride. The street was real. And it was barely a street. It began at the intersection and then crumpled into a open lot about a hundred yards down. People used the open lot as a short cut to the main road. There had been a huge tent on this lot where lively evangelistic crusades were waged every night. The church was now a building about a mile down the main road.

She watched the house and felt nothing – no sense of belonging. She wanted to leave. She wanted to drive as far away from everything as possible.

She had come there with a vague hope that she would feel some comfort in looking at the evidence of at least this piece of success in her life. But the comfort did not come. The emptiness remained. Chikita had tried, called her fool to worry about the lumps of blood that the dogs had been going after. She fed her ginger tea and some mashed yam, bland and insipid. "Better you just try again," she had said, casually. Then she added softly, "Baby, they know which time a woman ready for it, you know?" Sandra felt the gloom gathering around her. She wanted to be somewhere else. Before Chikita left the room, she looked at Sandra with something like a pitying reprimand.

"You must go up to St. Ann, you hear?" Sandra did not answer. St. Ann was too far away. She wanted to manage this alone. She had made her bed.

Leslie had phoned that afternoon and she had told him everything. He said nothing and then he said something about it being for the best. She hung up on him. He called back to ask about the Carlisle case. She gave him the details in clipped business-like tones, and then said good-bye. Ellen called next. Somehow she had heard. Sandra's doctor cared for a few other women in the church. Ellen wanted to encourage her, to assure her that the Lord knew best and that the church was praying. She started to quote a scripture about chastisement when Sandra assured her that she was doing quite fine and might be at service that Sunday. Ellen seemed uncertain about how to handle this. She was expecting a more broken and penitent tone, or something hysterical. Sandra, tiring of the little game, said good-bye abruptly and hung up. Nobody else called. After Chickita had gone for the day, Sandra ate some crackers but then could not stand to be in the house any longer. Now she sat in front of her new house for a few more minutes. Then she left, looking at its crude white façade fading to black in the rear view mirror.

She drove through Ensome City into Spanish Town proper. Then, instead of turning west for Kingston, she turned north towards Bog Walk, and kept driving. A thin mist fell in the valley before Flat Bridge. Sandra drove steadily as if certain of where she was going. By pure instinct she crossed the hills and valleys that divided the island, everything around her in thick darkness. After the damp, winding road of Fern Gully, she could see the dark stretch of sea. Ocho Rios was packed with light.

In Ocho Rios, she stopped at a jerk chicken kiosk and bought a piece. She asked for it to be extra spicy. The grinning vendor, sweating profusely, brought it over with a soft drink she had not asked for. "You gwine need this dawta."

"Thanks," she said paying him.

"You nuh fraid, sister?" he asked, counting out the change. "Even out hereso, tings rough, yuh know? Nice ting like you. Huh."

"Life," she said casually. She didn't want to see his eyes, the leer she knew would be there.

"Irie." He pulled back, shaking his head, as she drove off.

She turned west on the coast road and drove towards St. Ann's Bay chewing tart chicken flesh. She could feel the burning discomfort in her stomach already. Acid on acid. She kept driving.

Somewhere before Runaway Bay she saw the opening in the road leading up to a dirt track that disappeared into the darkness. She slowed, turned in, dimmed her lights, and waited to see that no one had followed her. Then she turned on the lights and began the slow tedious climb up a very rocky and steep incline. The rains of the previous months had eaten away at any semblance of firm surface that might have existed in the road. The headlights bounced against the thick foliage, and the van stalled on a particularly sharp bend. She reversed, accelerated, and with the momentum cleared the gradient; crashing into some bushes on the other side. She did not slow until she had climbed to a flatter area a few yards ahead. As she went further up the hill, the road narrowed and trees leaned into the roadway, branches brushing against the windshield of the car. It was always that way – for a few seconds you were convinced that the road would narrow into an impassable density of bush and would be swallowed up completely. It was at this point that she heard the dogs barking. She was close now. They would know that someone was coming up. Somebody would already have the gun out and everybody would be awake by now. She drove past an area that seemed unusually clear. She could make out the lights of the house. They must have cleared away all the trees. The last sharp turn before the long steep climb to the house fell steeply into a large pimento barbecue. The headlights caught the startled eyes of two cats sitting on the barbecue. Sandra could smell the harvested pimento thick and fragrant in the air.

She reached the house and parked. The moonlight washed the warm hood of the van. She waited. Then the front door opened and a middle-aged, fair-skinned man, wearing shorts and a singlet stepped out onto the wide verandah.

"Sandra?"

She could see the bulge of the revolver in his waist. His white hair was ruffled. He peered through his thick, black-rimmed glasses.

"Mr. Johnson." She was suddenly very tired. She was too weak to step out of the van. She felt the dampness in her underwear.

He came down to the van shooing away the dogs. Mrs. Johnson – Lola – was now on the porch. She was shorter than her husband and moved with precision, almost at a march. She leaned forward, trying to make out who was in the van.

"Sandra. Is that you?" she asked. She looked older. Her eyes were tired.

"She doesn't look too good, dear. You lucky, girl. Good thing I cut down them trees; we could make you out from here. Chikita said you would come. I wasn't so sure. We ready for World War Three up here, you know," he chuckled. "Poor thing, eh?" Mr Johnson opened the door and guided Sandra from behind the wheel. She moved slowly, as if in a dream.

"Lola," she said, "Lola, I am sorry, I should have called, but I just needed to… I just decided…"

They carried her inside with the help of Leyland, the Johnsons' adopted son, who ran the farm. Lola shooed everyone from the bathroom except Myrtle, a very old woman who had worked for the Johnsons for nearly forty years. Myrtle no longer worked. She was retired, now, she would say, retired with a pension.

The two women undressed Sandra and placed her in a warm bath spiced with mint, and other herbs. Sandra felt gentle hands caressing her body as she lulled in and out of sleep. Myrtle kept humming as they worked, while Lola clicked her tongue. After the warm bath, they washed her body with cooler water from the outside well, then they wiped her down with bay rum, covered her body with a large cotton shift, and poured her a cup of cocoa. Sandra moved through the ritual as if in a dream. She gave herself completely to these women. As she drank, they talked, but asked no questions. When she was finished, Lola led her to the bedroom and tucked her in. She prayed over her in psalms and songs. Sandra fell asleep to the soft intonations of Lola's prayers.

She slept.

"Speak the dream, the positive desire. You have to at least give it voice, you know. That is my lesson for today." Lola was holding a glass of fresh orange juice for Sandra. There was a mess of paper, sheets of poems written by Lola, on the bed.

Sandra had been reading all morning. "Even the impossible, speak it, the impossible desire. That's all, you know. It is like a prayer, then it becomes this very possible thing. Something you can touch. Palpable." She let the word resound for a while. Her eyes were bright. "Baron's in the garden right now. Cutting flowers for you; you'll see them later. He just sat up in bed this morning and said 'I'll cut some flowers for Sandra. She needs roses.' I said, 'No, she needs some breakfast.'" Lola laughed quietly. "When they come, feel the petals. Caress them in your fingers. Sometimes, to really feel them, you have to close your eyes and dream. Then you touch them and they are there. Faith."

Sandra looked at Lola's tiny hands. They were scarred with the wounds of tending roses and other delicate things: babies, dreams, hearts, souls. Lola wrote poems and travelled around the islands healing women. Sandra had met her years ago at a camp. Lola had walked up to her and in her tight, school-mistress whisper, had declared: "I think I am your mother. Prove me wrong." They became friends after that. At each critical moment in her life, Sandra found herself on the hill. She had taken the step to have the child alone. Now she was retracing her path. Lola asked few questions. She just waited, and waited. Then she listened, almost always in the bathroom while Lola washed in the tub.

The hill was whole. Away from the sordid fragmentation of the city she could think clearly. From the porch she stared into the Caribbean Sea, stretching out in multiple shades of blue. She began to regroup, pull together the scatterings of her mind. She felt the guards barricading her body relax their defensive postures, felt the calloused, protective layers of skin peel away, her pores open. Here, with the Johnsons' oblique, guarded questioning, their protective but permeable wall of silence, the barriers fell way. She could think. She laid out the game with God. Each move, like the post-mortem on a chess game, dissected, analysed. She was losing, and yet she was winning. She realised she had not counted money for days, subtracting, dividing, hundreds of figures stored in her head, adding, hustling, finding balance, losing balance: they all fell away in untidy useless heaps on the floor. She read poems through the days and slept with the sun. Here, the hill made instinctive the backward glance.

On Thursday of the next week, Lola came out onto the porch and stood beside her. They watched the sea silently for a long time. Then, Lola spoke quietly.

"You have to go back down."

They were silent again. A hawk crossed the sky flapping steadily, then dipped quickly into the trees.

That night, Sandra drove home, travelling westward, the long way around the island. As she drove she counted the impossible hopes she had, tasted the sweetness and comfort of contentment, and then imagined the texture of grace, her fingers feeling the soft petals. Her body was stronger now.

Kingston began early. The dust and heat, the complications that awaited her gathered around her like the evening's humidity, and yet she could sense that the restlessness that had consumed her for months and months had been replaced by a calm, as incomprehensible and impossible as an answered prayer.

FOREPLAY

FOREPLAY

The reason he slapped me was because I did not want to have sex with him. This is my summary. The drama of the moment was more complex. I said no. He said why. I said I didn't feel like it. He touched me. I pushed his hand away. He grabbed me. I pushed him away and pulled away. He asked what was wrong. I told him to go to hell. He slapped me. The reason he slapped me was because I did not want to have sex with him.

I hate having sex. It doesn't hurt. I just hate having sex. What I do like to do is make love. There is a difference. Men say – ah women… I say there is a difference and I know it. In making love there is love, foreplay, romance, intimacy and not necessarily in that order. There's a softness that remains even when you're twisted and looking ridiculous and smelling like sex and sweat, howling like a wild creature or grunting instructions. It's a softness that you know will take you when you're finished and lying there – and you still want to touch.

I hate foreplay with him. His idea of foreplay is a bit of prodding and fingering of the goods beforehand. Foreplay should be a game you play, something that's mutual, something that just happens. It's like talking about the noise the bed makes while you are sitting there watching television and doing your own thing. And then laughing at that and saying you'll try and keep it real slow and quiet tonight. And you feel the stirring, the damp softness. That is foreplay. Sometimes it can last for weeks, like that, because it's always there, stirring away.

I let my husband sex me (as he likes to say), but no foreplay. Sounds harsh, but that's just the fact of it. There's no orgasm. None of that jerking around, and falling like water. That would be a mockery. No feeling of pleasure. It doesn't hurt. Sometimes you can just be a hole.

Sometimes I pretend to be doing it with someone else. Then I don't feel like a hole. Then I feel like I'm travelling. I stay still, though. I never let him know that inside – in a small room – I'm shivering with the sweetness of it. To him I'm a hole. That's fine with me.

Last week he broke a cupboard full of dishes and told me to get the hell out. That hurt.

I started to take my trips to the country the day after that. The first time I wasn't sure where I was going. I just stepped out of the house and found myself walking in the hot sun towards Hope Road. Hope Road was busy as always. I stood on the corner and waited. A mini-van stopped and a conductor shouted, "Parade!" I never go downtown, at least not alone. It's too dangerous, part of Kingston that scares me. I used to go downtown years ago. I liked the adventure then. I used to take my father's material to his tailor – he had a shop on a street that faced the Parish Church downtown. I'd give the man the cloth that he called a pants' length. I would then go walking down Orange Street and King Street, then down to Harbour Street where a woman sold sweet oranges. I'd eat oranges and walk down to the sea wall and stare out to the sea, watching the big ships unloading at the docks. Then I'd make my way back to the tailor. He would have a brown paper package tied with a bit of string for me. I'd relish the excitement of hustling to get on a packed bus that would take me uptown to Red Hills. But that was before I married, before I left home, before my father died, before my world became this small space in Mona where nothing happens and all news is about somewhere else.

But that afternoon I jumped into the van full of people and we made our way to Parade. Nothing had changed. People were going about their daily lives. No one noticed me. I walked aimlessly until I came to an area that was clogged with vans and buses. Someone shouted, "Port Maria!" and it re-minded me of somewhere I'd been to years ago to visit a friend. The trips started just like that. Someone shouted Port Maria, I ran to the bus, climbed in and we drove off.

Before long we were deep in the hills. The smooth-looking slopes kept changing shades of green – from a brilliant lemon green to a dense mango-leaf dark green. The bus was empty, and I sat in the back, in a corner, rocking into half-sleep and sometimes crying. I was thinking, *This is how people disappear. This is how people vanish without a trace.* We passed small villages with tiny children sprinting after the bus and screaming. Sometimes we passed people who just looked through us. They had the look of a people who had stood in that spot forever.

When we reached Port Maria, I stepped out into the smell of rotting fish and the thick smoke of bush burning. I walked into a small café where they sold "home-cooked" meals and where a television repeated American movies and soap operas. I ordered curry goat that was too oily and peppery – the rice was perfectly cooked, the grains fine and firm. I ate the food knowing I could get sick from it. But I didn't think about it. I stared at the television watching a movie with men and women having perfectly choreographed sex in half-light, with an American cityscape blinking through huge glass windows. It all seemed funny to me. I wondered what Julia Roberts or Sharon Stone thought about while they opened their mouths with their orgasms. Did they think about other women and the way they had seen other women do it, or did they do it all from memory, the way they wished they themselves looked – or did someone tell them how to look? Whatever, it didn't really matter. I didn't believe them.

Coming back, it was completely black outside the bus, with the occasional spotting of lights. I didn't know whether I felt comforted or wounded by the fact that no one knew me. I was crying profusely now, and I couldn't stop. I didn't want to stop. Nothing happened to me in Parade at ten o'clock in the night. I found a bus to take me up to Mona. I walked into the house.

The broken glass was still scattered on the tiles. He was snoring on the bed, his arm tossed around my pillow. I pulled the pillow from under his arm and went to the boys' room.

Todd stirred and rolled over, his leg falling across my thigh. I left it there and slept. I did not dream much that night.

He still sexes me now and then, and I pretend about the whole thing. It keeps things quiet. That is all. But I take the bus more often these days. I'm learning this country in ways I never knew it. I think about the island as if she's a woman with so many tender armpits where I can rest my head and sleep. I read somewhere of a woman from Honduras saying that the land is like your mother, she can't be sold. It's a fancy idea, and normally I'd laugh at it, but when I am travelling around the island, my head is different – I think of things like that and they make sense. The woman from Honduras said that you come from her and you'll go back to her when it's over. My own mother is dead. She died before I needed to go back to her. Now I wish I could go back to her. I wish she lived in a small bungalow down in Hagley Park, with mauve awnings, and dark rooms full of dark mahogany furniture; rooms that smell of food cooking and her gentle perfume. I wish I could just ups and go down to her house, and see her kneeling on the hard earth tending to some flowers in the garden. Wish I could just go inside the soft cool of the house and find my own room there where I could close the blinds and lie down in the bed and sleep and wait for her to come and sit on the edge of the bed and say, "How yuh doing, love?" I don't even remember what my mother looks like now.

Now I'm travelling around this island and learning the names of villages deep in the hills and tiny, simple towns on the deserted coasts where tourists have not found the conveniences of America. I leave without telling a soul and I come back quietly. No one really notices. Todd is happy. The helper looks after him. He thinks his mother is strange. She is.

My husband has not hit me since. I know he wants to. I also know that he wants to sex me all the time. I let him, as I said, now and again – enough to keep the peace. But he knows that I'm never there, really. So he has nothing to say. I can hear how sick he feels with himself after he has come and rolled over. How else can he feel? He's getting sex only because he's my husband and that can never be enough. Am I punishing him? Maybe it's more than that. Punishment is rooted in a reaction to a particular thing. Punishment, apart from hell, is finite. This is like hell. It is a condition of our relationship. I am not punishing him. I am simply being, and what I am is someone who feels nothing for this man. Nothing at all.

People in Parade have started to recognize me and sometimes, when I go back to a village in distant parts of the island, people call my name and sometimes invite me home for meals. I accept. They don't know my real name. They know my new names. I have a list. It's not a clever list. I just take the names of characters from Shakespeare's plays and then I try and see how surprised people will be by the name. They're never surprised. They like Desdemona. They've started calling me Mona, which is nice. Next time I'll be Bianca. I may never use Goneril. I'd have to keep repeating myself and anyway, the name sounds like an antibiotic medication.

I never know when I'm going to go. I just get that feeling. It's like desire. It comes on me and then I get my bag and I step out. It's good for me. I am now able to think. I am able to fantasize. I fantasize while I'm travelling on the roads at night. They are gentle, faceless fantasies of men and women standing on the edge of a cliff looking out to sea, or men and women swimming in secret rivers in the crooks of the hills, fantasies of me walking through a thick bamboo grove, my skin filigreed with the filtered sunlight. The pictures I paint are like foreplay. Imagine what it will be like after another year of this. I'll be a wild woman for some unsuspecting soul, and when I come, I'll look ugly as sin and grunt like a horse in labour and it will come tumbling down after this long waiting. That's my dream, anyway.

EVENING SONG

I had it all worked out. It was five-thirty now. It would be dark in another hour. If I got back to the main road before that, I would be just in time to catch Tony's bus. Two birds with one stone. I would have a free ride home – and Tony. He would have some clever thing to say about my dress. It was an old uniform from last year. I was lazy the night before and didn't bother with washing my newer skirt. I did not realize how much I had grown in a year. The old skirt hugged my hips. Candice asked me if I was trying to catch a man that night. I laughed. I thought about Tony and what he would say.

The truth is, I should not have liked Tony at all. Even though he did not touch, he looked at me like those men on the corner, staring and sizing me up like they would a mango dangling on a tree:

"It ripe?"

"It nuh look ripe yet."

"A few more day."

"It look ripe to me"

But it was the way he talked, I suppose. There was always something playful about that smile, something harmless. I liked him. I thought he was cute. His eyes were brown and always wet. And he always looked at me. When he made his jokes, his comments, he never looked around to get approval; they were for me. At first I would cut my eye and scowl. Then one day I half smiled. He liked that.

One time, he was staring at my chest. "Yuh gwine have to buy a new blouse, girl," he said.

I was laughing.

"That one popping up. Cyaan manage the baggage." Then he grinned and stretched over me, reaching for some coins from a passenger behind me. "Fares, man, fares."

I knew I was special because I was one of the virulent mass of pests labelled "schoolers" by minibus operators. "Schoolers" were an awful burden. They paid less fare, had no manners and would overrun the vans like plagues every evening and early every morning. The conductors would have to drag them out of seats to make room for paying adults. "Schoolers" were scum, and treated like scum. But with me, it was different. I rarely stood in the van.

"Yuh better stan' up schoolers," he would grumble. Then he would squinge his nose. "This van too hot already. You ever notice how school pickney stink? Jesus!" Then that laugh.

But to me, he would lean over and whisper, "Yuh looking fat, babylove."

"Just move a gweh, bwai," I said mildly. It was all deliciously playful.

Sometimes he liked to make his jokes loudly. It was his way of showing how much he liked me. Candice thought it was scandalous. She was jealous. It was not always easy to know whether his comments were directed at me or at Candice. He rarely got so bold when she wasn't around. But two nights ago, Candice was not with me as the van rolled up to pick me up. He hopped off the moving van and ran towards me, his face lit up in a grin. As I moved to climb into the back of the van, he blocked me and pulled open the front seat door.

"Yuh better sit down right upfront, loveliness. If I make yuh stan' up over one a dem man, is no telling what commotion will go on. Yuh know?" Then he swung onto the side of the van, slapped the top with his open palm and shouted, "Press driver."

Style. He had style. The night before he saw me in the distance and began to look very thoughtful. His eyes stayed on my chest as I walked by him to climb on the bus. Then almost to himself, he muttered, "Thirty-two? No. Thirty-six? No. Forty? Yes. Forty inches of explosive dynamite! Girl, yuh packing heat." I laughed. I did not want to laugh, but I had to laugh. For some reason I felt sure it was safe to laugh. It was a safe place. You always looking for safe places in this country

110

as a woman. Somewhere, away from the eyes, the grins, the groping hands pulling at you, at your clothes, your skin. Tony was not like that. With Tony, I didn't mind looking like I did today. I wanted to hear what he would say, seeing me in this skirt that showed so much of my legs.

The sun was slowly defining itself into a circle of orange as it sunk behind the giant breadfruit trees that leaned out of the gully, spreading speckled light over the weather-worn road. I was singing and kicking a stone, trying to manoeuvre it along the narrow strip of asphalt, being careful not to let it fall either down the steep gully on one side, or the concrete gutter cut into the side of the hill on the other. The stone came to the edge of the gully and stopped. I walked up to it. I wanted to be daring. I kicked hard. The stone bounced on the asphalt and then after a curved flight disappeared completely into the gutter by the mountainside. I ran to the spot to search. It had disappeared.

Everything depended on Uncle. If he would simply take the watch and ask me to pick it up in the morning, that would be perfect. No discussions. I would be out of his yard and back on the road in seconds. I would even have time to kick another stone on the way back to the main road. But I was afraid that the damage to Mummy's watch would be such that he would want to fix it right away. This would give him another reason to have me around him so he could say the things he liked to say to me about my body, my sinful ways – the things he said he knew I was doing. If that happened, I would have to resort to another plan if I wanted to get to the main road before dark and catch Tony. I would have to cut through the gully and sprint through the bush to make it to the main road with time to spare.

I turned off the road and trotted into Aunty's yard. Everything was quiet. Their mongrel Flash was curled up in the dirt in the shade of a hibiscus hedge, licking his balls and snapping at flies.

Uncle had given up his ambitions to train Flash as a guard dog. Flash seemed grateful. Those days gunmen were simply

111

shooting dogs stupid enough to howl when they came by. Dogs learnt quickly. Jamaican dogs all knew to sprint quickly when a person bent over to pick up something. They knew night-time visitors were to be avoided. Flash played dumb and avoided certain death by gunshot wound. Now he could languish in the shade all day, licking his parts and eating flies.

There was no movement around the bungalow. The place was in complete darkness. The shadow of the looming hills mellowed the entire valley, softening the edges of the old house that Uncle had built himself, doing all the ornate woodwork around the large porch with painstaking care.

For a moment, I allowed myself to hope that perhaps he had finally capitulated and agreed to go to Bible Study with Aunty tonight. But this was not likely. Uncle did not go to church.

Aunty said he had not seen the inside of a church since they had gotten married. He did not make an exception even when his close friend and long time mistress, Hilda Tennant, was buried after her dismembered body had been pieced together – bits salvaged from the bloodied tiles of her bar and hardware store. Uncle stayed outside for the service, sipping a flask of rum and weeping; his eyes flaming red, his mouth moving, not uttering sound. But though he avoided the church, he was there at the graveside. People were scandalized at his behaviour. He was drunk and bawling as if he had lost his own wife. Aunty stood stock-still, staring at the coffin, ignoring everything around her.

I felt sorry for Aunty then. I even felt sorry for Uncle.

I knew he had to be somewhere else other than at church. I was not going to call, though. I stood at the bottom of the ornately carved steps that led to the verandah, counting slowly to fifty. After that, I would leave.

I was somewhere near forty-five and already backing away, my body gearing up for the quick sprint out of the yard when I saw him step from the side of the porch. He leaned on the railing and stared at me puffing slowly on a cigarette. Smoke concealed his face. There was no questioning, no surprise, as if he expected me, as if he had been waiting for me, as if we did this every day.

112

Scratching himself, he spat into the bed of flowers in front of the porch. It was as if I had been caught – that was how I felt.

I walked forward, searching my pocket for the watch while trying to juggle my books. The two pockets were filled with tissues and change. The watch was not there. I put down the books and heard him grunt as I bent over. I quickly squatted, facing the dog. Suddenly the short skirt seemed a mistake. The watch was in my folder. I got up and turned to face him. He was grinning. My stomach felt heavy. This happened whenever I was close to him, or he was close to me. He became "sir" not "uncle"; he became a stranger, someone I met on the road. I never smiled with him.

He sucked in the smoke, then blew out a thin line of white against the orange sky. The sun framed his head, masking his shadowed face. His unruly silver-grey hair waved in the slight breeze. Somebody told me that it was from him that I got my good hair.

I grew up with the feeling of having been chosen to carry the silvery black strands that always shone as if they were greased. Girls would admire the manageability of my hair and before my breasts came, before people started to talk about my hips and the way I walked, my hair was my one redeeming feature. My nose and lips carried the trace of my father's African features, and my skin, though never as dark as his, was darker than my mother's light skin. My hair saved me. Everyone wanted my hair. Uncle said I had the hair of a Jezebel – a slut. But others named me a saint because of it. Sometimes I felt I had to live up to it, that I'd been given a gift I had to become worthy of. "You will always have good hair, girl, yuh lucky," my mother used to say as she combed in scoops and scoops of sweet-smelling hair oil to preserve its quality. It was never cut.

For a long time, my hair assured me of my value. But the novelty wore off the more I realized that we, Uncle and me, were the only two left in the family with that trace of our Scottish ancestry.

In pictures of him as a young man, in his baggy khaki trousers and close-fitting button-up shirts, the sleeves rolled up to reveal muscular hairy arms; his hair, black and slick, always undulated like the hair of film stars. He was dapper, his skin shades lighter than his wife's, a "country" looking peasant-type in conservative church garb, standing there apologetically beside him – never smiling while he grinned. People called him handsome. I thought the man in the pictures was handsome. But he was a different man. The man in the pictures was in Panama. The tacky painting of coconut palms and quaint wooden houses that served as the backdrop for most of these photos transported him to another place, another time – somewhere more romantic and, strangely, more accessible to my mind than this old house.

I imagined him, this other handsome man, living a life as far removed from the squalor and dullness of our district as anything I had read in books. I could never put the two together. "Uncle" with a stomach, with thin grey hair, and eyes as old as sin, was another man altogether. So I credited the man in the pictures with the quality of my hair. He was the clear evidence that my mother came from good stock. She was less fortunate. She had the same stale yellow complexion, but her hair defied the inflow of light blood; it simply reverted to the tangle and density of some older, darker ancestry. She had bad hair. But her brother was proof that good ran in the family. She was proud of her brother, always introducing herself as the sister of that white man who fixes watches in Felicity Valley. She was also proud of me and the promise of my hair.

I remember once, when I was still young enough to have dreams about him, dreaming of him as worldly-wise, charming, impossibly romantic, speaking Spanish and roaming the streets of Panama with American GIs (the only people, he said, who he could relate to in that godforsaken place, because black people would always bring you down with them. "Show me your friends and I will show you who you are"). I remember once, while he worked on a watch, picking at its intricate viscera till sweat stung his eyes, staring hard at his hair, wanting to reach out and touch it, to feel it, to know if it was as silvery soft as I imagined it. I never did it. But I virtually felt the slick in my fingers. He had turned to me and asked sourly what I was looking at.

But that was a long time ago. Long before he started to look at me with the eyes of sin. Long before he started to worry about my waywardness and slack walk. Long before he became this body with a head of smoke and a tarnished crown of white thinning hair. Long before he became "sir", not "Uncle".

I stepped closer with the watch in my hand. His eyes were bloodshot from white rum or weed, both of which he consumed with religious regularity. His stare remained steady, taking me in, and yet somehow he seemed to be looking somewhere else, somewhere far away. His eyes dropped from my eyes, lingering at my chest, then to my skirt, like light crawling on the skin. I shuffled uncomfortably. Then he smiled. It crept into his eyes like a fresh idea pulling at old memories. I heard the splat of his spit as it landed on the leaf of an aloe vera plant.

"Mama say I mus' give you her watch, sir…" My throat was dry. I held the watch out to him. "She askin' if yuh can fix it … She seh it stop," I said quickly.

He did not look up from my skirt.

"It stop work," I said again. He seemed to be calculating something. I could not tell if he had heard. Instinctively, my right hand reached to pull my skirt down. When I realized what I was doing, I pulled the hand away and moved it to my pocket. Then I was not sure what to do with it. I pulled the books down over my stomach. He sucked the cigarette, then opened his mouth into a round "O", letting a slow, lazy twist of smoke hang in the air. A red hole, dark, obscene. Then he looked in my face. I looked away.

"What?" His voice, soft and high, came from somewhere else.

"Mama say if yuh could fix it," I said.

"What happen to it?"

"She say it stop… again." I stretched out my hand with the watch.

115

"Come, give me," he said, not moving his hand out. He stood there, waiting. The words were coming from some soft place in him. Light glinted off the yellow blotches on his moist eyes. I could see straight up his nostrils from where I stood. Two more dark holes.

"Come, child." This time, somewhat impatient, with an edge of definition around the loose softness of his phlegm-filled voice.

I moved to the steps, climbed a few and then stretched my hand again. They say dogs will bite if you let them know you are nervous. They can smell fear, primal fear. It gives them a sense of power; they can't help themselves. They must pounce at this smell to be what they are. I had learned to fake bravado, to control the smell of fear from emanating from my armpits in the presence of dogs. I could smell the sweat breaking through the day-old talcum under my arms, and I could tell that he was smelling it, too.

The tension of this moment was familiar and my dislike of it as intense as ever. For the previous few months this is what it had been like coming to this house. I would drive the anxiety back every time I had to come here on an errand, but my stomach would betray me.

All day, as I thought of coming here, my stomach would turn over. I would try to forget this thing, but like an old septic wound the sensation lingered. Now the familiar sensations were returning; the terrible sweating, the churning of my stomach. I disliked myself for showing him this, for letting him know, but I could do nothing about it.

"Come, give me the something, girl." His voice was impatient, playful, stern, teasing, toying. "What happen to you? Yuh look nervous."

I moved towards him holding out the watch. His eyes scanned my body. They stopped at the edge of my skirt, and I stopped. He tossed the cigarette stub over the railing, looked into my face and turned his back on me, making his way lazily towards the front door. "Come," he said.

I watched him move slowly inside the house without looking back. He moved as if he did not doubt that I would follow. In that one action he managed to drain the tension from the moment. I felt silly about the way my stomach had been churning. It was as if there was nothing to this pounding in my chest. He had a way of doing that. It was like being toyed with. One minute I was expecting impending disaster – my whole body tensed and waiting for a blow – and the next, nothing. I followed him into the cool of the living room.

"Cyaan see a damn thing in this place," he said as he switched on the lights in the front room and moved behind the counter.

He had transformed what had been the dining room into his workshop. It was simply furnished: a couple of wicker chairs, a scattering of wooden crates, and a large shelf filled with books and magazines that spilled onto the floor. His workbench stood in the middle of the room. Behind it was a large, roughly hewn mahogany cabinet with glassless doors. This rose to the ceiling and its wide shelves were filled with an assortment of clocks. The rest of the room was littered with tools, small metal boxes filled with watches and tiny screws and what I knew to be the mechanical parts of watches. He always boasted about knowing where everything was and he liked to abuse Aunty when she tried to clean the room.

This was his haven.

Uncle was never short of work, despite the tiny size of the district. Even though, around here, time was a fluid thing, defined not by the precision of watches and clocks, but by the task to be done, by mood and by the sun, people still carried watches like talismans, and they still tried to maintain their many ornate clocks with the same pride and care that they gave to their good furniture and family heirlooms. Uncle kept time moving. It was his gift, he said. A magical ability to peer into the belly of these machines, and discern their ailments. Then he would, with his knobby fingers, touch, prod, tickle until the thing came alive. Sometimes he would work on a piece for months, but everyone knew it would work one day. That was Uncle. His hands, always trembling because of the drink, would magically grow still, steady as a surgeon's when he came near a clock or a watch.

117

He walked over to his bench and turned on a shadeless lamp. The raw white glow flooded the room. I winced, looking away. On the walls were clocks of all different sizes, hands moving, hanging circular disks swinging disturbingly.

Interspersed haphazardly among these clocks were old, yellowing photographs in delicately crafted wooden frames. These were people I should have known. They were relatives from another time, standing there with the shock of the camera in their faces. They all had the look of dead people. Their gazes were always beyond the camera, beyond the frame, towards some other place, like the solemn distant look in pictures used in obituaries or funeral bulletins at church. They all had that gaze. Dead. And for each of them there was a story. Each picture carried a tale. My mother had pointed to each face, constructing a narrative about each one. I could not remember what story went with which face; who was the alcoholic who eventually killed himself after eight of his goats were poisoned by an old, bitter lover; or who was the missionary who travelled to Africa to save the souls of Africans on a Baptist Mission – who came back a very old and tired woman with nothing interesting to say about Africa except that demons were real; or who was the girl who died of pneumonia when she was eighteen and pregnant; or which one was the real estate man, who everybody knew made a lot of money, but when he died, nobody could find any of it. The list was a long one, and the faces had all become a blur to me. These were my family; all with the sallow transparency of the skin and the lightness of hair. I felt as far from them as I did from Uncle.

He watched me now from behind the counter. The brief respite was coming to a close. I could feel him gearing up for another of his comments. His body seemed to slouch slightly, as if it was looking for a posture that he had been told was sexy and mannish. I could feel the mood changing again. Suddenly his eyes seemed to glaze over. I could see them losing focus as his mind drifted from me, from the room. He held the watch in his hand.

I decided that I would just leave the watch with him and come back for it the next day. I would bring Candice with me. She knew how to deal with Uncle. She had a way of keeping control of things. She was the brazen type. The kind of girl who could read the motives in men's eyes and then dare to let them know that she knew. She had a way of making what they were thinking seem absurd. We would laugh and the men, slightly uncertain, would laugh too and all would be well. She could do it to Uncle. Once she asked him whether he thought he had x-ray vision. He stuttered after she said this. She laughed boldly and said that she knew she was right, he did wish he had x-ray vision so he could see through her skirt. The next day Uncle told my mother that I was keeping bad company and I would be fat with child before anybody knew it. I wished Candice was with me, to diffuse all of this.

"So what wrong wid it?" His voice was barely audible.

I wasn't sure what he wanted me to say. Then I began to wonder whether he had asked me what was wrong with me.

"Nothing," I muttered.

"What happen to de watch?" he said in a louder voice. "Open yuh mout' an' talk."

"I don' know... Mama seh it nat working..." I looked around the room, trying to avoid his eyes. "She say you mus' fix it and then tell her when it ready."

"So yuh don' know what happen to it, eh?" He was smiling.

"It stop," I said, feeling very foolish.

"It stop eh? But I will show you. Come, see something here. Come. Come here." I hesitated. But there was something different in his voice, something very playful and non-threatening. It was as if the watch, and the business of fixing it had switched his mood again. "Come, come, come..."

He had already started to pry open the back of the watch, so his head was down as he beckoned me. "Come look at this..."

I moved to the bench and stared as he lifted the silver cylinder to reveal the intricate belly of the watch. Circles, thin lines of silver and gold, cogged, interlocking wheels, all

119

glowing in the naked light. I looked quickly at his face. There were beads of sweat on his forehead. His grey irises, like those of a cat, were consumed by the vision of this naked watch, bare before him. I looked down at the clock. One of his fingers touched the gleaming innards.

"Sometimes, all yuh have to do is touch it," he said, then he leaned forward and blew a gentle breath into the watch. "And you blow into it. And maybe if yuh do it right, it will start again, just so." He looked at me. He smiled with just his eyes, stretching the heavy, swollen bags under them. There was genuine excitement in his eyes.

"Heeh," he said pushing it towards me. "Give it young breath, and watch what happen. You blow into it. Go on." He pushed it towards me again. I leaned forward and blew gently and uncertainly. I felt his hand on my cheek, rough, like a lizard crawling over my face. I pulled back quickly and backed myself into the semi-dark.

"Still dead," he said. I heard his wheezing giggle. "Sometime it don't work, eh?"

I began to wish that Aunty was home. At least when she was around, he never behaved like this. The last time she was not here and I had come to bring her some flour, he was full of his lewd jokes, laughing himself into fits of coughing. Then it was my expanding titties. He kept warning me about boys who loved to touch big titties, about how Candice's titties must be rough with so much manhandling. Yet even then, he kept his distance. But now, there was something slow and deliberate about his playfulness, his mood changes. I did not like it.

"Aunty not here?" I tried to be casual. Maybe a reminder about his wife would help.

"Church," he answered. "She praying for sinners like you and me."

"Oh." I said, avoiding the trap. I did not want anything to open the door for that kind of talk. He set that kind of trap all the time.

"What happen? You want her for something?" he asked.

"Jus' wanderin' if she was here…"

The place was so quiet. It was getting dark outside. If I were to make it to the main road for Tony, I would have to run at full speed through the gully. Uncle was bent over the watch, tinkering with a thin silver screwdriver, picking at the belly of the thing. I could tell that he was planning to keep me here as long as he could. I wanted to leave.

"How long it gwine tek?" I said. The words sounded almost impertinent as they came from my mouth.

"What happen? Yuh 'ave somewhere fe go?" he asked, looking up.

"No, no… I was just wonderin'," I stammered.

"Dyamn liaad!" His words came in a thin sharp whisper.

"I was jus' wonderin', maybe yuh wan' me come back." I stopped. My nervousness suddenly made me feel guilty. That I was lying made it even worse, made it seem like he was right.

"Huh! I watching yuh, yuh hearin' me, girl?" He still stared down into the watch. "From yuh start swell up in yuh lickle frock, yuh start behave like yuh is big smaddy, eh? Yuh start gallivant wid that prostitute Candice. Yuh tink yuh can match Candice? Yuh know what Candice doing wid her lickle self, eh? Yuh stay dere. I watchin' yuh like a hawk, yuh hear? Which man yuh chasin after now, eh? Uncle can see everyting, yuh hear?"

"Uncle, it getting dark. Me nuh like walk a road when it dark."

"Don't tell me no lie. You think I don' know what going on? Yuh tink I cyaan see?" he asked roughly.

Without realizing it, I was backing towards the door.

"So which part dis bwoy gwine carry yuh now? Eh?" He was grinning up at me. "Bush? Bush, right? Bwoy don' have no class. Dat is Candice style, yuh know? Bush. A lickle feel up an' rub up a bush."

I was at the door now, looking out at the darkening green of trees and bushes. I decided it was better not to say anything. To ignore, let him get tired of talking to himself, and then maybe, he would let me go. I would have to run quickly.

"I just looking out fe yuh, yuh hear," he continued. "We is family and I don wan yuh mash up our reputation in dis town,

121

yuh hear? Nobody in his family don' need to pick up no bush-rub. And we nat ready fe no expansion yet, yuh follow?" He laughed at his joke.

Despite my nervousness, I was growing irritated, even a bit annoyed at what he was doing to me. I was annoyed with myself, too, for standing there waiting for him to dismiss me, especially since I knew that he had no intention of doing so. But leaving without permission was not much of an option. My mother would be on my case, she would throw at me his accusations of my waywardness, my rudeness. And I would have little to say in response. There was no way to explain that I was afraid of what Uncle would do. And beyond all that, the truth was that I wanted to leave to see Tony.

So perhaps they were right about me. Perhaps Uncle could smell that thing in me, that feeling that I carried inside me, the stirrings that I knew should not have been there. The way my stomach would unfurl itself when I heard the thump and rumble of the big sound system on the bus; waves and waves of dancehall music causing everything to undulate with a sensual rhythm. And Tony would do his thing while hanging precariously on the side of the van; his hips rolling, a blatant show for me. These were my pleasures, secret pleasures and I knew they were not good thoughts; not the kind of thoughts that anybody, not even Candice, would imagine that I had. But sitting there on the mini-van, lost in the consuming sound of the music and the lewd lyrics, I would allow my mind to roam along paths forbidden.

And the confusing thing about standing there, awaiting Uncle's permission to leave, was that I knew the path in my mind was in some muddled and infected way entwined with the path his sordid mind was taking. I hated that, as he toyed with his own lewdness, my mind was slipping back to Tony. I wanted to get away from the pressure of all this. I was angry with myself for letting my mind drift like that.

The smell of cigarette smoke drew me back. I could hear his laboured breathing, interspersed with short grunts and long sighs as he straightened himself to stretch his back. It became clear to me that there was a rhythmic pattern to everything he did. The pattern of his breathing marked his every movement.

But when he spoke, I was startled. I had gotten used to the lull.

"Ah gwine need me glasses. Cyaan see a blasted t'ing," he said.

At first, I assumed he was talking to himself. But he continued, slowly. "Look inside the room, by the dresser." I looked blankly at him, trying not to understand. "Look inside the room, by the dresser," he repeated. "Wake up girl!"

"Look for what, sir?"

"Glasses," he said impatiently.

"What them look like?" I had never seen him wearing glasses.

"Jus look by the bed," he said, as he looked down at the watch he was working on.

I had no choice really. He simply ended the conversation making it hard for me to argue or protest. He remained a humped back, old, bowed over his workbench. His grey hair had fallen away to reveal a large bald spot in the middle of his head.

I turned on the light in bedroom, a dim, yellowish light glowing through lampshades that had grown opaquely yellow with age. I looked on the old mahogany dresser with the painstakingly crocheted mats on which Aunty's collectibles – tiny pennywhistle-blowing boys with rosy cheeks, porcelain dolls, dogs, and cats, and an elaborately painted relief of a graveyard, complete with tombstone and overhanging willow. This is where she kept her candleholders, brass and silver vessels that she never used at all. It was like a shrine. There were no glasses on the dresser. I looked around the room. I could find nothing on the chest of drawers where they kept their combs and brushes and medicines. I walked over to the bedside table and searched among her needle cushion, her unused stockings, more brushes, her bay-rum bottle, and crumpled bits of used tissue – there were no glasses. This was her side of the world, and it had a distinct scent of bay rum and Bengay liniment for her arthritis.

It was an old smell that brought back memories of when we used to come here for the huge outdoor parties that Uncle would throw. During those days, he thought nothing of slaughtering a goat and currying the creature for the crowd that would gather there. These Sunday affairs would take place after an estate cricket match. The sugar estate manager would come by with his family, and they would sit on the porch with Uncle. But the party really began when they left with their starched personalities and polite society manners.

Then, we children were allowed full freedom to roam the house while the adults ate and drank and danced and played dominoes. I remembered always hiding in this room. The cool of it, shaded by the thick Bombay mango tree that spread across the only windows that looked into the room. And the sense of a grotto, a veritable vegetative darkness, was enhanced by the forest of plants that Aunty kept inside the room on her side. She had extended the windowsill until it became a wide counter on which she placed her pots and trays. She grew fledgling crotons and aloe vera, delicate African violets and an assortment of other bushes and vines that crawled towards the sunlight with uncanny and unruly tenacity. I would tunnel deep into Aunty's sheets, heady with the scent of bay rum, Bengay and Uncle's Old Spice. Sometimes, I would fall asleep in that safe place, or I would simply lie there until I could start making out the images of another generation of my family on the wall.

The pictures, faded and mute like those in the other rooms, were fascinating to me. There were more pictures of Aunty and Uncle in this room. Pictures of them together, courting days, early married days, the day he bought his first car. There was one of them standing before an ornate doorway; she in a flowing white dress, her hair done up in that forties fashion, tidily pressed and full of body. In her arms was a bundle of white cloth almost concealing the barely discernible head of a baby.

Uncle stood with his hand in his pocket, half-grinning into the camera. He did not have his belly, and his eyes were clear and bold; the eyes of a soldier giddy at the thought going to war. He wore a fedora, tilted jauntily to one side. Aunty's half-smile looked saintly. She had blessings in those eyes, a sweet sadness of deep knowing. For years, until I had my own child, I thought that that was what new mothers felt like – like saints, at peace with themselves, with God, with the world. She had that look. The baby had died two years later from a cold. They had no more. I remember how I used to cry for that cousin I knew would have been my best friend. My mother tells me that I used to talk to her when I was much younger – this was years after she was dead. I would tell everyone that I had seen her and talked to her. They kept the picture in the room, hidden away. Aunty never talked about Shirley.

I decided to try and find the glasses inside the drawers. I fumbled through Aunty's hair clips, rollers, more combs and brushes, tarnished and stained make-up compacts, older photographs with torn, chewed-up edges, or large stains like coffee stains across the surface, water marks, aging everything in the pictures. I found her tattered Bible, the one that simply crumbled in her hands one day from overuse. She had finally picked up the new leather-bound engraved one that our Sunday school class had bought for her. She wore it to church like new shoes. She kept complaining about how hard it was to find things in the new one, and she kept suggesting that the versions were different, that it read differently from her old one. She would never throw away the old one. It was testimony to her devotion, to her diligence as a reader of the Word.

I tried his drawers. Notebooks, handkerchiefs, leather laces, and watches. Watches of every assortment and size, none of them working. Watches with colourful numbers, watches with digits broken off the face, watches with cracked faces, watches with huge knobs, watches with leather straps, watches with gold straps, watches without straps – a veritable graveyard of time-pieces, all frozen, some gutted, but silent – very silent. But there were no glasses. I found his cigarettes hidden in a corner. He was not supposed to be smoking, but he did when Aunty was not around.

I surveyed the room again, trying to find the glasses. I had never seen him in glasses. She did not wear glasses either, at least as far as I knew. I looked at her picture; she smiled down: "Bless you child." I smiled back.

Then the room went dark. I turned to see him silhouetted in the doorway. He had turned out the dim yellow light and the harsh white light from the worktable framed him. I could see no features, no face. I moved instinctively towards the door. He shut it. I heard the keys jangle as the lock slipped into place. Even as he followed me around the room telling me to relax, his breath short and uneven, I could not admit it was happening. Somehow my brain was unable or unwilling to do the simple calculus of the moment. His hands would reach for me, I would pull away and he would say, "What happen? What happen?" Then he would sit on the edge of the bed and look at me. At one point he made a speech about playing hard to get, about how silly it was and how much easier it would be to relax and enjoy it. All this time, I said nothing.

I wanted to ask him to let me out. Inside me, I felt that I was reaching a point of clarity – that place where you know you can say anything to anybody, regardless of who they are. Like the time I spoke up to the netball coach who wanted me to lie about a foul I had committed. After the game, she came at me when we were alone. I told her that what she wanted would be unfair and wrong. I said that even if she could lie, I wouldn't. And when she started shouting at me, I shouted back and told her to shut up and kiss my ass. The thing is, she was not startled or taken aback. She said something else and walked away. The next day it was clear that something had happened. We talked differently. I stopped saying "Miss". I just called her "coach". We had crossed the line.

And here in this dark place, I knew we had crossed the line. I knew that by doing what he had done, he had crossed the line, and yet I was dumb. I had no words. I couldn't even say please. Then the ritual of him following me around started again.

126

Suddenly, he had a burst of energy and moved faster than I expected he could. He cornered me near the plants. His breath was coming in sharp wheezes after the sudden exertion. As I pulled back, I felt my foot knock over one of Aunty's plants. He moved closer and started to grope at me. We wrestled, me pulling at his hands that reached for my breasts, him twisting and trying again, twisting and trying again. Finally, I pulled away and moved to the other side of the room. I stood there trying to breathe. He sat on the bed again, watching me.

We stayed like that in silence. Finally, I found words. "I will tell Mama," I said softly.

"You mother?" He chuckled. "Girl, you must be a real fool, eh? How your mother gwine believe that? Don't play the ass. Anyway, you better have something good to tell her then," he laughed.

I suddenly felt weak. I was unprepared for his complete nonchalance about what I had said. I was not prepared for the shock of realizing that my mother was not going to be my protector. He knew it all along. I had just started to realize it.

He was walking towards me, talking softly: "What sense it mek to tell them what a wicked bitch me is, ef nutting nuh happen, eh?"

I backed away slowly.

"But after you taste this, you won' tell a soul. I promise you," he said.

I knew I had moved in the wrong direction only when it was too late. I was at the foot of the bed, and he lunged at me, pinning me down on the bed. I screamed out for the first time. It was a startled kind of scream, not an exertion of power, just sudden fear. He reached between my legs. He kept muttering, "Relax, relax."

From far away I could hear myself saying, "No, no!" I could feel the cool air on my thigh. I felt totally naked. My legs locked together. There was a dull stabbing, and the strain to pry my legs open, then the stabbing again. I shifted my pelvis; he missed and grunted. My mind focused on every muscle in my thigh, keeping them together. The stabbing and grunting continued and then quite suddenly it stopped.

There was a few seconds of stillness. And then he grunted, "Oh rass!" and collapsed on me, jerking softly, as he made choking sounds.

I felt the wetness on my thighs. He stopped moving. I waited for his breathing to grow steadier. For some reason I knew it would, I knew he was finished.

I quickly pushed him off me. He turned onto his back. His eyes were half-open but he was not moving. He looked dead, there on the bed. My mouth filled with water. The thought of vomiting on him crossed my mind, but I turned away quickly and threw up on the floor. It was when I was retching that I realized that I was crying and trembling uncontrollably. I sat on the edge of the bed and cried until I felt completely empty. Then I turned to him. His eyes were open and he was watching me. There was an uncertainty there, a peculiar look of confusion. I reached to his belt and unhooked the key.

"Wait deh, wait deh. I soon ready again." His voice was a far way away.

I continued to get up. He did not move. I walked towards the door.

"Who gwine clean that nastiness, eh?" I heard him ask. I turned to look at him. He was sitting up, his body leaned over, his pants still undone and his shirt unbuttoned. His teats hung dumbly from his chest. For the first time his smallness struck me. He seemed so small, so pathetically small and old in that moment.

I walked quickly into the living room, picked up my books and ran towards the door.

Outside, clean air cooled the sweat on my blouse. By the time I walked past Flash, I could feel the smear of his sperm hardening on my thigh. I let the darkness swallow me. I could not see myself. I tried not to think as I stumbled through the gully in the half darkness. Behind each tree, I could hear sounds, people watching me and whispering. I started to run. Everything in me was in pain, hurting. I kept running.

That night, alone, I washed the skirt. I washed it again and the again. The smell remained. So I poured nearly half a bottle of bleach on it. The blue dye of the material coloured the basin and when it dried, it was a pale powder blue. I put it to my nose. The smell was still there. I burnt it in the backyard.

Mama was angry with me for months because I would not go to Aunty's house. Her anger turned to a terrible depression and a bewildered sense of hopelessness when I cut off my hair, leaving a crop of short curly hair where my hair once flowed. No one understood. Candice thought it was stupid but still sexy. I would not let it grow. It is still short. I wear it like a habit.

When Mama asked about the watch, I was abrupt and a rude. I told her she would have to get it herself. That was the beginning of my rudeness phase. That was the beginning of my period of being an out-of-hand child. Uncle's words were repeated in the house all the time. My mother would admonish me for playing with Candice and coming in at all hours. She read waywardness in my sullen disposition and flippant tongue. She was especially angry at my attitude to Uncle's words of wisdom and warning. She told me that he had been threatening to withhold my inheritance money, to change his will. She reminded me that it was important to be decent to Uncle.

"He can keep his damn money!" I shouted. She slapped me in my mouth.

I didn't care. But she did, though. She just sat there and cried.

I could have explained, but it was pointless. She would not believe. I knew she could not afford to believe. And what would she do if she believed? How could she cope with the way it would change her life? She could not protect me, she could not punish him without destroying her own life and the life of everyone else. She would have to call me a liar, call me a slut. I was only fourteen then, but I understood that completely. I understood it as well as I understand it now. She had failed me, but not because I could not tell her that her brother

129

had raped me, but because long before that, she had made it clear that he was her source of value, that he gave her dignity. I did not know how to take that away from her because I did not want to hurt her. It was not about her. Not really.

I still saw Aunty at church, but it was hard to smile with her without feeling a sense of betrayal. It was unfair, but I always pictured her as being there in that room with me while Uncle stabbed at my thighs. Sometimes at night, I would scream, not because of the shock of a nightmare, but simply because I needed to convince myself over and over again that I hated it, that I did fight, that it was not my fault. As for Tony – it is the way of trauma, isn't it? – that evening ended everything. I look back now and think how everything was so thoroughly poisoned by what happened with Uncle. It was impossible to think of Tony without thinking of Uncle. The images belonged to the same terrible narrative. I could never unsplice one from the other. It is the way of trauma. Everything you touch, smell, see or think about at the depth of trauma is tarnished forever.

I walked home after that, kicking stones, trying to avoid the gully and the gutter. And for years after, at twilight, when the sun sank like an orb behind the dirty green mountains, time stammered.

Vershan II

LET ME GO

Vershan II

LET ME GO

A wash of cymbals and the lights dim to dark blue. Coming out of the deep shuddering is the walking bass-line, so fat in its roundness that it wraps around the body like a blanket. The one drop is simple, a way to count time. How sweet is the harmony that carries into this softness – a terrible sweetness that makes the body shiver and bumps pimple the skin.

The lead singer stands still, but manages somehow to make his waist speak another language. This is a Ken Boothe, Alton Ellis, Gregory Isaacs kind of groove, this is Slim Smith trying to complain about the girl who holds and tries to control – this is a man knowing that he is about to sing a love song, that the people will fall into its sweetness without knowing what has brought him to this song, what makes him want to weep when he sings this song.

This is a song about exile, about the way that love can become a dream. It is the song that he can't live. How a woman will take you and make you write psalms. He sees the faces of the women who have made him sing this song as he stands on a hill over Kingston, looking at the marvellous layers of blue rising from the deep blue-black of the ocean, rising slowly through the tender shadings from cobalt to the brilliant aquamarine that makes the heavens seem as otherworldly as they are. Only jewels give this colour. He stares at the sky and sings this song. He has come back. His body is tender after another orgasm and another woman's lament is carrying to him across the divide. This song is about his quest for some-one to hold him down, keep him here. He will keep running so that he can be held down, kept here.

This love sweet like the earth after the rain
It's falling, falling down.
I come to you in the wetness and everything is still the same
Yuh hold me, love me, turn the niceness back on me
Guide me, draw me, wrap your sweet sweet love around me

But yuh got to
Let me go
I can't take it no more
Please let me go
Don't know what you have on me, girl
Let me go
I pleading with you please, child
Let me go…

She's waiting for me over there in another country
You know this, you know this
So how come you calling me back to you with your sweetness
Want to caress me, groove me, want to rub a dub with me
Balm me, bless me, heal me with you sweet loving

The bridge is a complex of chords, minor chords clashing with major chords – the dangling lament of sorrow with the sweet seduction of hope in major chords. He makes the cliché come alive, seem so special and fresh, as if a man is calling the name of his woman for the first time.

Yuh have me under control
Yuh are deep inside my soul
What you have on me soh
Let me go, gial let me go

Don't blaze your fire, girl, don't stir your pot
What am I gonna do when
You tie me up in the night time with your bad gial talk
I am falling, I am falling
Yuh hold me, love me, turn your niceness on me
Caress me, groove me, want to rub a dub with me

Gial,
Let me go
Yuh don't know what you doing to me
Let me go
I keep coming back for more
Let me go
No more, no more, no more
Let me go

Then the music turns into a blue dub, and the world is caught up in the grind of the moment. This is slow easy lovers' rock, bouncing the hips, and every man knows the draw of a woman, calling him out of himself, making him crawl into the night, travel for miles, just to find that sweet woman who knows the language he wants to hear, who knows how to make him moan with contradictions. He holds his woman and grinds her, trying his best to beat back the wail of the Sirens, trying to beat back the madness in his head. On this bed of sound, his voice carries the sweet agony of the bedroom, the freedom to fall deeply into the pain of pleasure. He sings, and remembers as he sings:

I carry water in cupped hands,
I have found thirsty lips,
I pour, she drinks quickly,
her throat rolling, her eyes grateful,

I dip again, she is waiting,
I feel the soft of her lip
Flame my finger tips.

Her tongue cleans my palm.
she makes water with her eyes,
beckons me to taste the salt.

I am the water carrier.
I feel the burning sweetness
of my giving, and the bright

alertness of this salt
touching my tongue.

Then his voice rises high and with such a terrible desperation it fires the room. He sings now, from deep within –
calling beyond himself, far beyond himself...

Oh giver of water
Dry my stream
Before I drown
In this pooling
Of our better selves

There is a woman in the song, a host of women who stand
at the doorway and wait for him to come. He has been running
from woman to woman, it is true, but he knows that he is
looking for a hand on his hand. He likes to lie between their
legs and smell the slow cooking of their wombs, and he wants
to be drawn into that space head-first, as if there, there in that
warm place, he will find something that will hold him and
make him weep. He knows that as he sings this song he smells
the earth of this country, this country that has such a hold on
him.

When he is away, he thinks about Jamaica as if she is a
woman. The smell of the land, the way the sun hits her in the
morning, the way she argues with him about who he thinks he
is and the way she can grab him with a look. The way that a
woman, any woman, can make him turn and want to be with
her by just saying something thick with the earth's language.
This is the sweetness that consumes him.

How can a young man keep his way pure. As he sings this
song, there is the strange fear of damnation, the fear that
haunted him when he lay with a woman for the first time,
when she stood there and looked at him, and when she
showed him himself and he fell into her and felt himself
drowning. When he sings this song he remembers how he had
to come and confess all this to Aunt Josephine, to confess his

136

failure, to confess his triumph, to confess that he had tasted the sweetness of the island and it had totally consumed him. He confessed that he wanted his mother the moment he came, even though he did not know who his mother would be. And the memory of her, that girl who was kind to him, who was gentle with him and who stayed with him until he felt his death upon him, she fills his head as the music pulls him in…

> *Oh giver of water*
> *Dry my stream*
> *Before I drown*
> *In this pooling*
> *Of our better selves*

FLIGHT

FLIGHT

Hugh was in a bad state. His chest felt tight. He wanted to run outside, he wanted to breathe deeply. Something heavy was upon him; he would start to see things. The feeling was familiar. He would normally take his medication at this point. This time, he was going to fly.

Next day he left his room in Spanish Town and climbed up to Blue Mountain Peak. He had to do it, needed to do it. A year ago, revelation had come to him as he climbed this mountain. It had come in the wind. In the smoke on the reddish edge of a slope of earth and bramble blackened by a bush fire he had seen that vision. In the wide, open silence of the hillside, the voice of God had spoken to him, making sense of his past, his separation from his family, the problems with Ruby. Maybe God would speak to him again.

This time, though, there was no sun. It rained. The rain was vicious and constant. He took a bus as far as the bus would go in the driving rain. The driver decided to turn back when the bus reached a sharp hook in the road where the mountainside had crumbled, making the road virtually impassable.

Hugh stepped into the driving rain and plunged into the swirl of muddy water, crossing the barrier. He then continued uphill and walked until pain rushed through his legs. He could hardly breathe. He could not see beyond the thick green of the bushes on the path, a muddy stretch of stone and sucking wetness. He was shivering as he panted up the mountain, not sure whether he would make it to the top, not sure why he was going there. The rain stopped suddenly and a heavy humidity weighed on him. The clouds loomed darkly overhead. He began to sweat. His thighs flamed with a terrible chafing from the roughness of the wet khaki on his skin. He began to smell himself, a sickening smell that seemed to seep from his pores.

Each turn in the path was the same turn come again and again. Each goat he saw on the slopes was the same goat. A naked boy ran beside him laughing and then disappeared behind bushes. He reappeared some miles further on and then vanished. The naked child kept doing this, laughing, staring at him, sprinting, swinging his hands and pumping his little legs. Hugh wanted to talk to the boy but he knew he could not. The boy kept coming and going.

He was not going to make it to the top of the mountain that afternoon. His body was going to have to rest. Wasn't there a hut somewhere about? As he remembered it, there was a path that led to a small clearing where a stand-pipe stood. Not far from that clearing should have been the hut. He had rested there with an old girlfriend once. He kept expecting the path but did not see it.

Darkness was coming on though it was not yet four o'clock. His temples were pounding. He imagined his heart growing too frantic, shattering his body.

Then with immense relief he saw what looked like the path.

He walked down it, stumbling as the gradient pulled him into the clutch of bushes that slapped his face and chest. He was in a clearing, but there was nothing in it. Leading from it, however, going upwards, was a smaller overgrown path. There was nowhere else to go.

He dragged himself up this path, further into the cold of the mountains, and then deep into a cluster of trees in an upland valley. It was not the same place of a year ago. He was sure he was lost now. He kept walking.

As he entered what seemed like a grotto, a riot of birds startled and sprang into the sky, screaming, fluttering. The green and deep purple sky was suddenly filled with a blur of greys and whites, and then, just as suddenly, the thick dark green was in place again. Above, a john-crow circled, alone in the storm. It was calm, dangling there, turning slowly, unperturbed by the violent movement around it. There was something dead in the area: the smell of decay, but not unwholesome – more earthy. It was strange, though, that there were no other john-crows in sight. The bird was undoubtedly scavenging on something dead. Hugh could not explain it, nor could he explain the blue mist that was coming over his eyes.

It was cool here, but he was still sweating. He could feel the burning of chafed flesh between his thighs, and a heavy pressure on his left ankle. He couldn't understand this heaviness because these days he could feel his body diminishing the precise moment another pound melted away. He felt at his body. He had lost the taut protrusion of his stomach, but it had not gone flat. He had the loose flesh of a woman who had just given birth to child. He had imagined that without the excess weight he would be handsome, but the last time he stood in front of the mirror, he did not see handsome. He saw a fierce creature with small eyes that were bloodshot, lips, once full and damp, now cracked with dryness and a forehead that receded into the middle of his scalp, untidy knots of hair scattered over his gleaming pate. He felt the weight of his nose; its size was monstrous against his gaunt face.

He walked with the sense of his monstrousness. One foot after the other. The air was thin.

He saw the hut at last. It was a sturdy hut. Stumpy, squat, like a short boxer. Everything was tightly squeezed into place – totally efficient, like an assassin. The hut looked like those so perfectly proportioned short people who made taller people seem deformed. It appeared to have been carved out of a massive chunk of wood placed there by God. Just like that.

Hugh knew that he was going to stay in a hut with remarkable cosmic properties. The door was made of thick rough wood. He walked in, shut the door. He was in pitch blackness. He could hear the rain beating hard on the roof.

It was cold, airless and there seemed to be tiny bones all over the floor. Something crawled over his leg. He kicked. It was not heavy like a rat. Lizards. He sat there and felt the chemicals changing in his head.

He started to talk to the lizards after he had been there several hours. And sing. Soon he was taking short runs around the room. He was not sure why. He opened the door and looked outside. It was pitch black. He would have to stay there until there was light. He walked and trotted around some more until he was sweating. When he was tired, he sat down and pulled off his trousers. He used the tip of his fingers to touch the tender and lumpy inside of his thighs. The fire from the chafing was fierce. The skin had blistered. He sniffed the fingers; they smelt like burning hair.

He had to think.

He could hear the thinking going on in his brain. He could hear his mind working. He sat there and felt the way his body was doing the thinking as well.

He knew that if he thought hard enough he could fly.

After a few hours, he felt himself drifting to sleep. He was hungry but thought it best to save the remains of the fruit and bread he had brought until the morning. He was going to finish the hill. Then he heard what he was sure were footsteps outside. He opened his eyes and heard the faint chattering of a transistor radio. Its tinny sound carried the news of the murder of some old women and child in a home for the elderly poor. The home had been set ablaze. Several old women and a child were feared dead. He could smell the fire. In the darkness he was no longer sure whether he was sleeping or awake. The radio passed. He got up sluggishly and stumbled through the dark to the door and looked out. He could see nothing. It was still raining. He closed the door and stood in the room.

The silence in the room consumed him. He began to talk to the lizards again, and then he began to cry because he knew that he was responsible for the deaths, for the killing of the child, the old women. He was responsible. He saw the deaths of the women sitting in their own squalor and watching the flames consume them. He could see it all. He could see people pulling the bodies out into the street. He could see the crowd looking on and shaking their heads, spitting to cleanse the

144

stench from their mouths. His chest pained him and a sharp stab ran across his right wrist and down into the bones in his fingers. He squeezed his hands and winced as if something had broken. But there was no break, though a deep-down pain was sending sharp pangs up his arm. He was tired and he was crying.

It was time to fly.

He tried. He sat there and waited for flight to come. When it did, eventually, it must have been about three in the morning. Then it occurred to him that were he to fly, he could not see where to go. So he decided to wait for light.

They did not come into the room until six o'clock in the evening the next day. Someone was wondering aloud whether he was still alive. Someone laughed and said that he would undoubtedly lose weight this way. But their talk was nervous.

The lizards were talking. They had come for him.

He closed his eyes and then opened them again. The door was splintered and streaks of light filtered through. The lizards stopped talking. They had forgotten about him. He walked to the door. He waited at the door for a few minutes. Then he opened the door. He flew out.

He flew out and was soon somewhere far beyond the hut, beyond the thick grotto, the path, far beyond his plans to climb to the peak. He was going back into the belly of the city. He felt a sense of disappointment that God had not spoken to him. But he was flying and that could only be a kind of prophecy. Maybe he had the power to go back down and deal with it all.

He was going home and the chemicals in his brain were telling him how to make his way down. As he swooped he felt the wind in his face, his belly rising to his throat and sinking to his bowels. His legs trembled with the excitement. Sometimes he would walk and then fly a few hundred yards, then alight in an open area. He did this all day. He could not understand why he was still flying and alighting on denser and denser paths without coming across anything familiar. He felt no hunger, no thirst, just an incredible lightness.

The sunset began to dazzle him as he took to the air again. His lungs were filling. His mind was sharper and he felt that everything was clear. Although he could not pinpoint exactly where he was, he knew where he was going: down into the belly of the city.

This time when he came to a new spot, it seemed familiar. He saw the naked child sprinting into the bushes. He found it funny, the naked backside of the boy, jumping, catching the sun, and the yellow flash of his soles. He followed but found no sign of the child.

This bothered him. Flight, he expected, would take him down faster. But it did not work that way. The mountain forests seemed to go on and on. The sea remained far away – brimming blue in the distance.

It took him most of the day to come off the mountain and make it to a road that twisted down the foothills to August Town. It was a hill town where a community of farmers and poor people worked for the wealthy producers of the famous Blue Mountain coffee and where some wealthier people from the city built houses and buzzed around the steeply inclined roads in their Land Rovers and SUVs.

When he got there, the community was closed down for the night, except for a rum shop called "The World End Café". He walked in and asked an old man in a stained white shirt and a blue turban if they had any food. They had some food, some nice shrimp and if he had the money to pay, he could have it in a stew with some yams and rice. The man had gold in his mouth of broken teeth.

Hugh put money on the table and the man brought the food. He told the man that he was a genius. The man smiled knowingly. His skin was like the inside of tangerine peel, his eyes brown and transparent with the evidence of mixed ancestry staring back for all to see. His mouth was a flat thing, a "mash mouth". Everything he said sounded like the sloppy wetness of mud. He listened as Hugh described, quite casually, the business of flying and how it worked.

"You don't lift your arms or anything like that. You don't jump. If you jump you will find yourself where you started. Not going anywhere. Flight is not about jumping. Flight, you

146

see, is about knowing you can fly. When you know you can walk, you don't jump to propel yourself forward. You simply do it. You have the assurance and the confidence that your body will respond to the command in your head. That is what flying is like." As he spoke, the man looked at him with very wet eyes. For a moment, Hugh thought the man was drunk.

"Are you drunk?"

"No, man. Not drunk. Yuh jus' bring tears to my eyes. When I see strange things I feel like crying. The las' time I go church, that is all I was doing." The man was crying profusely now, with a huge grin on his face. "The people dem start praise the Lord the more I cry, and the more they jumping and praising the Lord, the more I weeping. Not because I see any revelation, but because the music stir up my flesh, you know. Mek me have to say, 'Jesus, people is something else'. That is just what I was saying when you start talk. 'Jesus, people is amazing.' You, my bredda, you is amazing. Look on you, a young man, and look how you talking bout flying like is the simplest ting in the world. I call that genius. You born for brightness. That's why I crying like dis. I know you from somewhere…"

"No you don't," Hugh said. He did not know the man.

"Yes man. Kendal? Grange? Negril? Little London? Dog Park? Vineyard Town? Water Street? Molynes Road? Canewood Crescent? Cardiff Crescent…?"

The names had a familiar ring to Hugh, as if he was travelling along paths he knew. But the places did not register logically. He kept saying, "No, no, no, no," as the man spoke these names like a mantra.

Then the man stopped.

He watched Hugh, smiling.

Hugh seemed also to be in tears, because of the copious flow of sweat from his nose, not just beads of sweat, but a flow, a gleaming flow from the pepper – and from his allergic reaction to the shrimp. But he did not know this then. So he kept talking and eating and soon he was promising the man that he would reveal the secret of flying to him. The man, curiously, was not interested.

"I don't want to fly," he said, pouring more water for Hugh.

"How come?" Hugh asked.

"That woulda spoil it. No good reason, really. You fly. I watch. Hell, I don't even have to watch. You fly and talk it. I feel good."

"Like that," Hugh said.

"Like that," the man said.

They went silent for a long time. Hugh kept eating and staring out into the night. He was getting his body ready to fly. He did not have much further to go to get to Papine where he would catch a van to Half Way Tree. From there he would get a bus to take him along the Boulevard that ran through a stretch of wet cane lands and a few scattered communities, including a treacherous village just on the outskirts of Spanish Town where men lurked by the roadside to pounce on hapless drivers who had broken down. Through that dark stretch of highway and then onto the amber-lit streets of Spanish Town. Home.

When the meal was almost finished, as he was scraping the last grains of rice onto his fork, he began to feel a terrible heat at the back of his neck, a strange prickly heat that made him slap his neck hard. Then he started to rub it.

He felt dizzy but was not sure if it was dizziness or just the way the light flickered when moths danced across the naked bulb. The heat was spreading down his neck across his back; it was spreading into his scalp as well. He began to scratch his scalp. The burning sensation was becoming an intense itch that suddenly consumed his groin. Underneath his balls, he could feel a flaming itch and he reached for it and started to scratch at it. The man stared at him. He wondered whether he should call someone to witness this remarkable happening. The heat was devouring Hugh. His body was on fire long before the terrible pain of stomach cramps knocked him from his chair. He bent over and stared at the man.

"What you put in the food, man?" His body was battling with an invasion. He knew it was the food and yet he was sure he had not been poisoned. He had the idea to strip naked. It came to him in a revelation. Soon he was down to his

148

underwear and then that too was discarded. Hugh could see his face in the man's eyes. Not a reflection, but in the way the man looked at him. Hugh reached for his face, mirroring the gesture of the man. He felt his skin protruding from his body. His skin felt dead, like the numbness of his face under anaesthetic at the dentist's – that feeling of uncertainty about where the face began and ended, about whose face he was touching.

But he knew that his face had swollen beyond anything that had happened to him before and that the old man was worried. He was worried that he was watching something that no one would believe when he told them about it. He desperately wanted company; his mangy dog was just not enough – it was lying still as death at the doorway, staring into the night, a fly eating the yellow matter in his eyes. The man decided that he had to get someone to see.

Hugh took water from a jug, poured it into his cupped hand and began to wash his neck with it. It was helping the heat on his body but not helping at all the feeling of contraction in his throat and the pain in his stomach. He sat down, and then he stood up. He started to walk around the room. He could feel things spinning now. He was spinning and he could tell that this thing could kill him.

He looked down on his body: the stomach protruding, the large round thighs, the hands like yam, the teats, full and pendulous. His nose, he could tell, was twice its normal size. It felt so heavy on his face. He was standing in the light when he saw massive welts literally growing all around his body. He could see them spreading across his skin.

It fascinated him.

He felt the weight of his balls and when he lifted the penis and balls to see what was causing so much heat, he saw the lumpiness of his skin, stretched and swollen beneath the fleshiness of his member that was growing erect. The sight amused him. But he had no time to laugh. He got the water jug and began to pour water on his body, on all the welts, and he began to talk himself down. He began to jog on the spot, thinking that the sweating might force the toxins from his body.

He did not notice the old man returning with a woman, much younger, who was really not supposed to witness the nakedness of a grown man at her tender age. But she saw him and she could not stop staring at the man and his hugeness and the strange patterns on his skin. She could not close her mouth, could not think to cover her exposed breast where her nightdress had slipped down her shoulder, could not think to seem even slightly coy. She was looking at a cow born with two heads, a goat giving birth to a kitten, a plantain with five fingers glued to each other like a webbed hand, a donkey-drawn cart with two crows on top while three were laughing – or some such monstrosity.

She came closer, staring at him. They recognized each other at the same time. Her hand covered her mouth.

She was a nurse Hugh had met when he had taught a graphic art class at the University Hospital for many years. That was five years ago; he had felt better looking then and fitter. It started with him staring at her everyday he passed her on the spine of the labour ward. She always stared back at him. Then he began to smile just when he realized that he was timing his arrival at work and his lunch break to match her schedule. Soon he knew when she would not be there, those days when he would keep looking for her, hoping to catch sight of her. He would feel heavy when he did not see her. And on those days he would daydream about her – they were unfair dreams of lust and desire and she was always giving.

Then one day she played a joke on him. She hid behind one of the columns on a day when he expected her to be there. As he walked past the column, slowly, looking behind him, she stepped into the corridor and with her arms akimbo, asked, "You los' something?" His mouth did not form the words quickly enough to make him feel cool, but he managed, "You," and she laughed harder than she ought to have. They started to lunch together.

She talked to him whenever they saw each other. He liked

her strange distance and her ability to say forthright things. The first time she told him a secret they were standing under a rusting almond tree outside the nurses' residence, smoking and staring at one dog mounting another. They remained silent staring, aware of each other. Finally, as the bitch pulled away with a yelp and trotted off, leaving the male hopping away in some discomfort, she chuckled.

"Yuh bitch yuh, she done and what yuh gwine do wid dat?"

They laughed. Then she said softly, "I's a shame when them thing excite you, eh?"

"Not really," he said, looking at her and smiling.

"Yuh right, no shame in dat." And they kept smoking and waiting for the dogs to return.

Now seeing her, it came to him that for years he had imagined her harbouring secret feelings for him. She was a subject in so many of his wayward fantasies. Her face was one of four that he could conjure at will, while masturbating or trying to will his dreams towards pleasant sexual encounters at night. The things he had done with her! It was the same face – she had not aged at all – the same low haircut, the same subterranean Indian features in her thin nose bridge and the olive sheen of her skin.

She had been transferred to Mandeville six months after they met. They had done little else but talk about incidentals, peppering them with sudden and inexplicable secrets. Like when he told her he had stolen money from his grandmother and had lied about it to everyone, or when she told him that she was sleeping with three men and all were looking after her, or when he told her that he sometimes felt like a bastard, or when she told him that she had had an abortion. Then she simply left and that was the end of it. Still, she was stored in his mind as an object of tender desire.

Now she was half covering her face, half peeping at him, with a shy sensuality as if she knew what he had done with her all these years. She seemed to want to apologize for being so lewd and forthright.

"Oh God!" she said, and then she chuckled that chuckle.

Maybe she had to do that to assuage her sense of guilt and sinfulness for staring with such fascination at his monstrously swollen penis, which was like an animal that could make a sound and crawl around on its own – monstrous, yes, but with a disturbing beauty.

Icilda, which was her name, the name she preferred, she had told him, though everyone called her Icy, ceased to be a viewer at that moment, and became one with Hugh as he poured water on his body, trying to calm the heat, trying to get himself together so he could fly. The chemicals, he kept saying. The chemicals. The chemicals. They were causing him such trouble.

She helped him with the water.

"More, more," he said.

"It going down," she said, looking at the penis with what he could tell was a hint of disappointment.

"Yes, it look soh," the man said.

Hugh felt his penis draining of blood. The pain seeped out of the taut skin – a sense of intense relief like the rush of nerves during a much postponed piss. The flame was still crawling across his shoulders.

"The shoulders…" he said to Icilda.

She poured water on his shoulders.

"Jesus, have mercy," she breathed as she stood behind him. She was looking at islands of huge welts across his back. "You allergic," she said.

"Him need a purge. The man full a poison," the old man said. He disappeared behind his counter and then reappeared with a glass of dark fluid.

Hugh saw the fluid coming towards him and he suddenly felt like opening his arms and flying again.

"Come, bredda. Drink this. Stout, and a lickle senna pod. Come."

Hugh did not want to drink, but when Icilda took the glass from the old man and offered it to him, he took it, staring into her eyes. His mind was scattering across the hills. He listened to her cooing. She looked like Ruby, his girlfriend. It was a

152

truth he had resisted from the moment he saw Icilda step in the room, but he could no longer fight it. She looked like Ruby.

"Ruby," he said.

"Drink it."

So he drank it. It made him grow weak, a drunken kind of weakness. Then he felt the heaving of his stomach, the pressure in his bowels. Icilda knew when to help him to the latrine at the back. She sat him down and held his face as he released his insides into the dark hole.

Afterwards he slept.

He dreamt of Ruby Williams lying on a table, her long black plaits spindling off her sweaty head, and she was bleeding from her vagina. He dreamt of Ruby making love to him. He dreamt of Ruby with her head bandannaed, preaching a mouthful of revelations to the sky. But in all the dreams, Ruby was alone. He was merely watching Ruby. He was not with Ruby.

In the morning, he woke to see that he was lying on a burlap bag at the doorway of the store. The wall of the store was painted an off-white colour and was stained with the markings of muddy feet. He stood up and realized he was naked. His clothes were neatly folded beside him, laundered and dry. He put them on. On the counter was an enamel plate decorated with brightly coloured plums and leaves. On the plate was a sandwich of thickly-sliced bread that seeped with oil from the spillage of ackee, saltfish, tomatoes and onions. He ate the meal quickly chewing on the soft egg-like texture of the fruit, flavoured with hot peppers, thyme, onions and sweet coconut milk.

After, he walked outside into the cool morning. His eyes hurt. His body hurt. His stomach muscles hurt.

There was no one around. The dog was pissing against a post at the far end of the street. Hugh wanted to call to someone but thought better of it. He began to walk down the hill. After five minutes, Icilda appeared, climbing up the hill with a covered basket.

153

"How yuh feeling?" she asked.

"Fine."

"You look better."

"Yes. Thanks."

"That woman dead?"

"Who?"

"Ruby… All yuh deh pon is Ruby, Ruby, whole night? She dead?"

Hugh panicked at the thought. Did she know something? She couldn't know. Ruby is not dead. The baby died, not Ruby.

"No," he said. It was almost a question. Icilda smiled. He felt reassured.

"She lef' yuh, den." This was a statement.

"Yes."

"Den yuh mus' run her down," Icilda said laughing. "Yuh love her bad. She turn yuh fool."

Hugh was not sure whether Icilda was laughing with sympathy or mockery. "Yes," he said. "Anyway, I gone. Tell your old man t'anks…"

"My old man?" She laughed. "You mean my *man*."

"Yes, yes." Hugh smiled with her, trying to cover the pang of jealousy that he was sure she recognized in the way he averted his eyes.

"Walk good. I like you. You big. And you tender, too. You know from I leave you to go Mandeville, I dream you – whole heap a night I dream you, big same way," she said softly, as if she was trying to sooth him. "Ruby is a lucky gial." She smiled slyly and climbed past him up the hill.

Below him, hidden in places by dense stands of trees, Hugh could see the two rivers of the Blue Mountains, Hope and Mammee, meeting in a v – like the uterus, fed by fallopian tubes, opening out into the winding Hope River into the city. Hugh closed his eyes to avoid the image of blood in the river. He opened them again and the air was exploding with a rush of colours.

As he stood there on one of the rock bridges that traversed

Hope River, he saw a woman sitting on the far side of the bridge, her sandals dangling from her dust-white feet. The rest of her legs were shining with sweat, a black gleam of health and vigour in her skin. She wore a yellow dashiki dress and cradled a large guitar on her thighs. He could not see her face because the sun was a ball of energy behind her, round, even against the pale blue sky. But he could see the spot of gold in her hair where the sunlight spilled. She was humming, her feet swinging in rhythm. As Hugh drew closer she spoke softly.

"Look," she said. "I see heaven open before me and the Son of Man standing at the right hand of God." Hugh felt a strange flaming in his neck. He hurried along. He could hear the smile in her song, sung in a deep contralto, a song that had the cadence of a mento: slow, rural and oddly ironic.

All night long in my bed
I looked for the one my heart loves;
I looked for him but did not find him,
I will search for the one my heart loves
I will search for the one my heart loves.

He continued walking down the hill, planting his feet carefully, as if he was not sure if the road might not give way if he pressed too hard on the ground.

At the bottom of the hill, instead of heading home, he turned down the road that led to the University Hospital where he had been admitted in the past. He found his doctor and explained to him as calmly as he could that he needed to rest, he needed some medication.

Hugh leaned against the wall and felt himself slipping.

What happened after that remained unclear to him. He called it a long sleep because he could not remember any of it, except as one remembers dreams. Three women kept coming to visit him: Ruby, Icilda, always with a bucket of water, and the woman with the dashiki and a mouthful of scriptures.

155

But one mid morning – a brilliant Kingston morning – he found himself standing on the concrete ramp outside Ward Twenty-one, the psychiatric ward. They were letting him go. Not that they thought he was fine, but well enough at least to go home.

What he remembered, as in most dreams, was that he was trying to go somewhere and everything was working against him getting there. That is what most of his time on the ward had been like. He could not go; they wanted to stop him from going and he fought to go. Fought and fought until he was quite exhausted. He also remembered that his tongue had been heavier than he had ever known it to be. He could distinctly recall an argument with his doctor who was quibbling about his assertion that the tongue actually weighed ten pounds. The doctor was adamant that it weighed nine pounds and twelve ounces, no more than that. They had argued and there might have been a fight. He was not sure about that. He just recalled the argument.

He found walking difficult. The sun was relentless, oppressive. It made most things seem white. He saw faces but could not make them out. By the time he was on the bus, Hugh was drenched with sweat, panting, trying to get a good breath in. He was nauseous and did not think he could make it home.

On the bus, he realized that no one had asked him to shower or to change his clothes for a while. An intense smell was rising from his crotch like the stench of a dead thing. He could smell it. He quickly closed his legs, but could tell that the scent had escaped and was spinning through the van, overpowering every other scent. He stunk and he could tell that his whole body stunk, not just the crotch, but his armpits, and more than that, his skin. The stench was seeping out of his skin – a kind of purging of toxins. He smelt himself and was repulsed. Yet no one asked him to get off the bus. He just had a whole row to himself, and in his heart he repented of every cruel word he had spoken about his people.

They forgave him this stench of death that came off his body.

Kingston's heat bore down on his bare head. Now he missed the hills with their timelessness. Here, he was afraid to think, so many dangers in the sounds, the noises, the faces, the smells, the relentless light. He had to seek shelter in this place that had not changed at all. He thought that perhaps it would be different. But it was as if he had never left, had never flown, had never vanished into the belly of the asylum with its chemicals and white relentless light and emerged triumphant with the warm awareness that a woman had looked at him and loved him.

He made it home to Spanish Town. He made it just as the postman was riding away from his gate. The helper was staring at him and kept asking him if he was supposed to be there or somewhere else. She meant the asylum. He said nothing. He knew that he had arrived home and all would be well. He knew this, as he knew things that involved faith, as he knew that he was not going to die young, as he knew that he would find love and lose it and live his life remembering what it tasted like, as he knew where he would sit on his fiftieth birthday (in the shade of a brittle orange tree, black with blight, standing there on the slope of a barren hill). He would sit there and stare into the sea; the sea would be south of him. He knew these things. He knew that he would ignore the helper, go into the room, lie on the bed in the gloom, and feel his body drifting slowly.

There was a letter from Ruby. The envelope held a pink bill for the procedure and prescription painkillers, and a brief note saying, "Hugh, you need to pay this. Ruby."

He slept and when he woke it was as if he had not slept at all. As if the day was the same as it had always been.

SINATRA

Angela knew what she was talking about. She had been in the court every day during the trial and they enjoyed her flamboyant flair for description and her insider knowledge. Anyone who frequented the area near the courthouse knew by the shouting and cheering when the day's proceedings were over. Angela had, indeed, become part of the proceedings.

She wore a different business suit for each day of the trial, which had gone on for two weeks. She was always accompanied by a tall and very black man called Pencil.

Pencil had a huge face with ballooning brown eyes. His hair glistened with grease and conditioner and was cut in the rebel style – shaved sides and craziness on the top. When Pencil smiled (which was constantly) the brightness of his large teeth under his heavy, wet lips was intimidating. Pencil also slicked-up for the trial. The three-piece-suit he wore was tailor-made: bulging trousers that narrowed dramatically at the ankles, a loose jacket and close-fitting waistcoat with a watch and chain of gold curved stylishly across his torso. Several gold and silver chains hung about his neck. His accessories were completed by the knob earring on his left ear and reels of bracelets on his right wrist. Pencil was impressive. If his attire did not impress the observer, the clear bulge at the waist of his trousers demanded respect.

When they came to the gathering of people each day, Pencil touched no one, he simply stood behind Angela grinning and repeating, "Easy man. Easy, man..." Pencil was cool. At no point did he seem worried that his "bonafide breddren" would be found guilty. She watched him stride through the world as if he owned it. When she panicked, he said, "Just cool..." and somehow she was beginning to trust this confidence.

But faced with the press, faced with the crowd, Angela had to talk – it was just her way. She was animated in her descriptions of the trial. She complained about the judge's rudeness to Sinatra, and expressed relief that it was the jury – decent law-abiding Jamaicans – who would give the final verdict. Angela was confident that they would do the right thing. Pencil assured her that that wasn't a problem. He had heard this from the MP in the area who said that he knew the members of the jury well.

After each day of the trial, a regular crowd would join Angela in a tiny kiosk bar that was tucked into a small lane near the court and listen intently to her commentary, adding their cheers, groans and threats through it all. Most of the people lingered on the sidewalk, sat on boxes, steel drums and the rusted body of a burnt out Ford Cortina drinking beers and listening to Angela. With Pencil beside her, she felt safe, and Ophelia, the thin black woman who owned the bar, was protective of Angela because she had ensured that the trial of Sinatra brought her good business.

Here was a writer, an uptown woman with plenty of style, and she was writing about one of their own.

Invariably, as the evening wore on, the mood would become one of celebration and joy. The huge tapedeck that Ophelia commandeered from her son and placed in an oil drum at the doorway of the bar would be fired up and people would start to dance.

Some of them really did like Sinatra. Several of the women there had been very close to him. Babsy was his current baby-mother. He was with her when the police kicked down the door to her boss's condo, a large, three-bedroom, stylishly furnished place which was part of a complex of duplexes tucked into the rich green crotch of Beverley Hills, where the well-off had built monstrously elaborate homes on the prime real estate that overlooked Kingston. Babsy had the key for the condo because her boss, a contractor, assured her that the

162

place was hers as long as she was there when he wanted her to be.

How the police knew to find Sinatra there that night remained a mystery. Of course, there were theories. Babsy's boss was now working in Seattle with his family and he did have good connections with the police force.

They came quietly, kicked down, tipped him from the bed and shot him casually in the foot. She screamed for mercy. They ignored her. They didn't even touch her.

They dragged Sinatra from the bedroom, through the living room, leaving a trail of blood on the fluffy white carpet. She followed them out into the streets in her nightdress.

The entire neighbourhood of well-to-do professionals and "decent people" came out to see what was happening. They stood behind their ornate cement fences and watched as the notorious Sinatra stood stark naked in the street with the remarkable assured manner he had, as if he had called the police to talk to him. Sinatra had been brought to account.

Few would have believed that Sinatra virtually lived in their neighbourhood. The scandal was unnerving and Babsy's wailing, complete with rolling on the grass (revealing her underwear in the process), did not help much.

That had been about five months, several headline stories, several top-level resignations, several arrests, and several retaliatory deaths of policemen ago. Sinatra still walked with a limp, but he was a confident man. Letters had been published in the newspapers praising his community work. It was he who had organized the series of "Shock Out" reggae shows that raised over $10M for approved schools and places of safety. Sinatra was a community leader with heart. He might have killed, they said, but he only killed those who deserved to die, those who were intent on destroying the unity and peace in his community. Sinatra was no thief. He was well-known for his disdain of thieves. Indeed, he would organize trials in the gully and execute thieves himself. He did this, they argued, because the police didn't care about the ghettoes and did not see it necessary to treat those areas as a part of their constituency.

The community supported Sinatra because he protected them, brought a semblance of law and order to the area. The community tribunals and their justice might have been swift and ugly, but they were efficient. National death statistics never included these areas. The trials, and the burials that frequently followed, mostly went unreported. People from the area always boasted that their local crime rate was lower than most other parts of the city. They had few burglaries, few rapes (as understood, of course, by the tribunals), no muggings to speak of. It was safe there. He was *their* Don. So they liked him.

Women wrote letters to the papers declaring that Sinatra was a good father, that none of his children starved. Admittedly, he had a weakness for women, but it was only natural because he was a handsome and good man and many women threw themselves at him. There were a few negative letters and interviews that focused on the alleged victims of Sinatra's notorious posse during the two-month spate of killings and robberies just prior to the general elections of the previous year. The descriptions were brutal and those who had witnessed the violence were convinced that Sinatra was insane. Sinatra himself responded to all this by saying: "Election time is war time in Jamaica an' people mus' get hurt, yes? An' nuff a them who dead was criminal said way. Don' feget that." His apologists in the upper ranks of the Party asked doubters: "When America invaded Panama you know how much innocent people dead? Well, for every liberty them have a price and sometime the good suffer."

Sinatra never actually admitted to killing anyone and the Crown was dealing with only one genuine murder charge that they thought would stick. This killing had happened about four years ago when he was working for a politician. Such cases rarely reached the courts, particularly when the politicians who paid for the executions were on the side that won the elections. But this particular politician had found Jesus soon after coming to power, had resigned within the year and, to show that he was properly cleansed of his sins, had penned

a tell-all book. These confessions contained enough melo-
drama and scandal to spawn one radio series, an aborted
television drama, and publishing interest in the United States.
He made a heap of money on the book, and thanked God for
his bounty. It was in this book that Sinatra was first implicated,
and while the police and the government had initially chosen
to ignore the entire episode, the public, especially those who
called up talk shows and wrote editorials, found the book's
content far too tasty to be ignored. Everybody started calling
for Sinatra's arrest, everybody, that is, with a big mouth on the
radio. One St. Andrew middle-class talk-show host put in his
two bits:

"Nobody should be outside the law in this country: no
politician, no policeman, no soldier, no ghetto don and, by
God, no sorry-ass (excuse my French) criminal murderer
with the name of another criminal gangster singer from
Babylon up north. This is an avowed criminal wanted for
extradition in the United States, whose notoriety everybody
seems to know but the police. No. Even that kind of scum
should be placed before the mercy of the legal system so that
justice can be done. And may the defence lawyer who takes his
case rest well at night with such a heavy conscience."

Who cared that this clarion call came from one who was
himself a lawyer, who had made most of his substantial wealth
and reputation defending equally conscience-wearying mur-
derers and drug barons? The thing was, they had at least one
admirable trait: they paid on time and well.

So the police acted. Sinatra was picked up and the excitement began. Most people knew that the charges would not
stick. What jury could be found that was beyond Sinatra's and
his protectors' reach? The fact that Sinatra did not spend any
time in jail during the investigation and the trial hardly
encouraged a different view.

Few knew better that he would be cleared of all charges
than Sinatra himself, and no one could have been more brazen
than he was about it.

He wrote a book.

Remarkably, he had no ghostwriter. The raw quality of the language, the pedestrian grammar, the creative punctuation were all retained from the original manuscript. Here was a man of the people speaking to the people.

The book sold even more copies than the born-again politician's book had done. In his book Sinatra declared that the police had nothing useful on him and that he and his children and supporters would be vindicated. God would hear their prayers.

So what subject should have been more attractive for an ambitious and radical writer like Angela? What better way of anatomising the state of the nation than to write about this court case? The politician's and Sinatra's books were the work of amateurs – though Sinatra's had of course a grassroot's authenticity – but neither, argued Angela, had analysis or art. They had shown, though, that there was a book-buying public with a healthy appetite for this particular story. So Angela turned up every day of the trial, acquired Pencil as a very cool fashion accessory and discovered a talent for dramatic re-enactment and instant commentary.

The trial itself lacked drama. Sinatra's former Rollick Town accomplices were to have been the prime witnesses. They, it was rumoured, still held a grudge against him for leaving them leaderless and penniless when he decided to go solo and work closely with politicians and then embark on the lucrative drug trade. But none showed up for the trial, at least not as Crown witnesses. Angela witnessed the spectacle of a young lawyer trying to make a case out of nothing in front of a witty, but increasingly impatient judge, and a clearly bored jury.

When Sinatra was acquitted a party erupted in the streets just outside the courthouse. "Spontaneously," was how Angela put it, though she had noticed the sound system being set up earlier that day. The curry-goat, jerk chicken and fish sellers had already started cooking long before light. She had noticed all this, but the line was too rich to be avoided.

The police drank beer and the sound system played Bob Marley's "Duppy Conqueror" over and over again.

Technically, Sinatra had not really been set free from jail. He had actually stayed in the Commissioner's office, furnished with a bed and a kitchenette, for the one night – or at least the last two hours of darkness of early Sunday morning – after he had been "picked up". A doctor had come to look at the foot, and the policemen who had arrested him came in one by one and apologized for the way they had behaved. They explained that their instructions had been to make a spectacle for the neighbours, and that the guy who had shot him just got carried away. That policeman, a young, thick-necked boy, came into the room stammering, his eyes red. He said he did not know who they were dealing with, that nobody told him. He said he was sorry and hated what had happened. Sinatra simply said, "Fuck you." The boy stood there for a long time not sure what to do. Eventually, one of the officers came and took him out. Sinatra kissed his teeth and asked for the boy's name. It was the way of the world.

At six in the morning Sinatra had been released on bail. The paperwork was done on the Monday. He had not seen a cell since that time. Nevertheless, the Marley song was felt to be properly symbolic, a larger statement about the Babylon shitstem and its imprisonment of the souls of Black sufferers like Sinatra.

To complete the scene of the Prometheus unbound, Babsy stood outside the court with their baby in her arms, the true queen of a returned hero. It was all quite spectacular, and people were entertained.

That night, three of Sinatra's old friends from Rollick Town were found with their genitals in their mouths and their eyes gouged out; a killing that announced that the men were "batty-men". Sinatra, Angela learned from Pencil, sent flowers and cards and promised to make it to the funeral.

For a time after the trial, even more blood flowed in the belly of the city than usual. About the quality of this violence Angela and her circle of friends had theories in abundance but no real conclusions. How could one put one's finger on it; how not just see the open wound, the raw, exposed flesh?

What was a writer to do? Pontificate like the leader writers in the papers? Pretend to reasoned analysis in a world gone mad? Apply ideas of fairness, right and wrong in a situation where both sides were blatantly corrupt? How tell a story which appealed to readers whose attention could be caught only by ever more sensational reports of ever more outrageous acts of violence? Perhaps all one could do was simply record the madness, to respond to it in an instinctive and emotional way. To Angela, the choices seemed so limited. In the end she did what most Jamaicans did: made a piece of entertainment out of the whole business. It was a way of coping; it was a way of being.

So she was partial to Sinatra because he was cool – nice-looking and sexy. She knew this criteria was facile, completely lacking any moral focus. She knew this, and she also suspected that many of her judgments were that way nowadays. Taking sides with the police would have been equally absurd: they had no moral authority on their side and besides, they were rarely cool or good-looking. A policeman as hero? What was his cause? Protecting a social order that led back through colonialism to slavery. The criminal as rebel? His defiance of that order gave you something to admire, but was he really doing anything more than finding his own niche in the food chain? So, it was the entertainment value of each character in the case that made her decision for her. If they made for dull fiction, they were lost.

She worked on and off on her book for the best part of a year and then became bored with it. Sinatra faded from the scene and stayed in relative obscurity until news came of his arrest in America for credit card fraud. She did not feel any interest in writing about that piece of news. She had seen a picture of him as he was being arraigned in America. He had lost that look, his head was bowed – heroism was harder in America, no one knew who he was or cared. He deserved all he got.

She reread the first few completed chapters of the book and was embarrassed at how dull Sinatra seemed, how shallow her attempt to make an epic narrative of his squalid occupation.

But most of all she had to admit that his genius was a myth, a storm in a teacup. The clumsy but well manicured fingers that were shaking the teacup were the true story. There was the genius – the politicians who were still quietly in power, untarnished by the mess. Sinatra was what? A grand hero in his little world, but an insignificant tool of others in the grander scheme of things. There was not enough there to salvage, and besides, he did not make her tingle any more.

IN THE GULLY

IN THE GULLY

She scrambled down the gravel path, her bag bouncing against her bottom. The path was dusty and her shoes lost their sheen as she skidded on the steeper slopes. Near the bottom of the path she slowed herself down by grabbing onto a hanging branch. Her feet gave way and she sat down suddenly on her bag. She laughed to herself, then looked up the hillside to see if anyone was watching. She saw no one, just a haze of slowly falling dust particles landing on the thick clumps of bush that barely survived on this stony slope. To her left, the sound of Kingston's evening traffic was faint above her.

The sun was no longer overhead; her shadow was longer in front of her. She looked at the gold watch on her wrist. Her mother complained that it was just too expensive for such a young child, but her father wanted her to have it – he said they could afford it and that he was not going to deprive his daughter of anything. She wore it everyday, wore it to sleep – it never left her wrist. It was three o'clock. She could take her time. No one would be expecting her until five o'clock.

Carefully, she regained her footing and continued to move down slowly, keeping as close to the wall as possible and trying not to look over the edge until she was almost at the gully bottom. As she got closer, she increased her pace until she was sprinting at full speed onto the gully's cracked concrete floor. Her footsteps echoed in the empty space.

She stopped in the middle and then looked around. From where she stood she could see the line of the gully for a few chains until it vanished around a sharp corner. She knew that it stretched for miles until it came to the sea.

Just above the corner was a bridge. People walked across it like tiny insects.

The gully walls rose fifteen feet above her. There were huge cracks where shrubs and trees had pushed their way through the concrete. Enough silt and topsoil had accumulated from decades of rains to sustain a series of small forests. At the sides of the gully larger clumps of thick bush grew, some with vines that crawled up the sides of the grey walls. These had so weathered that their surface was pocked with holes big enough to take the toe of a man's shoe. Grass poked out of these holes. In the middle of the gully was a smaller canal that ran its entire length, also disappearing around the corner. It too was filled with debris and sand, in which more trees had started to grow.

She moved quickly to the clump of bushes to one side of the gully where there was a huge boulder, about her height. Under it she found her pile of brightly coloured books, hidden there on her way to school. She read them as she walked to and from school but couldn't take them in with her because it was a Catholic school and they did not encourage that kind of literature.

She might have defied the school and taken the books to class had she not been working to impress her new form mistress that she was a good student. This teacher had said that such books were silly and only filled your mind with nonsense, ideas about love that were not true. She agreed with the teacher, but still enjoyed reading her Mills and Boons full of panting men and women, women with dreams of their ideal man, Europeans living exotic lives in manors, mansions, and beach houses. She was transported by the stories and she liked where they took her. She liked how they made her feel.

As long as the teacher did not know, all would be well.

She picked up the books and stuffed all but the one she was reading in her bag. She opened the book and began reading as she walked along the gully towards the hills. Violet, a black haired vixen, was racing through Germany with an Italian lover, totally smitten by her cruel ways, following her in his convertible. The clean German villages, the smooth valleys and hillsides, the quaint cottages and the billowing clouds in a blue sky filled her head. She read quickly, devouring the images, hurrying to the moment they would have to meet and he would hold her and touch her and Violet's legs would feel weak, her heart pounding, her body melting into his.

She rarely looked up because she knew her way so well – where to stop reading and watch the path so as not to step into black balls of goat droppings. Then she would continue reading.

Whenever she came near the police station, she would always stop reading. She had heard that the high wall that loomed just above the gully with barred windows was the back wall of the police lock-up. Sometimes she saw hands hanging from the windows but the holes were too dark to make out faces. Here, on the stretch of concrete above the gully wall, was a thick mass of barbed wire that rose almost as high as the windows. The wall was a faded orange colour, with patches where raw concrete had been smeared as if to fill holes in it.

She walked quickly past the police station and where the post office had been before it was burnt to the ground. She walked past the wall that protected the horses in the paddock beside the post office from falling into the gully. Next, the gully bisected a small housing district. She had to walk under a footbridge that hung over a roadway that ran through the gully. Usually this area was busy and quite a few cars used this roadway, uneven as it was, as a short-cut from the main road on the police station side to the residential area on the other side. She would sometimes walk into this district and buy sweets. She had a few friends from school who lived there and whenever she did not have swimming practice they would walk along the gully together. She would continue along the gully while they went home via the roadway.

She knew quite a few people in the district. There was Caddy, and the gardener who looked after their yard who lived in a small hut just beyond the footbridge. He had the reputa-tion for being wild and violent, but she knew him as a friendly

175

and gentle man. He would sit by himself on the gully wall, smoking herb. When he saw her, he would smile and nod. She was always afraid he would fall off. He never did. Sometimes he would come down to talk to her. She also knew some of the "rude" boys who hung around the bars and the side shops in the area or played cricket in the gully. They had been her schoolmates in primary school; the ones who failed the Common Entrance and were not bothering with school again. She was amazed at the way they suddenly seemed to mature. Some were growing moustaches and beards and their voices were deeper, more manly. They had been friends with whom she had stolen golf balls from the golf course and eaten unripe mangoes. Sometimes they greeted her, sometimes they didn't. She never tried to understand why; it was quite normal. She knew she was more fortunate than them and that some of them thought she was just a spoilt girl. But then they had always felt that way so it didn't bother her. Caddy, though, was always glad to see her.

After passing through this district, the gully was narrowed by thick forests on both sides for a few hundred yards. She enjoyed this area most because it was the quietest and most isolated. It was the only place where she felt safe to pee by the concrete wall without anyone seeing. Doing this in the wide open was somehow exciting, even though she only did it when she felt she couldn't wait until she got home.

She would read along this stretch, occasionally looking up to watch the dart of birds from one side of the gully to the other. She walked under another bridge that was never used by cars and then she came to the tributary that passed just behind her backyard. She climbed up the thick concrete slope, walked along the edge of the tributary for a few yards and then turned up the path that led through the short patch of bush onto an open lot. This was owned by the people who had built the house in the lot beside it. It was the largest and most elaborate house on the avenue, and the houses in the avenue were all quite large. The owners of this particular house were rich. The man was a politician and his sons all worked in the family business. All except one: Felix. Felix stayed at home.

She put her books in her bag and began to run through the open lot to the avenue. A dog from the politician's house began to bark and to paw at the fence. Felix looked out through the grill. His face was red and full of pimples and sores.

"What you doing in there?" he shouted over the dog barking.

"Nothing," she said, slowing down. She was frightened.

"I will set the dog on you, you know," he shouted back.

"Sorry," she said, moving slowly towards the avenue.

"I will set Charles on you, you know," he shouted again.

"Sorry," she said as she reached the road.

She began to run up the road. The dog chased her along the fence, jumping, barking, with a mouth full of foam.

"Get her, Charles, get her, get her!" Felix stood behind the fence screaming.

She hesitated a little near the gate. She wasn't sure if the dog could jump the gate. She started to move and the dog was there snarling. Soon dogs from the other houses had joined in the noise. She was terrified. She stood still, almost in tears.

"Get her, Charles. He can jump the fence, you know!" Felix was still screaming at the top of his voice.

"Call your dog, please," she said, still unable to move. "Please."

"Felix! Felix!" A woman's voice came from the back of the house. "Felix! Felix!"

"Yes, Ma."

The woman was on the verandah now. "What are you doing? What kind of nonsense is this?"

"She was trespassing. I set Charles on her. He can jump the fence." Felix was much taller than his mother. He looked down at her, his face glowing with great intensity.

"Oh, God. Felix…" She saw the girl in the white uniform standing transfixed in the road.

"Go on, little girl, the dog won't trouble you… go on. Come, Charles… Come…"

The dog stopped barking and moved towards the girl,

177

wagging its tail. As the girl moved for the first time the dog suddenly barked again, but this time it was at the woman. The bark became a playful whine as the dog wagged its tail so aggressively that it seemed about to dislocate its spine. The girl did not wait. She ran at full speed towards her home. She did not look back.

That night she promised herself never to walk though the gully again. She would walk along the road and hope that Felix did not see her. She told no one about it, but the incident really frightened her.

But the problem with Felix and the dog did not happen again, and soon she began walking through the gully as usual, waving to the gardener and Caddy and watching the crazy crows circle dizzily above the dry gully walls.

2

They said he was mad. He had heard that all his life and while he didn't believe it, he grew to live it. He wasn't mad. He was slow. He was different; he knew that. He was the only person who dared to kill john-crows with his catapult. Most boys said it was illegal to kill the sleek black buzzards but Caddy wanted a close-up look at this huge crow so he shot one and showed it to his friends. They were all amazed at its size and the smooth texture of the pink bald head that had buried itself in so many carcasses, but they were even more convinced that he was mad.

He was aggressive; he knew that.

The other boys expected it from him. He played cricket aggressively. He never learnt to bowl properly but he flung the ball with more force than anyone else. He batted well and so very often he spent most of the recess time batting. Few boys dared to go after a ball while he was going after it. He threw his size around and kicked, pushed and punched while trying to get the ball to bowl. His greatest pleasure was to hear the loud bang of ball on the metal desk that was their makeshift wicket.

Caddy was a black child with half-brothers and sisters who could pass for white. They, more than he, with their tattered clothing, skins reddened from walking miles in the sun, and the thick patois they spoke, were targets for bullying and abuse. They were self-evidently a worthless lot, squandering the advantage of their skin, so useless that even with their whiteness they remained hopelessly poor. There was a more deep-seated reason for their targeting for persecution. Their poverty was a threat to the almost comforting article of faith among their black neighbours that race and race alone was the cause of their poverty. If the poverty of Caddy's family was the result of their hopelessness, what then of theirs?

The bullying, though, was more intended than carried out. Caddy saw to that. He worked hard to protect his siblings, took great pains to ensure that they lived a remarkably spoilt life at school. They would complain to him and he would punish those of their friends who were unwilling to comply with their wishes.

He wasn't always called Caddy. He was called a lot of other things like "Blacka", "Last Night", "Midnight", "Bigga", "Tar Baby", "Maddix", "Toughas", and a variety of other names referring either to his size, his colour or his temperament. He fought his way out of all of them. He selected "Caddy" because he wanted to play golf himself one day and the little girl who used to walk home with them everyday said the boys walking with the golfers were called caddies. So he named himself Caddy and was soon substituting the title Caddy for words like "I", "me" and "mine" until it became clear that Caddy was the only safe name to call him.

Caddy knew he wasn't very bright. He liked to read, though he read very slowly, but he hated maths and really made no effort to understand. His mother said that his father was like that too. He knew everything about his father because his mother was not the type to hide those things from her children. His father was dead. He died in jail in America, she said. He was a big construction worker who did not speak much but could fight. She was a higgler in front of the building

179

this man was working on. They got along well, she said. She was the only person who could control him. They never lived together, but he used to visit her. When she was pregnant he went to Montego Bay to work. Then he went away to America. He got into some dark deals up there and they caught him. He died in jail. She said he was a very black man and she should have known that anything too black was worthless. Caddy, she said, was just like his father and he was going to get into the same mess if he wasn't careful. She hoped, though, that the other children would take after *their* father. He was white – a successful businessman who gave her money now and then. She had been a servant in his house. He did not care about his outside children. He was quite clear about that.

But she didn't dislike Caddy. In fact he knew that she loved him and depended on him. She used to beat him a lot because, according to her, his skin could take it. He didn't mind that. She didn't expect him to do very well in school and so when he repeated a few grades she did not punish him much. She just forced him to find work cutting lawns and painting houses in the afternoons. She argued with him a lot but she was rarely surprised by the things he did. Even when he said he wanted to go to extension school downtown, she said it would be okay as long as he still worked.

She heard about all the things he was supposed to have done. She knew half of them were stories – though some were true.

It was true he used to sneak into the paddock at night, lead one of the horses out and spend a good portion of the night riding it on the golf course. He stopped doing it when the owners got complaints that their horses were causing girls in the convent, which was beside the golf course, difficulty sleeping at night. He found out that most of the girls in the school had heard about his cowboy stunts on the golf course. The little girl who walked through the gully mentioned it to him one day. He was pleased that she was amused. She just laughed and said: "Boy, Caddy, you are something else."

It was also true that he was the most remarkable mango

thief in the district. He went to places that most boys dared not enter. He went into the most affluent residential areas where the dogs were the fiercest, the yards the largest, but mangoes most abundant and sweet. He picked only pedigree mangoes: Julies with their blandly sweet, subtly aromatic but large, chunky fruit; Bombays with their tangy, fleshy fruit, and the hood-ended East Indians that that were the sweetest, juiciest mango anyone knew of. It was also true that he had killed a few dogs with stones and had gotten in trouble with the police because of this.

It was also true that Caddy was one of the boys who had burnt down the post office. When he heard that the boys wanted to cause some trouble as close to the police station as possible he was happy to join them. They wanted his help because he was daring, not to say crazy. He was the last person to leave the scene. He was impressed with the blaze. He had been pleased with himself for being a part of it, because the little girl had complained to him that the post office was inefficient and she wasn't getting her letters on time. She wasn't pleased when it had burnt down and that had upset him.

He made friends with some of the golfers, the richer older men. He became caddy for Mr. Ernest, the politician, who hired Caddy to do his lawn and garden as well as be his caddy. He encouraged Caddy to play golf and gave him his first two clubs. They were old and Mr. Ernest had gotten a new set. Caddy thought Mr. Ernest was a good man though he never allowed Caddy to get familiar. He knew Mr. Ernest was also a very powerful man, not afraid to walk through the district and talk to the people because he had men there who looked after his interests. Caddy hoped that Mr. Ernest would make him one of those men soon. The men lived in Mr. Ernest's yard. They came from the district but he insisted that they stay in the small house behind the big house. They were guards for the house and they got along well with the dogs that were always chained to the twelve-foot chain-link fence behind it.

Mr. Ernest asked Caddy to befriend his son, Felix. Felix

was retarded. He was the only one of Mr. Ernest's sons who was not working in his garment factory. Felix said he wasn't born that way, but the pressure was too much for him. Felix said his mother and father were wicked and ever since he was a boy they had tried to dump him. He wanted Caddy to understand this. Felix talked a lot about his family. He claimed he only told these things to Caddy but Caddy doubted it.

He would watch Caddy mowing the lawn from the grilled verandah as he squeezed his pimples and wiped the little worms that curled out of his face onto his clothes. He would call Caddy over to talk.

"My father," he began, "my father said you are a dangerous guy."

"Your father say that?" Caddy asked, after emptying a bottle of water in a few long gulps.

"Yes."

"Uhmm." Caddy looked into the sun, squinting his eyes. "Hot."

"Daddy, my father… he had another woman, you know…" He waited for a response. Caddy said nothing.

"You don' believe me? Ask mummy, my mother. She knows. It's a woman who works at the factory. A young girl. He have more than one woman but my mother only knows about her. And guess what?"

Caddy looked into the sun again. He said nothing. Felix pushed his shoulder.

"Guess what?"

"What?" Caddy said without conviction.

"Sherlock screwing that same woman too…" He laughed a very strange and loud laugh that was too sudden and too energetic. He kept laughing until water filled his eyes. Caddy smiled because he did not know what else to do.

"Yes, Sherlock screwing her too. And Shane used to screw her. You know that? The men in this family love women. We love women too much. Like Daddy. He's like that. We love women. Me too… I love women."

Caddy chuckled slightly.

"You don' believe me? You think I am a battyman, nuh, like you?" He said stepping back and laughing.

"Daddy said you are a battyman, you know."

"You better mind your mout', you hear?" Caddy was not amused and did not really care if he found himself punching the little fool in the mouth.

"What happen? Is lie?" Felix said, still laughing.

"Shut yuh mout'! You hear me?" Caddy turned sharply on Felix. "Don' call me no battyman, you hear?"

"Aright, aright... is jus' a joke." Felix was noticeably shaken. "So you like girls then. Me too, I like girls. I screw that woman already: Myrtle, the helper. I screw her right in the living room. She never want to do it, but I screw her and I know she like it. And I tell her if she tell mummy, my mother, she would lose the work. Screw her right on the sofa."

Caddy got up and started towards the lawn. Felix followed.

"You ever screw yet?"

Caddy did not answer.

"You know who I want to screw now? You know who? I want to screw Mrs. Marshall, Shirley, who live next door and that same woman in the factory. I want to screw all of them."

Caddy went to work on the lawn again. He started the mower and drowned out Felix's fantasies. Felix went back to the verandah and sat there watching Caddy. His eyes slowly glazed over and his mind drifted far from the verandah. He continued to squeeze the huge red blotches on his face. His other hand rubbed the thin red hairs on his chest. Caddy continued to mow.

The girl came up the gully path and walked quickly through the open lot. She saw Caddy. He saw her too. He figured it was her by the uniform and as she came closer he was sure of it. She waved to him and he waved back, watching as she moved past the verandah, then by the front gate and disappeared up the road. Felix saw this. He walked to the front gate looking after her until she turned into her yard. Then he walked over to Caddy and shouted.

"I want to screw her too!"

Caddy wanted to ignore him, but he continued:

"You don' want to screw her too? Nice girl, you know. Nice little girl. She like me, I know that. Hey, you know how you can screw her? Well, she walk in that gully everyday, jus' wait for her and..."

He did not get the chance to finish. Caddy slapped him across the face with such force that it threw him to the ground, then he punched him in the face with both fists. Felix struggled to get away, screaming at the top of his voice. One of the guards came from behind the house and pulled Caddy off. Felix was still screaming at the top of his voice.

"I gwine screw her. I gwine screw her, you watch, you watch, battyman, battyman!" He went into the house and returned with a gun.

"You wan' me shoot you, you wan' me shoot you? I will shoot you, you hear, you little battyman!"

He pointed the gun but didn't fire it. He just stood there looking around distractedly as if waiting for someone to stop him. The helper came out and took the gun from him and then guided him into the house. He threw his body on her and started to bawl loudly. The door shut on the noise of his screaming. The guard told Caddy to go home. He asked no questions, he just said, "Go home."

3

Five john-crows circled, each on a different level, swooping and swerving under slowly moving white clouds in a still and strangely peaceful blue sky. From afar the black crows looked glorious.

Faint smoke from a fire in the forest beside the gully slowly drifted upwards and then vanished in the still sky. The sun was directly overhead and it beat down relentlessly.

One of the john-crows swooped down gracefully just below the tree-line and then just as languidly flapped its wings twice as it swayed back into the sky, joining the circle dance. They waited for stillness before they would land.

184

The forest was silent.

In the gully a strong stench of rotting flesh filled the air. It was so intense that it seemed visible.

Three men, two in uniform, stood in a triangle around a clump of bushes. At a distance, a woman, plump, with shining skin, stood holding the edge of her dress to her face. The policemen were continually spitting and waving flies away with their hands. One of them moved towards the clump and disappeared behind the thick bushes. He came back out stumbling somewhat and dragging a rope behind him. The rope was taut for a while, then suddenly became slack. He dropped the rope and turned away from the clump with his handkerchief over his mouth. He walked quickly to the opposite wall, leaned on it and began to vomit violently. The other two policemen, one in uniform, the other in white short sleeves and black trousers, held their stomachs and watched their friend with grim faces. Suddenly the plain-clothes officer was retching just where he stood.

"Jesus Christ! Jesus Christ! Man!" the third policeman said. "I tell you, I tell you, man… Jesus Christ, man!"

"Where them guys with the masks, man?" the plain-clothes officer said, wiping his mouth with the handkerchief and putting it to his nose.

"You radio them?"

"Yes sir." The third policeman watched his companion leaning on the wall.

"What I tell you? You see what them do to her? You see it? Jesus Christ man, I never see nothing like that yet? Jesus Christ, man?" He spat.

"Stop it!" the plain-clothes man said. "We have to bring her out of there."

"Not me, sah! No way. That is… Oh God, is only a little girl," he said shaking his head.

"I cyaan tek the smell, sah. When the mask them come. You want to see her?"

"I have seen her. You alright, Jones?" he asked the officer who was sweating by the wall.

"Is not the first dead body you see. Or is the firs' one you never shoot?" The officer laughed nervously.

"Is wickedness... wickedness... poor ting." The woman standing afar off still held the skirt to her face. "I never know it was somebody t'row down here, but when I look... the john-crow them pick out her eye them... Oh Lord, have mercy, why them do dat to this lickle girl. It is a nice girl, yuh know... nice girl."

"You know her?" the officer in plain clothes asked.

"She live up the hill," the woman said. "She walk this way everyday. She just go to that school up so..."

"I see the uniform..." The officer turned away.

"Come, Jones, come man, pull the body out here so, come man."

"No sir," Jones said, leaning on the wall. "Cyann look at that, sir. Is a lickle girl."

"Jesus Christ man, Jesus Christ!" the third officer was muttering. Then he put his handkerchief over his face and moved to the clump of bushes. He picked up the rope and began to pull...

"Maggots, you wan' see maggots..." he said, his voice muffled by the handkerchief.

The woman gave a small scream when she saw the black shoes and the blue socks with the rope tied to it.

The officer dragged the burden onto the clear concrete area leaving a trail of moisture and white worms where the head bobbed.

The girl's hair was splattered with blood, but the thick plaits were still somehow intact. The crows had made craters where her eyes should have been, dark holes with red lining and worms crawling around. Her skin had darkened in death. In her forehead was a huge hole. Her mouth was still clearly formed and her teeth stuck out under the tight lips. Her right arm was twisted behind her back and the navy-blue ribbon was hanging loosely on her neck, and under it her white belt was pulled tightly around her neck, embedded in her flesh. Her white dress was dirty with mud and dust. There were

186

black and red holes across her chest. Four of them. The dress was torn where the wounds were. Her dress was lifted above her waist. She had on no underwear. The area that was her vagina was a massive wound lined with a slippery dryness that was cracked like the dry blood around the wound. Her thighs were marked with black bruises, round blotches of black. Her knees were dry and cracking with the same slippery dryness. Her bag was still around her shoulders but it dragged through the lines of moisture and maggots coming from her head.

The flies danced around and inside her body.

The plain-clothes officer moved forward to look and stood still for a few seconds. Slowly he began to shake his head. He spat as fluid began to gather in his mouth. He wiped his lips and covered his nostrils, standing very still. Fluid filled his mouth again and he spat to his side. He tried to distance himself from the child, but the wounds glared back at him.

Stab wounds… strangled to death with her belt… gagged with the ribbon, her mouth sore at the edges; those flies, why don't they leave her alone…? John-crows ate her eyes. They eat the eyes first. Why? Why not the largest wound, like the small mouth torn open. Strangled to death perhaps. Stab wounds. Stabbed to death. Bleeding: insignificant. Did they rape her before or after? Approximate age 14 years, maybe 13. She hasn't got breasts. No hair. Who the hell could do a thing like that? She is about Clarissa's age. Haven't ever seen Clarissa's stomach, not since she was two. We should cover her body. Those flies. Flies give birth to maggots who in turn become flies. They eat the eyes first.

Jesus Christ!

He turned to move from the body and his stomach twisted violently. He moved towards the woman, holding his mouth. She turned away as he began to vomit again.

The third officer watched, almost wanting to gloat but feeling absolutely sickened by the sight and the stench.

"You have the sheet?" the plain-clothes officer asked, his mouth sour with vomit.

"Yes sir." The third officer said.

"Cover her up," he said. "Blow away the flies firs'..."

The third officer moved to the pile of folders and briefcases and took out a stained white sheet. He walked up to the body and waved away the flies with the sheet as much as he could. Then he picked up a small stick and moved it towards the hem of the girl's dress.

"Don't touch it...her..." the plain-clothes man said sharply.

"But, officer...she..." The policeman still kept the stick on the dress.

"Alright, alright," the plain-clothes man said. They had already moved the corpse, disturbing the crime scene. They had taken the photos. That was enough. It would make no difference. The position of the body did not matter in these cases. Someone would come forward, someone would know. It was just a matter of time.

"Cover her," he said. *Cover the poor child*, he said in his head.

The officer pulled the dress over her stomach and legs. Then he covered the body with a sheet. Climbing over the body he walked behind the clumps of bushes grunting through his nose and spitting. He came back out with two books and an immaculately white pair of panties. He held the panties on the stick while keeping the books between a folded piece of brown paper.

"Put them there..." the plainclothes man said pointing to the briefcase and folder. "Nothing else?"

"Cyaan see nothing else, sir." The officer said. "But we coulda look."

"Yes... Jones... Jones."

"Yes sir?" Jones straightened up and moved towards the officer.

"Jesus Christ, man. Jesus Christ! How man coulda be so sick, so damn wicked. What she coulda do...?" The third officer was moving through the bushes looking for evidence.

"You said you know her?" the plain-clothes man said to the woman.

"Yes sir. I think she live up on Radial Drive. That is jus' up so and she normally walk this way and she use to go to school with my daughter... my daughter..." She was crying.

188

The crows circled, hanging above the dry gully. The sun was relentless in the blue plate of sky and the clouds hardly moved or changed their shape.

4

When Caddy heard that the girl was dead he knew who had done it. He said nothing. He just disappeared for a week. He ran away to his grandmother in the country because he was hurting. But the story followed him on the radio and in the newspapers. If he had stayed he would have killed Felix because he knew that Felix had done it.

He spent a week hiding out in the woods during the day, only coming in late at nights to sleep. He did not eat much and he did not explain what the problem was to his grand-mother. She knew Caddy was strange and she assumed he had fought with her daughter again. She suspected that if Caddy couldn't run away to her little house in Mandeville, there was a risk he would do something dangerous. Here it was cooler and he did not have to deal with so many people, so it was less dangerous. She asked him no questions. She moved slowly about her business, cooking for him, washing his dirty clothes and sometimes singing hymns in the hope that he would hear and be transformed. She knew that only one thing could help him but she didn't know whether she had the strength to confront his demons.

After a week Caddy knew what he was going to do.

5

Caswell ran. He always ran. Sometimes they caught him, sometimes they didn't, but he always took the chance and ran. He knew the gully area better than any of them so he knew he could lose them. So he ran when he heard them.

His work demanded that he could run. Sometimes he picked mangoes, ackees, cashews, breadfruits, sweet sops, sour sops, guineps, tamarinds from the trees of the wealthy people who lived in the hills. He would go around with his fourteen foot pole with a wire hook at the end, and he would pull down fruit which he would place in his basket and carry the booty down to Constant Spring market where he would sell the stolen goods. Sometimes he had to run from dogs, from angry homeowners, and sometimes from the police. But this was what he did.

If Caswell was not running from them for that reason, he was running from them because they knew he sold weed which he harvested from an old Rastaman's plot of land high in the hills. He knew how to run and how to hide the weed in places that he could return to later. Running was something he was good at. He could clear fences, leap into gullies, skid around shacks and houses and disappear from the best of them.

He knew when to run, knew when they would start running, too. He could size up the police, work out how strong they were as runners by their size and he would pace himself accordingly. He knew when to stay far away enough to avoid angering them; he knew that sometimes they might want to shoot, but he also knew that most times they would give up easily because he was a petty thief. He was petty; he was not worth the effort.

When he was not running he was looking for quick work cleaning out gardens, bushing yards, running errands for helpers, trying to make a quick money whenever he could. Then he would not run much. But he also used that time to work out how best to break into a house, to work out what was valuable in a house. He did not always use the information for himself. Sometimes he sold it to his friends, a few of whom were really committed thieves. He did not like to steal, not like that. There was nothing he feared more than the death of a thief at the hands of an irate Jamaican mob. They killed thieves. They tortured thieves and then beat them to death. It was the most horrible thing to witness. He had seen some of his friends bloodied by these mobs – they turned on you quickly and with clear-eyed viciousness. Once he had to run from a mob. He outran everyone but a short stocky boy who gained on him and then lunged at him with a stone, trying to bring him down. Caswell had avoided the boy and then kicked him in the groin. The boy fell over in pain and Caswell ran away, his heart thumping. He did not like to steal. Sometimes he had to, but only if there was some righteous reason to do so. He would steal from thieves and from those who he regarded as unscrupulous. God's mercy did not extend to those.

"Hey bwoy, stop! stop!" a policeman shouted from the car parked in front of one of the shops that overlooked the roadway that traversed the gully.

Caswell ran.

The two policemen jumped out of the car, slamming the doors. The plain-clothes officer in shirtsleeves stepped out of the back door with a pistol in his hand. He followed the other two officers, who carried a submachine and a shotgun, along with their revolvers.

"Don' shoot him, you hear!" he shouted after them as they took off down the gully after the short black man in khaki shorts and a red singlet.

The plain-clothes man stopped running and went back to the police car. Two women stood beside the car.

"Is him, officer. Is a little bad boy. I know is him do it. Caswell, 'im name. A damn t'ief. And 'im wicked, too," one said.

"Wicked, wicked. A girl say him rape her already," the other said.

"Which girl?" the first woman asked.

"Elsie… you know Elsie…?" the other woman said.

"That is a little bitch. Anybody can rape her!" The first woman laughed.

"Well, she say him rape her." The other woman laughed too.

"Dat gial cyan rape. Dutty gial love buddy too much. A longer time she a try get dat Caswell bway fe ride her," one woman said laughing.

191

They were now laughing, both of them.

The officer was doubtful about these two women. He did not think they were reliable. But the old man who lived on the edge of the gully and a few other people said they had seen this short black fellow in red singlet and khaki shorts walking through the gully towards the hills on the day that the girl must have been killed. They said he was carrying a long pole with a wire hook at the end and a huge bag. He was probably going to pick ackees, but he also carried a very sharp-looking machete. They said the girl walked by there a few minutes after and so he must have done it. He was the kind of fellow to do something like that. The officer wasn't sure, he just wanted to question the man. He was looking for someone who was insane, not a hardened thief like this short black fellow.

Caswell was breathing heavily now, but he did not panic. He knew the limits if his lungs and he knew that he could continue at this pace for a long time. He could hear their footsteps on the cement floor not far behind. He knew that he did not have to stop because they were not supposed to shoot him and they wouldn't catch him at the rate things were going. He was sweating. He had reasons to run. Normally, he would have stopped if he heard instructions not to shoot, but this time he would have gotten into trouble.

Caswell reluctantly pulled out the lump of newspaper filled with dried ganja leaves and tossed it into the bushes to one side. He noted where he had thrown it. Then he discarded his knife, a huge two-edged weapon that he claimed he used to peel oranges. Then he threw out the four gold chains in the other pocket. He couldn't see where they'd gone, but he'd return and find them later. He was still running as he reached for the gold watch at the bottom of his pocket. He had to discard all these things because the helper must have suspected him of taking them and told the police. She had not seen him, but if she did not point at somebody, she would lose the job.

He hadn't been back to the house for a few days after the girl's body was found, and they hadn't tried to find him to ask him back or pay him after he'd spent most of the week cutting the hedge around the house. So he had slipped back and gotten something for his work. There was no point in trying to get them to pay. They wouldn't. They were all like that. They worked people because they could. He would go and ask and they would say they did not know what he was talking about. Anyway, he did not want to go back to that family. The mess with the dead girl and the crazy son was more than he wanted. He would find something better. He just knew he had to get some pay for his work and this was a simple way. The dogs knew him well now and they let him walk by without raising a stink. He knew when the helper would go down the street to pick up some groceries every day. He watched her from the corner as she walked hurriedly in the stark sunlight, her faded blue and worn shin length denim dress flopping in the humid breeze. Then he went in quickly through the back grill he knew she would have left open.

Caswell got what he needed and left through the thick mango grove behind the house that stopped at the edge of the gully. He jumped down into the gully and trotted away, his fingers toying with the gold watch he had found in that crazy boy's room, sitting there like a plea for attention on his dresser. It was a woman's watch and it made him wonder why the son would have a woman's watch in his room. The room itself was bare and seemed unoccupied, as if someone had moved out recently. The bed was stripped and the pillows were piled to one side. He pulled open a few drawers and finding nothing, quickly moved to another room. He calculated rapidly what he thought was a fair wage for his labours. He took only a few things. A few small items.

Now he knew they were onto him. The helper must have suggested that he was the one. Maybe she saw him. He was not sure about much now except his running. He was focused, aware of his body, of the fluid action of his arms, of the calm pace of his breathing; he gauged that he had enough stamina to last a long time at this pace, enough strength in his legs to burst into a sprint whenever he wanted to. He liked the feeling of power that came over him as he felt the earth moving under him, the way the wind hit him in the face, the way that space was eaten up by his strides.

He kept running.

The policeman caught sight of the red singlet bobbing its way up one of the concrete slopes and about to disappear into the thick bushes just above the gully. He was sure that this was the guy who did it. He knew this boy. He was a tough and wicked fellow and he would rape a girl and do that to her. He stopped suddenly and lifted the revolver. The other policeman stopped and looked at him.

"I gwine kill the dog. Jesus Christ, man. I gwine shoot the dog," he said slowly, aiming at the bobbing red patch.

"He say don' kill..." The other policeman was suddenly silent. He couldn't do anything.

The shot echoed in the gully. Birds rose above the trees. The red patch stopped suddenly and the short black man fell over the gully wall landing heavily on his shoulder.

"Bitch!" The policeman smiled with the gun still pointed. "Bitch!"

They walked up slowly. The short black man was groaning loudly on the ground. The bullet had disfigured his head. He was dead but unwilling to die. He was groaning and clawing at the concrete as if reaching for something. They found the gold watch in his pocket. It was the same watch described by the girl's mother.

"Stinking dog!" The policeman said, spitting.

"I don't give a rass. This dog fe dead."

They dragged the body by the feet to the bridge, leaving a trail of blood on the concrete. It was all very untidy.

"Felix not here," the helper said, through the grill. Her face was shining with sweat. Her head was covered with a floral scarf. "Felix gone weh from las' week."

"Mr. Ernest there?" Caddy shouted from the gate because the other dogs were unchained and lying in the driveway. The three vicious ones were lying harmlessly looking at him. The less ferocious, Charles, was barking himself hoarse and spewing foam all over the concrete.

"Him say him don' need you to work today; the grass cut two day now." She kept looking behind her.

"Mr. Ernest in there?" Caddy shouted again.

"Him say him don' need you today." She was almost pleading with him. "Come back nex' week. Alright?"

"I wan' see Mr. Ernest," Caddy shouted. "If him in dere tell him I have to see him. Is about Felix."

Mr. Ernest stood in the doorway. He wore white pants and a white shirt carefully tucked into the pants. He wore a pair of white brogues and a black belt. His hair was slick against his head. He had a fresh, clean look about him, as if he had just showered and shaved. He said something to the helper that Caddy could not hear. She bowed her head and walked into the house. Mr. Ernest walked into the light on the verandah. His clothes glowed in the sunlight.

He unlocked the grill and walked slowly towards the gate. The three sleeping dogs got up and followed him to the gate, growling.

"Sit down, sit down, man!" Mr. Ernest said. They hesitated. "You don' hear. Sit down. Go back, go back!"

The three dogs moved back to almost the exact same spots they were in before. They circled the area slowly, their paws clicking on the concrete ground. Then they lay down and watched. Charles was silent but he kept prancing about.

"What you want?" Mr. Ernest asked, standing a few yards from the gate. One of the guards had come from behind the house. His waist bulged with a gun. Caddy could see a black object sticking out under the shirt. He stood at the end of the driveway, watching as if he just happened to be passing by. Mr. Ernest did not seem to notice him.

"Sir… sorry…" Caddy started.

"Jus' talk man, come talk." Mr. Ernest used the same tone that had used on the dogs. "What you want?"

Caddy began to have doubts about doing what he intended to say, but he thought about the girl and decided to go ahead.

"Is Felix, sir," he began.

"Felix not here," Mr. Ernest said. He sucked his teeth trying to dislodge a piece of beef. Then he stuck his finger into his mouth to pick it out.

"I know, but… Mr. Ernest, is Felix kill that girl, Mr. Ernest," Caddy said quickly.

Mr. Ernest barely reacted. He stopped poking at the tooth for a split second and then continued. He pulled the finger from his mouth and sucked the tooth again while wiping the finger with a handkerchief. Then he pulled the dark glasses from his breast pocket and began to wipe them slowly with the handkerchief. He looked down at his hands as he spoke.

"Who tell you that?"

"Him say him was going to do it, Mr. Ernest. Ask Myrtle, she hear him," Caddy said quickly. He wasn't sure whether Mr. Ernest was upset or not.

"Yesterday they kill the man who do it. You never hear?" Mr. Ernest put on the silver-framed dark glasses. His nose twitched a bit.

"Is not that man do it, sir. Is not him, is Felix…" Caddy said.

"How you know?" Mr. Ernest spoke slowly and calmly.

Caddy felt awkward. He was sure it was Felix but he wasn't sure he could convince Mr. Ernest if Mr. Ernest was intent on not being convinced. In an odd way, Caddy had expected Mr. Ernest to find a solution based on the simple truth that Felix had done it. But now it was clear that Mr. Ernest had made up his mind. He would demand evidence from Caddy. Mr. Ernest always wanted facts. Immediately. He always asked Caddy to give his own estimate of what he should be paid for any work he did. He knew Mr. Ernest did this to ensure that the payment was low. Mr. Ernest knew that people would underestimate the cost of their services when they were dealing with him. Caddy knew what Mr. Ernest was doing, yet he always charged less than he deserved. He always felt cheated. Mr. Ernest always wanted the estimate on the spot.

"He said so," Caddy said uncertainly. "Right here so."

"That's how you know?" Mr. Ernest asked, looking directly at Caddy. Caddy could not see his eyes.

If Mr. Ernest had been there that day he would understand why, he would believe, Caddy thought, but he couldn't prove it. He began to feel it was a bad idea to tell the man.

"So tha's how you know?" Mr. Ernest said a little louder than before. Caddy knew he was getting upset.

"Yes sir…"

"Hmmm." Mr. Ernest shook his head. Then he waited, still looking at Caddy. The sky and earth were evenly divided in black and white in the reflection of his dark glasses. "So what you going to do?"

"Well… I was goin' tell the police, sir," Caddy said quietly. He looked at his hands.

"Police?" Mr. Ernest said, in a tone that seemed to sneer at the absurdity of Caddy's statement. "You going to tell the police that my son murder that lickle girl who live up the road from us. You going to tell the police that…"

Caddy was silent.

"Eh?" Mr. Ernest shouted.

"Yes, sir," Caddy said quickly.

"Go home and sleep, boy, you hear me? Go home and sleep, you hear?"

"I have to tell them, sir. I cyaan do no better, sir." Caddy now realized what he was doing. He realized that Mr. Ernest was very angry. "You ask Felix, sir? You ask him if is him, Mr. Ernest? Ask him, sir, jus' ask him an' see…"

"You hear what I say, Caddy?" Mr. Ernest stepped closer. "You hear what I say?"

"But…" Caddy started.

"Go home," Mr. Ernest said.

"I have to tell the police den, sir." Caddy was stammering. His heart was sounding through his entire body.

"Oh," Mr. Ernest said calmly, "oh…" as if he had received a pleasant revelation and had arrived at some simple conclusion.

"Yes sir." Caddy pulled back from the gate. "I gone, sir… But you mus' ask him."

Mr. Ernest said nothing. He watched Caddy walk down the road into the open lot. Charles chased the boy along the fence barking madly. Caddy was unnerved by the barking. He walked unsteadily along the path into the gully. As he disappeared past that sign that read "No Trespassing. Trespassers Will Be Prosecuted" and into the bush just above the forest, Mr. Ernest called the guard to him. They stood talking for a while, then Mr. Ernest went inside and the guard disappeared behind the house.

7

Above the gully, five john-crows circled, swooping into the gully occasionally and soaring upwards, flapping noiselessly in the very still sky. Caddy smelt the residual stench of rotting flesh in the air. As he reached nearer to the area of the gully lined with the thickest trees the stench increased. The crows circled again closer to his head and he remembered the peculiar texture of the crows' bald head and rough feathers. He kept walking, the stench thick in his nostrils and heavy in his stomach.

He heard footsteps behind him, but he didn't look back.

The crows dipped and circled in the still blue sky. The sun was relentless on the cracked cement of the gully.

Vershan III

CHOKOTA

Vershan III

CHOKOTA

Like the wilderness sound of Burning Spear, the horns announcing the arrival of the prophet – an Isaiah speaking into the barren world – the music comes. This music is the wind in a desert somewhere in northern Ghana, and a man is searching for his past, searching for some meaning in that past. On his feet are the worn red and black sandals of earth-walkers. There is dirt in the air, there is a sun, relentless in the air, and somewhere in the forest on the other side is the voice.

Sometimes songs came to Kwaku Blue in dreams like this. He did not know his father. Yet in his dreams he was always walking through a desert searching for a kraal, a village where the elders are gathered and waiting for him to return, to be welcomed.

Kwaku Blue always felt a stranger in Jamaica. His name. His statement of difference. "I am Kwaku Blue. I am from Ghana. That is which part I was born." And his nicknames were always mocking Africa, mocking him: Unka, Cudjoe, Tarzan Cousin, and on and on. At night he comforted himself with the dream of a long path through that desert land with sharp rocks marking a road that pointed him to the village where his father was always waiting:

Scratch, scratch, scratch the dust with a stick
Sand dance 'round the old man's head
African elder on the desert edge
Teacher from Togo say, "Look back,
Come back to the track."
Oh, calling me back
Oh, calling me back.

Kwaku Blue sang this song with the gritty, long-suffering lamentation of Burning Spear, and his voice would settle on the slow one-drop, the circular bass line and the dirge-like dreadness of the sound. He moved his hips with a slow sensual ease, as if beyond himself, beyond the dread truth of the music.

Wood already burn wid fire
Is black, blacker dan black
Firewood dat taste the fire
Ain't hard to catch alight
Ain't hard to burn so bright
Ain't hard to catch alight

He carried a dream in his head every time he sang this song. In the dream he is standing in Ghana. He is a tall man, and there, walking through the yoyi trees, is a man with eyes like his, with a nose like his, with skin, black and shiny like polished ebony, walking with his head upright, his chest bare, his shoulders firm and broad, coming towards him with a face of tender welcome. He sees the man coming and behind him a whole history of people, faces, eyes trying to receive him too. In the dream he walks to the man and they embrace. The man speaks in a language that Kwaku Blue should not understand, yet he understands it. The man is saying: *Welcome home. Now you can stop waiting for something to slow down in you, waiting for something to happen. You spent all your life expecting something to happen. It has happened now.* Kwaku Blue nods for in this dream the man knows him better than he knows himself. The man knows everything that is terrible about him, everything that is secret about him, every mystery he has not understood, every fear. This man knows all this, yet understands and embraces him. He no longer has to wait.

Chokota on the village soil
My ears on the noisy ground
Oh, black man, how long yuh been waiting

Oh my father how long yuh been waiting
For me to come on back

When others heard this song, they said it was a song about Africa as home, about Africa as the spiritual home of the black man. They watched as Kwaku Blue bent his face to the guitar and strummed out the slow beat of the tune as he began to sing, tentatively at first and then with more and more confidence, the song he had dreamt. In the studio in Ocho Rios, they nodded, acknowledging that something powerful was there. Kwaku Blue did not usually have the song's melody so sharply defined when he brought a song in, but this one was set, and he rode the guitar with an assured sense of knowing, eyes closed.

The bass player joined in first, trying to find something round and yet haunting, something that could ground this song, this journey to a past, all their pasts. But what no one knew was that Kwaku Blue was desperately depressed as he sang of this dream that was just a dream of something that would not happen. He did not know his father. The man he saw in the desert was a stranger. The man he asked for light, for direction, was a stranger.

Give, give, give gimme a light old man
I tell you how, how this journey long
My mamma tell me dat I've got your eyes
Your eye dem full up wid water
As you call me back,
I hear yuh singing…

Soon the rest of the band was finding its place. Kwaku Blue put the guitar down and stood with his hands clutching the microphone, his voice trying to transform the dream into something he could believe. The music washed over him. He stood alone before the face of this music and felt far from the rest of the world. In such moments he would pour everything into the singing, trying to make it real, trying to make his pain sound through.

I hear the message
Understand the message
I hear the message
Understand the message
Calling me back
Calling me back
Calling me back
Calling me back.

THE POET

THE POET

None of the cars could move. A VW squatted stubbornly in the middle of the intersection; the driver, a woman, glared up at the driver of the white minibus. He smoked lazily, the sun's reflection bouncing off his shades. A taxi driver tried to twist a way around the cars by driving onto the pavement. He had to stop when a pick-up truck driver tried the same thing from the other direction. A bicycle rider laughed his way through the pile. He was the only one that found it funny. The passengers in the bus were insulting the woman in the car. She was sweating, nervous, but determined; she was not going to move.

"What we need now is the police," Morris said, looking over his spectacles and rubbing his hairy stomach through his shirt. "Where the hell the police them is now, when you want them? Beating up some poor nigger, and you have traffic pile up hereso in the middle a town. Suppose a ambulance try to ply through? Could be a dead person…"

"You don' like it, Morris?" said a young man passing by.

"You like it?" Morris asked. He ran his hand through his greying thin hair.

"I like she. She kind a ol' but she have spunk." The man grinned. "You see how she have Johnson? Johnson is a violent man, you know, but it look like him like her, too. That man not even coming out of the bus. She have spunk."

"Tha's all you can think 'bout, eh? You see a woman standing up for her rights and all you see is boobs."

"Who bring up boobs, Morris? Still, she *have* nice boobs. You must write a poem about her." The man moved away from Morris while staying close enough to suggest that they were still talking. He seemed entertained.

"What we need is the damn police!" Morris shouted. People turned to look at him. He was dressed in a crushed and baggy pair of khaki trousers last washed two months ago when his sister came to see him from the convent, to do her duty for God and her conscience. She had also given him the pair of worn house-slippers. They were the type with rubber soles and straps. Now they were black with grime and hard to distinguish from his feet. He wore an oversized white shirt, stained brown around the armpits and down the front. This was stolen property. A week ago, he had "borrowed" it from the clothesline of some middle class suburban dweller. Stealing was a political act. The havenots should enjoy these occasional moments of rebellion against the haves. These days he was a havenot despite his complexion and pedigree.

But his poverty was an ill-fitting garment. His shoulders drooped slightly, forcing him to jut his head forward when he walked. His belly protruded alarmingly. He called it his "Biafran belly". He was one of those white men who might well have had a touch of black blood in their ancestry, who displayed it in the cool poise of their walk, and the ease with which their tongues rolled around the bounce and speed of the dialect. You could tell, too, by the way his skin took to the sun. The browning was relaxed and evenly spread, with none of the leathery toughness and discoloration about the face of those true ancient whites who still huddled in beach houses on the secluded coasts.

"What we need is the damn police to stop this foolishness! Hell, man!" His heavy black spectacles teetered on the edge of his nose. His eyes were bloodshot, so much so that it was hard to distinguish what would have been the whites of his eyes from the brown pupils that danced like beads in his head. "And what you think the buggers would do? What you think the stinking buggers would do, eh, Johnson? Johnson!" He pointed to the driver of the minibus who leaned forward with a slight grin tweaking the edges of his mouth. "Yes, you. You woulda go straight a jail, not because you wrong, not because you drive like a mad man, but because you harass the woman, you stinking black nigger. Because you harass a fair-skin lady. And you can't tell me a rass because you see *this* – which part the sun don' touch…" He was unbuttoning his shirt to expose his chest. The skin was noticeably whiter along the ribs and was freckled with blotchy brown spots. "Yeah. Yeah! I know what the privileges is. Yeah. Harass a white thing like that and is jail. Ask any police man that. Hell!"

"Hey Morris, you giving the woman a show, eh? I's like you want give her some juice, some white man juice," Johnson shouted from the van, leaning his body out of the open door. "Morris, yuh mad as hell!"

"Mad nuh?" Morris stood with his legs apart and began to make notes in a tattered note pad that he drew from his back pocket.

"You going into a poem, Johnson," a man laughed. "The man putting down you name. Book him yes, Morris. Shit."

Morris wrote steadily.

"*Tha's* why black people can't get anywhere," Morris said. It was as if he suddenly realized that he had something important to say, something new. "Where the police them is? Beating up some nigger, that is where. You hear that? Beating up some nigger and them can't come and look after the damn traffic. Hell, man!"

People laughed. The traffic began moving, the clot loosened. The pick-up van had reversed and the taxi was able to go through. Other cars followed suit and soon Johnson, tired of the game of out-waiting the woman and the complaints of his conductor and passengers, used the pavement to swing around the woman. Then she, smiling victoriously, guided her white VW down the road.

"Bitch. A little light-skin bitch! Why you move, Johnson? Why you back down? This is our history, right here." Morris was scribbling in his note pad, writing furiously. Sweat poured down his face and dripped onto the pad. He wiped away the droplets with his filthy hands, leaving a stain over the blank sheet. While others cloistered in the shaded areas, Morris took the brunt of the sun on his balding plate. People moved by, staring at him with indulgent amusement. Some tried to peer into his pad. He protected it with his body. A few greeted him as "Mr. Morris", but did not wait for a reply.

Morris thumbed back a few pages of his pad, sticking his thumb onto his tongue after each flick. He read, his mouth moving slowly without making a sound.

River turbulent, thick like blood. Coolade is thin, river is thick like blood beating against the rock, beating hard like blood against the rock. Cut the throat and river-like lumps of old drying blood stain the floor and the baton pulps brain on the dirt grey asphalt. Blood covers all. Jesus bleed blood on the concrete cell stones and let black hands, my hands turned black and blue with my suffering, be cleansed. How can I be white and free when my pain is black, blue black and bloody red? I will hide in the green and stare at the sky's unconcerned vacancy. Bottles lie empty on my cell floor, by God, my gut swishes juices and my eyes sway on the river swell yet there is no change, for when I wake the baton is at my head.

He turned the pages again.

Bitch.

Bitch.

Just because she think she white.

Where the hell the police are?

Beating some nigger, beating some nigger.

Morris stopped just before he reached the bar and turned to face the road, now flowing easily with traffic. His forehead wrinkled slowly, as if he was straining to actualize an image fermenting in his mind. He shook his head violently. Loose, greying strands of hair waved in the air, then settled unevenly on his spotted pate.

"I give it ten minutes, and we going want to know where the hell the police man them is, again." He looked at the flowing traffic. "Ten minutes and this going clog up like a damn bloodclot, car pile upon car, truck crushing truck, and people running round like mad ants. A veritable Tower of Babble, to rass! What the hell else? And who will give a damn for this still small voice crying out in this wilderness of concrete and steel?"

He stamped the ground with his left foot and stood to attention, rigid, a discarded statue.

Then he was marching towards the sound of men laughing their way through a philosophical discussion further down the road in a small bar. They shouted, grunted, slammed the table and then fell into conspiratorial whispers, like the dangerous drone of bees before they turn on some poor unsuspecting soul. The music in the bar was low and unobtrusive, old material from the fifties and sixties – a mixture of mento, rhythm and blues, and the occasional jazz number – Sarah Vaughan or something plaintive like that.

Morris stuck his hands into his pockets and sorted out the one-dollar and forty cents of change among the bits of newspaper and the two dirty handkerchiefs he used to wipe his forehead. He clutched the money in his hand without taking it out of his pocket. He walked into the bar, bowing his head at the door as if he were entering a church.

After the sunlight and glare, the darkness and cool of the bar was a haven. Morris could make out the shapes of the bee-like cluster of men at one end of the bar, their heads almost knocking in the shadows. A small brown man sat in the gloom at the far end of the bar counter, nursing a tumbler of white rum. He stared drunkenly at the red counter with the stillness of someone who could have been in the same spot for hours, not moving, yet not stiff.

The swarm of bees split into four swaying guffawing shapes, slapping the tables and each other's backs. Morris felt a twinge of nostalgia: memories of youthful laughter, rows and rows of bottles glowing their mute brown transparency on the slippery tables, bold metallic aluminium ashtrays smoking like pyres, a wallet fat with good currency and the assurance of regular pay cheques to come, the casual song of affluence in the sharp cut of car-keys in the pocket, and friends – whole, alive, no blood, no madness ravaging their eyes. Gradually, his mind drifted back to the smoky room. The men were huddled again.

The bartender was busy behind the counter. He had not

seen Morris come in. He was still in the doorway, trying to get used to the light and trying to muster up the right tone with which to approach the bartender. He released the coins in his pocket and they jingled slightly as they hit the gravelled bottom. He took out a grimy handkerchief and wiped his face with it after taking off the black-framed spectacles. He was thirsty. He looked at the man sitting at the bar. He had not taken a sip from his tumbler. He was sitting just where that red-headed white reporter fellow had been waiting for him to walk in. It was years ago but he remembered every detail; the way the nervous sweating reporter had scribbled so earnestly in his note book:

"Do you have a woman… a wife?"

"No time for a woman… you know it…"

Morris remembered his incoherence. He was still drunk from the night before. He had brilliant turns of phrase in his head, but they crumbled when they reached his mouth, crumbled into mutterings and grunts.

"You never feel like having a…"

"Uh…"

"You know…"

"You mean love."

"Yeah, love, that's it. Ever been in love?"

"Sometimes, uhuh… but… no time for that."

"A girlfriend?"

"I have my poetry."

"And that is all you need when you are… ah… lonely?"

"Sometimes I have a girlfriend."

"Yeah, yeah… uhuh… uhuh." He was writing quickly now.

"Yeah."

"When was the last time…? Last one?"

"Last one was forty dollars ago."

"Forty dollars? Ah, you mean…"

"She could really turn my world around… Shit!"

He was thirsty.

212

My thirst is pain in the throat, like a red wound inflamed by memory of lost balm. Sweet rum heals the wound and the memory and I cry to dream again. Bottles lie on my table, prepared for me in the presence of my enemies with batons at the ready to numb me to pain. I cry to dream again. If you walk far enough from the thick rush of blood that is the river you can find streams of crystal molasses that bite the throat and soothe like Limacol on the skin. When I sleepwalk it does not matter what I say; if they don't hear; if they won't hear; if I don't speak. Drowning is a balm. Is there no balm in Gilead?

His memory tilted like a hand-held camera shooting jerky, slanting images of his dusty feet and gnarled hands, his straw hat and the blazing white of his calico suit, sitting there, the poet already crumbling at the edges – but long before his death – expounding to the red-headed boy, who wrote and wrote until Morris began to feel as if he was stealing a part of him, sucking him dry. But the beers kept coming to the table and Morris let the picture continue to tilt, to grow more unsteady, until all the world could see the pink of his eye-lids and the cake of old tears turning to stone in his eye-corner. Somebody told him that the journalist's piece had been published and that Heinemann was interested in his next collection – but they gave up trying to find him. That was a long time ago. Before his death.

The words danced through his head as he stood there waiting for the moment to go in and speak. He wanted to write down all the words and images that flittered in his head. He had the instinct for a poem, a good story – maybe a good film. He knew one when he felt one. But he just stood there and the question mark grew large in his mind until it filled the page fully. He would write his next poem as a massive question mark. A graphic poem, one of those computer poems of Brathwaite, with bold lettering and witty distortions of the word on the page. It would just be a large question mark. A poem that would speak like a mouth trying to catch flies.

The bartender saw him and smiled wryly.

"Morris," he said. "Morris, what happening, man?"

"Ah, Stanley," Morris said, a huge smile on his face. "Ah, Stanley, I come to tell you marvellous news, my friend!"

"Marvellous news!"

Morris's hands opened wide, his shirt-sleeves hanging down his sides like wings. He threw his head back and said even more loudly, and with an elaborate wave of his hand: "Marvellous news!"

"You not serious, man!" Stanley said. "What it is now, Morris?"

"Not what is it *now*, but what is it." Morris leaned on the counter. His eyes sparkled mischievously. He had a look of desperate enthusiasm, as if he needed Stanley's indulgence and faith to take another breath. His words tumbled over each other. "This is different, this has never happened to me before, and it couldn't happen because the circumstances here are special, unique. My suffering has made it all unique. Like a well-crafted poem. The blood and flesh on the floor where the battle was waged before the coming of the poem. This news is news that would make any man, any artist, anybody who has a damned sense of pride in creation, proud of his education, proud of his apprenticeship, proud of his muse, proud of the suffering that has given substance to his voice. Proud to rass!"

"Damn good news!" Stanley chuckled with genuine admiration.

"It is marvellous news!"

"It sound good, fe true, Morris."

"Good? Good?" Morris pulled a stool under him, nodding a quick greeting at the man with the tumbler of rum. Had the fellow been drawn into the drama? He had not. He just stared at the counter.

"Marvellous, my friend, that is the word I used – and I don't mince my words – marvellous. It's not the money, you see…" Morris continued, trying to maintain the energy.

"Money!" Stanley exclaimed. The man with the tumbler turned lazily.

The multi-headed bees in the corner exploded again, arms

flaying with laughter, then collapsed into its mound of bobbing heads again. Stanley frowned like one irritated by pestering insects.

"It's not the money," Morris continued, as if he had not heard Stanley's exclamation. "Money is one thing. Money pays the rent, but who care about rent? The money I pay on that flea-ridden room downtown could just as easily be spent on a bottle of whites, and I would be just as happy. All I need are small comforts, friend, and any old campaigner knows that a bed is a damned comfort. Learned to sleep standing up in Burma. That is one hell of a lesson to learn."

"So what about this money? You know you owe me?" Stanley was toying with Morris. The bar was relatively empty. The men in the corner had enough beer to last them another half-hour.

"What I jus, say, man? What the hell I jus' say? Why people won't listen sometimes, eh?" Morris exploded, spinning around, making as if to walk to the door. Then he quickly looked around. "I said it's not the damn money! It's not that. It is that they have *seen*, my brother. Somewhere on this earth, someone's eyes have been opened and they have seen the need to allow the voice to continue, to allow the imagination to rise above the baton blows and the boot heels of conscript thugs in government issue. Keep alive, my angels said, and they heard. Hell, they are my angels to rass. I lay on the stone in front of the Kibbo River and listened to the gurgle of the river like blood from the throat and I knew I heard the sound of hope beating against the rocks. And see? They have understood. And even if they can't understand, they are damned impressed because a poem is like a gem stone. Even a fool can tell that it's got to be something precious. And I said to myself, I got to get the thing typed. Should use a clean piece of paper because the old one with my pigeon scrawl is stained with old curry and my rusted life, but then I say, no. If they cannot find the trace of my brilliant dreams among the squalor then they will never find me. So believe me, is not the money, you know? I got the letter today. That whore my wife say, 'Morris, Sherman

Morris' – even now the bitch can't say my first name without my las' name, like an insult – 'where have you been?' And like the devil with a hose between his legs, I say: 'Wandering to and fro about the earth.' And she reply, 'Why? It have news for you, good news, and you wandering around like you mad!' But the Jezebel is a damned Philistine, and you know what, Stanley, she does this twice a year. Drive up in her car, the tyres stained with the red dust from that criminal husband's plantation, blow me out of some good sleep just to remind me what I have lost. Like I give a damn. A blasted Philistine who could never understand the heart of an artist. I am a damn aristocrat, Stanley. But I make the mistake of giving up my birthright for that lump of pottage. She don't understand poetry, brother. She think poetry is Elvis Presley singing 'Love me Tender'. She can' even hear the poetry in the way she cuss me."

"So you happy then?" Stanley asked.

Morris was breathing heavily, trying to catch his breath, to regain his footing. Talk of his wife always stirred something histrionic in him, some gloriously vitriolic diatribe about her ignorance.

"Happy? Happy?" he said with a quietly incredulous voice. "I said I have marvellous news, man."

"But you don't tell me what it is."

The men-cluster laughed loudly again. Then a single shape emerged from the splintered shadows and moved towards the bar. He became a tall man with a white shirt carefully tucked into his black trousers. His chin was tidily void of even the hint of a beard, and his head was cropped in the funky squared stylings of the day. Stanley did not wait for a request; he simply put twelve bottles on the table. The man grinned and nodded. He was drunk, but he wore it well, nothing unsteady, just a peculiar fluidity of the arms and legs. He counted the bottles slowly then muttered, "Soon come," to Stanley and walked out of the bar pulling at the front of his pants. He wobbled slightly when the glare of the sunlight slapped his face.

"And him is just drinking a few beer," Stanley grunted. "Jus' beer. Yout'!" The last word came out like a curse. Morris said nothing until the man returned, still pulling at his pants and then wiping his hands on his bottom. He gathered six bottles, took them away, then returned for the other six. This time he nodded at Stanley. "You counting?" Stanley nodded.

"Good, good. Friday night, you know."

Morris watched him become one with the shadow-mound again, then turned to Stanley. The moment was lost. He felt the energy slipping from him.

"Give me a quart of whites," he said to Stanley in a subdued tone.

"You have the money?" Stanley asked, smiling.

"I just told you about the good news."

"You never tell me. You started, but you never finish."

"Them reprinting the book. Putting in a few more poems, plus a introduction by Walcott," Morris said with seeming nonchalance. He did not want it to sound like an exaggeration, a lie. "I got the letter today. Late because the bitch was holding on to it."

"Oh yeah?" Stanley sounded doubtful. "That mean some money, then?"

"Sure. Eastern Europe, India, China. They translating the damn thing. Hundred of thousands of people will be reading the stuff soon. Walcott using it in Boston as text. You know? The real thing." Morris ran his hand through his hair. "I just heard today. Thought I could celebrate. Hell of a thing eh?"

"Yeah."

"When a man could be so damned popular, so damned successful and he can't even drink a whites to celebrate. A whites that won't cost the price of just one of those books. West Indian life for you, boy."

"So, it's not no tricky business, like the last time, Morris?" Morris's casual tone was eroding his wall of doubt.

"The last time it was London. You can't trust the damn British. They still vex with us because of Naipaul, because of Clive Lloyd, because of Independence to rass. We beating them at their own game like a set of yuppie Calibans and they don' like it. No, this one not from London." Morris wiped his face wisely, and cleaned his spectacles.

"So the Russians decide to deal with you?"

"Eastern Europe, man. Not Russians. They don' have time for that now. I mean, they must be in on the deal, but..." He broke off. "Anyway, a man should celebrate good things in life, eh? Hell, some boys must be sitting there in Prague right now, toasting me to high heaven with some real sandpaper vodka, and look at me. Trying to beg a whites from a man like you. So, a quart is all I ask. I want to carry some to Clara. I told her. She so happy."

"Strange how you find her home," Stanley said. "Hear she lef' and gone Trinidad. Well, that is what she tell me."

Morris held his head down and shook it sadly. Then he looked up, like one caught trying to protect a criminal with lies. He spoke softly.

"You heard."

"Yes," Stanley said. His smile was smaller.

"I wanted someone to celebrate the news with. How I could come in here and have such good news and not mention her? After all she done for me, after all the rent that woman pay for me, after all I put her through. And I mentioned the other whore and don't even mention her. You can blame me for that, Stanley? It would look bad. I would lie for that woman." Morris looked down. "I have to celebrate alone, because I drive her away. My muse drive the woman away. It hurts, Stanley, because all I wanted was for her to see." He was crying.

Stanley began to laugh, slapping the counter so hard that the drunk man suddenly straightened up, his eyes blinking. He muttered something about a "nex' one," and continued to rock with his eyes closed. The tumbler was now empty.

"Jesus, Morris, you is something else, man!" Stanley laughed. "You is a shitty piece of work."

Morris looked up smiling stupidly, his eyes bright with tears. The smile grew into a laugh that seemed to be searching for a oneness with Stanley's mirth. He wanted them to continue laughing until Stanley would say: "Hell man, you is something else. Come drink this and go to sleep." But it didn't happen. Stanley stopped laughing quickly and turned towards the shelves behind him.

"You don' have no money, Morris?"

"I getting some royalties coming in next week. They doing my work at UWI now," Morris tried a standard line. He had used it in every bar on the strip.

"I's like them love to send you royalties, man. I's like you is Stephen King or something. Fast as it come, fast as it go. I bet you sink the whole a it into the villa you building in Granville's Cove, right?" Morris could not tell from his tone whether he was being indulgent. Stanley was like that, a games player. His bald pate glowed with sweat that collected in tiny beads in the folds of his thick neck. Stanley began to write something on a pad.

"Well, you know how it is…" Morris, said, trying to feel out Stanley's mood. He wanted Stanley to soften, but he could not rely on self-pity. Stanley abhorred self-pity. But he responded to self-deprecation, a thin line of difference that only Stanley understood. If a man walked in with the stump of his arm bleeding, screaming in pain, Stanley would be slow to react. But if the man came in and asked calmly, "You'all see my hand anywhere? Damn thing drop off and I starting to miss it so much my heart can't stop bleeding", Stanley would take this man to the end of the world, laughing all the way.

Morris needed a drink badly, but it was getting so that he was not sure if he could concentrate long enough on the game. He was moving towards the self-pitying desperate stage, knowing full well that that would mean catastrophe. He tried the pleading eyes. He let tears well a bit to give them a glow. Then he smiled crookedly, waiting for Stanley to look. It was the plea of a pitiful clown whose audience had moved from amusement to irritation and pity at his overused antics. But Stanley would not turn around. He continued to write on the pad.

"Hard boy, hard," Stanley was muttering, almost to himself.

"Dollar fifty," Morris offered.

"Alright," Stanley said, still writing.

"Dollar fifty," Morris repeated, this time letting the money fall on the counter. This was his last trick. Offer some money and hope that it displayed his sincerity. It was a last resort because he had hoped to pick up a few cigarettes with the change.

The men in the darkness burst into laughter.

"Alright," Stanley said. He put down the pen and picked up a rum bottle. Morris saw what he had been working on – filling in crosses on a "Spot the Ball" contest from the news-paper. It was a ritual with him.

"You think you will win this time?" Morris asked, speaking despite the discomfort of a mouth filled with saliva. Morris could fell the burn of the rum on his tongue. He needed it.

"Win every time, you know that."

"Yeah, yeah…"

Stanley placed a tumbler on the counter and poured a few drops into the bottom of the glass. Then he scooped the money into his palms.

"What is this?"

"Just the libation," Stanley smiled. "Go and pour it. The Gods gwine want to celebrate too."

Morris hesitated. With most men he would drink the droplet of rum because that could be all they would get. With Stanley you could not be sure. He stared at Morris, waiting – almost daring him to pour it out.

Morris spilled the rum to the ground, his eyes steady on Stanley. Stanley smiled. Then he placed a small bottle of rum in front of Morris. His eyes softened when he saw this.

"Thank you," he said. "You are a king among men." He had hoped for more, but this was a lot more than a dollar and fifty cents. There was still kindness in the world.

He drank with gratitude. He sat in a dark end of the bar that smelt of old, wet cardboard and drank the white rum, thinking of the gurgle of river water as the juice spilt down his throat. He began to pay attention to the shadows moving at the other end of the bar. What could make four young civil servants laugh so robustly on a day like this and in a city like this? He could hear snatches of their conversation and the more he drank, the more intrigued he became by their animated movements. He wanted to put faces on the shadows. He wanted to drink with somebody. He looked at the other man in the bar. He was slumped over the counter, passed out.

He had the distinct impression they had noticed him, had heard him plead for the bottle of rum. The boy who had collected the beers had stepped by him as if he wasn't there. Looked through him as if he knew he was lying and found him insignificant. This ability of the young to completely dismiss the existence of others irritated him no end. If the boy was amused, it was not an indulgent amusement, but the mocking laugh of derision that threatened to draw every bit of energy from you if you let it. Morris constructed the boy's history and type. A university type of the counter-revolutionary years.

They all sounded like university types, just out of school and into jobs that paid more than they were used to. The kind that would watch himself and Professor Spender, arms slumped around each other, rolling into the campus at nine-thirty in the morning after their rendezvous at the Chinese man's old bar – the one that had been burnt to the ground during the big riots. The bar was located in front of the university – a modest hole made of plyboard, cardboard and strips of discarded galvanized sheets. The men would bang on the galvanize until the Chinese man or his daughter, the whore-to-be, opened up and placed a bottle of scotch on the table before disappearing inside to get some more sleep or whatever they did in the silence of the paraffin-smelling house. In those days, Morris drank scotch. He could afford it then. They would speak of the pleasures of university employment and the pliable imaginations and thighs of the young undergraduate girls. Then they would wobble to their classes where they gave loud, sacrilegious and politically suicidal lectures.

Professor Spender's body was found in a plastic bag discarded in the mud of a river just outside town, and bottles and stones rained on Morris and broke his head. He was left for dead, but he lived.

It was students, like those four boys sitting there drinking and laughing, who had done it.

In their first year they were fascinated by the brilliance and audacity of radicals like Morris. He entertained their fertile minds and slept with the willing teenage girls who were bursting with their newly found sense of freedom and daring. In their second year, the girls wanted better grades and brought a stark pragmatism to the lovemaking and gallivanting – and Morris complied. The men discarded the Marxist label for that of moderate social democrat. By the final year, they thought only of jobs and friends in high places and the women, now feminist and angry, without friends in high places, sent telling letters to his wife and family before they packed off their afro heads to graduate schools abroad.

Some were friends. One boy was his protégé. A slim, olive skinned, half Indian boy whose family had sent him away from the cane fields to make something of himself. The boy's neediness seduced Morris. He took him in, read his poetry, taught him about the grace of the properly metered line, about the poetry of cricket. Then one day, Morris got the boy drunk. They woke up entangled under the ficus tree outside Morris's office on campus. Morris was naked. The boy vomited and ran away cursing Morris, calling him an anti-man, a batty-man, a faggot. Morris was not sure what had happened. He remembered that they had been laughing and wrestling, and deep inside, he knew that he found the boy to be a tender creature – something delicate and in need of cradling. But that was the poetry of it. The reality was drunkenness and none of it made sense.

Spender told him not to worry. He reminded Morris of their boarding school days when they learned that passion was always crudely pragmatic. That night, they drank in the Chinese bar, and then decided to go down to the river to swim and commune with the water spirits. They were both naked, stretched out on the pebbled beach when the stones rained down on them.

Morris was sure that the boy had led the students who came and hurled the stones – the first ones, anyway. But it could have been one of the women he had slept with regularly – the one who had written the letter to his wife. It could have been her, Ursula, a tall Guyanese with sloe eyes, who had demanded his resignation in the student-run newsletter. When he asked her why she had written that, she laughed and said, "You stopped asking me if I came."

He survived the stoning, and soon all the students had graduated or left. He was left alone. Spender was dead. No one talked to him. His anger lasted for a while, then one day, during one of his long binges, it dawned on him that he was attacking a bunch of children and colleagues who did not even know he existed. The years had consumed the legend of his indiscretions.

This pained him. He stopped drinking and disappeared for more than a year until people said he was dead. He was in fact living in the bush amongst a group of Rastafarians from whom he scrounged meals.

He wrote the beginnings of many poems under the heavy sedation of bush marijuana, pretended conversion and let his hair grow unruly – but they all knew that it was a sham. He finished few, if any, of the poems because he was afraid that when they were finished he would have nothing else to do. He contemplated the prison of the trees and the sky, the endless country spaces. When he finished the bottles of scotch he had bought before leaving the city, he drank bay rum and wished it would kill him. It just made him sick. Something had changed. He decided that living open to the elements had drained him of his irony, his sense of humour, his urbane worldly wisdom. So he came home like John the Baptist with a head full of lice. People still said he was dead. Finally he admitted it. Morris was dead.

The men exploded again and Morris rose from his seat swaying slightly. He walked slowly to Stanley, who was looking vacantly outside.

"You know them?" Morris asked, pointing to the men.

"Yeah."

"Happy, eh?"

"One of them just reach back from foreign. America, I think. Baltimore. Him full of talk now... Seen the promise land and thing... Lawyers, mos' a them. One of them is a writer, the one who come back. Like you. But I think they still publishing him. One day somebody might just beat up his rass too. I can feel it. That head just look like it shape for a nice bottle."

"You can tell, eh?"

"Of course. Coulda tell you that you was gwine get the blows, man. Coulda tell you that." Stanley nodded. "I coulda tell from the firs' day I hear you in here. After you leave, people start to talk 'bout high-flying white nigger, eh? I say to myself, that is a dead man. But you live longer than I ever dream. As for that one. They will finish him. Wipe the floor with him. Talk too loud. I know it."

"Writer, eh?" Morris muttered.

"Politician, if you ask me." Stanley hissed his teeth. "Only one kind a writer can get way with murder here and that is a reggae singer, cause everybody know that black reggae man don' have no sense, right?"

Morris's eyes swallowed what they saw. His mind slipped. *I gave birth to a poem and it bore no fruit for it feared the sunlight and the blast of gun-powder. My poem died with a cord wrapped tight about its throat. I sought to plant again, but could not find a hole to pour my seed. The hole that breeds a poem: poem from a seed, must be supple and soft, soaking and soggy with the thick stench of nether places. It lingers on the finger after you have tasted. But this land is dry and the earth hard. Stones, pebbles, rocks, boulders, eggs...*

Stanley was used to such moments. Morris would stand still, looking into the darkness, his mouth moving slowly – "catching flies" they would say – his brow twisting with the effort to remember or to form sounds that would not come. Then he would shake his head and relax. His eyes would see again. Morris grunted when he was out of it. He looked across the shadows huddled together again.

"I's politics them talking," Stanley said, nodding his head at the men. "Stay out. You don' know who dem is, Morris." It was too late. Morris was moving into the darkness at the other end of the bar. Stanley watched him turn into a tall swaggering shadow. He heard when Morris announced himself, standing a few yards off.

"I am Sherman Morris, the poet. Buy me a drink." Three parts of the shadow exploded at once. But one of the young men rose slowly and extended his hand. Morris was taken aback. He had expected the explosion of laughter, in fact, was pleased with it. He had meant for it to happen but he was not prepared for the look of admiration in the eyes of the half-Indian boy who rose and offered his hand. The young man smiled, revealing a row of small sharp teeth, as if embarrassed by the idiocy of his friends. Morris took the hand and shook it, not letting go until the young man's hand twitched slightly.

"We have done you wrong, sir," he said. "We have done you a grave injustice."

Morris swayed unsteadily as his brain tried to determine whether this was genuine or just a cruel joke. His half-smile reflected the uncertainty. The boy looked so damned sincere.

"Gentlemen, this is one of the few who have fought on and suffered the wounds of battle. This is one who dared to taunt the beast, the monolithic bureaucracy, with the pen. Here is one of the old campaigners who we have whispered about in our little holes in London, New York, Toronto and Baltimore. Morris, the poems-man. Whatever happened to him? It is you, isn't it? The poet?" There was a flicker of uncertainty in the boy's excitement. The beer had mellowed his eyes into damp softness. He was sweating dark round spots in his armpits and on the front of his white shirt.

"Yes… It's me." Morris smiled.

It began like that. They bought a bottle of beer for Morris. He drank quickly and then said: "I asked for a drink."

They found this very funny and ordered him a bottle of scotch.

Morris sipped his scotch and decided to impress them with his battle scars. As he spoke, he kept glancing at the Indian man, trying hard to determine whether he knew him. The more he drank, the less certain of himself. Maybe he did know the boy. The boy looked at him, not with intimacy, but with a certain familiarity; he laughed loudly at Morris's jokes and smiled just before each punch line, as if it, it seemed to Morris, he had heard them before. But he couldn't have. These are new jokes, new stories, new lies.

Morris insulted all the politicians – the most feared ones included – with vitriol and foolhardy aplomb. He knew more politics in one square inch of his brain than any of those men put together. He said he taught Lancaster in school and had dared to insult the little opportunistic runt to his face. He showed the blows he suffered for his honesty. He was that kind of person. He lived with the poor and shat in the same holes they shat in, drank the same stinking water, and slept with the same diseased whores. He was a poor man. A poet.

And the young men listened with some awe, watching this frail white man drooping with the mix of scotch and white rum, trying to convince them of his complete blackness – his beautiful black heart – as he sat there with his thick black-framed spectacles and his thin filthy hair. But Morris knew what they saw, he knew that they saw before them a battered stone, bruised by continuous flinging against a wall that was not even dented.

The half-Indian leaned forward, drinking in all that Morris said. His eyes shone. His fascination kept the others polite. They did not interrupt Morris's diatribes.

Then suddenly, in a brief lull when Morris dragged at his scotch, the boy asked softly: "Mr. Morris, tell us about the poet," he said. "Tell us about the poet, your friend, August Spender."

Morris moved the glass from his lips as if he was about to say something. He could have painted a glorious picture of the poet, then he saw the boy's eyes. The boy was looking for the truth, a poem, an honest poem. Morris placed the glass on the table and looked down. They watched his shoulders begin to shudder and they heard the painful indrawing of wind in his throat. They watched him place his hands over his face as moisture silvered his stubby fingers until they were wet and dripping. No one spoke. They watched his head shake and his eyes beg when he removed his hands, now muddy with the mixture of tears and old, old dirt. They did not seem to know what to do, though they knew what he was asking. They saw it in his eyes, red with rum and tears. Morris's shoulders shook and a strange low drone rumbled in his chest as he cried.

Morris knew it was him – the boy. It was him. He looked at the Indian's face, the strange quality of amusement, drunkenness and curiosity. The man stared back, steadily. It was obvious that he had not told any of the others. They had fallen silent with the uncanny sense of knowing that is hard to explain. Morris bowed his head again. He felt that awful sense of loss, that sense of failure.

In his head the images circled and then fell apart. He felt the large heaviness in his throat and then the tears would stop. It was a sweet sensation of complete weakness, like a weak bladder, out of control because of too much rum, or the relief of voiding at the first cut of the cat-o-nine on the corporal bench in the police yard. It was as complete as a long-awaited orgasm. As complete and as painful. He knew he had to leave the room. The boy with his desire for truth stared back at him in utter confusion.

They watched as Morris rose slowly, still making the awful sound in his throat. He moved unsteadily to the door. He looked drunk now. At the door, when the sun slapped his face, his head jerked back and his back went slack as he teetered backwards trying to gain some balance on very unsteady legs. He crashed hard against some tables. Then he lunged forward through the door. Even Stanley was silent. He did not laugh, despite all the tears. The half-Indian writer slammed his fist hard on the table.

Soon the noise of car horns and the shouting and laughing drew Stanley to the door of the bar. He suspected that it was Morris, but he was not sure what exactly to expect.

"Oh hell, Morris, man!" Stanley exclaimed, holding his head. "Oh, hell man!" Three of the four shadows rose and rushed to the doorway and followed Stanley outside. The half-Indian poet sat staring at the chair where Morris had sat.

Outside, Morris was kneeling at an intersection, his hands outstretched; one finger of his left hand jutting stiffly into the hard bright blue sky, and his right thumb pointing into the melting asphalt. His hands were so steady that people followed the direction of the finger and thumb with their eyes. All saw the silence of the sky overhead and the unyielding tar on the ground. There was a pile-up of cars around Morris who kept muttering, "Call the police, call the damn police…," tears still running down his face.

The sirens brought the half-Indian to the doorway.

Morris looked at him and he could tell from the way the man held his body upright and turned his face slightly askance that he wanted to see in this broken man being dragged like a corpse into the Black Maria, the image he had for so many years kept in his head about the poet. He wanted to see the tall, full-bodied man, skin browned by the sun, hair thick and wavy-white in the wind, sipping scotch and soda on a wooden verandah of some riverside cabin, talking about the struggle and the way forward; the teacher, wise after years of battle, with a head full of images, craft, words used and reused in incredible combinations, full of hope for the younger ones, with a thick heap of manuscripts waiting to get out at last. Morris knew that he had hoped for something less squalid, something that would make him think that that drunken night, whatever did happen, was worth it – was about art, was about beauty, was about passion. Morris understood this because he hoped the same thing.

But it was all a failure – and Morris's body grew limp just when the man's shoulders dropped.

"Damned faggot," he spat, and then led the others away.

Morris, the poet, did not struggle. He just kept muttering "See the bitch them here at last. See the bitch them here at last. Now crucify my rass, and make me a bloody legend."

The Black Maria drove towards the coast where the asylum reflected darkly over the ocean.

THE CLEARING

THE CLEARING

A sample of all the particles on the floor in the room would have revealed a curious assortment of tiny pebbles, bits of hair, balls of fabric, shreds of tissue of different hues, bits of tinsel from the Christmas party, dried up grass and plain old dust – anything that the soles of his shoes would have brought in over the past three weeks. There were clothes strewn all over the bed and brown-stained socks stank in a pile behind the door. His books and letters were scattered on the floor, where he had left them after the frantic search for a lost chapter of his thesis. He'd suddenly gotten the idea that this document contained the secret to the completion of his present project. He'd found it, but he was wrong. The writing was weaker than he'd thought and the only relevant aspect of the paper was a sentence that was, he now realized, a naive misinterpretation of the text. He'd stopped working for a week after that. He bought several cases of beer and stayed indoors drinking the depression from his mind. After the beer came lucidity and hunger; he had no more money.

He sat in front of the typewriter, a sheet of virgin paper in the machine. He kneaded his scalp through his unruly hair trying to massage some fresh idea into his brain. He had been moving from the desk to the bathroom and back for the past three hours. The same sheet of paper was in the machine. He reached for the coffee-stained pile of papers that constituted the first two chapters and went back to trying to extract a thought-line from them. The problem was that he had written these chapters over six months ago. He was now struggling with the realization that he had lost the connections completely, that he could not think with the same kind of clarity.

He stood and moved to the window, looking out into the wood-lot behind the plyboard building. The earth was parched. Huge tyre marks criss-crossed the lot. The mud, churned up by the tractor tyres, was now caked solid and almost pink in its dryness. The trees started uncertainly a few chains away from the building. First there were the stumps and felled trunks tangled among the brambles. Gradually the forest assumed a sturdier character and beyond that was darkness.

The sky purpled gently above the tree line. He could hear the faint sound of traffic on the highway about a mile away. It would get dark soon. With the mist from the mountains would come some rain and chill. He felt the burn of acid in his stomach. He was hungry and worried. He knew he had an ulcer but the pink anti-acid fluid that had warded off the pain for weeks had now dried up in the bottle that was lying on its side somewhere on the floor. He couldn't afford another bottle. Would he even be able to make it out to the highway? Even if he could, he wasn't going to break his promise. He had said he would finish the last chapter before he left and would to do so at all costs.

The food was finished but that was nothing to worry about. The stress of hunger would draw something out of him, the creative impulse he knew was there. As soon as the first words were written – the first paragraph – he would complete the whole thing in no time and the sheer momentum of productivity would drive the hunger and weakness from his mind. A day and half, once he got started, would see it finished. It was all in his head: the reading, the thrust of the argument, the eloquent phrases, everything – all he lacked was the angle. He walked around the room talking to himself. It was something that had started three days ago when he was trying to reassure himself that he could do without the beer. He had just finished the last bottle. He was only a bit unsteady, but he felt the charge of creative energy. It was something he had come to appreciate about his body. It would, as if by the secretion of some enzyme, feel creative. It almost always worked. He had gone to the typewriter and the first few words were full of potential:

```
    The crucible of the writer's mind is
fettered to the turmoil of his society. He
```

may try to flee the welling chaos in his
world, but must return to it if he desires
to describe the human condition in fiction.
Friction in diction brings restriction...

It was becoming a poem. He pulled it out and broke the
piece down into poetic phrases. He spent the next hour and a
half producing a mediocre poem about writing. By evening
the creative secretions had stopped. The fire of productivity
petered out. It hadn't caught. He went to bed early and did not
sleep until it got light. The ideas had flowed, but he could find
no moment of clarity to structure them. By the afternoon,
when he could think clearly, he could not recall his thoughts
of the night before. He burnt the poem and placed another
sheet of paper in the machine.

He watched the last spurt of orange light in the sky fade
almost abruptly to black. He was down to water now, and a few
fluff-covered sweets he managed to find in the mess of the
floor. He felt very weak. His eyes began to ache again. He
rubbed them and winced at the pain. They felt extremely
heavy and watery. A grating irritation like a tiny grain of gravel
under the eyelid cut into the eyeball. He held the eye open
until it dripped tears. He hoped it would wash out the particle.
When he let the lid fall, the pain was still there. He walked over
to the propped-up bedside table and picked up the lamp with
its naked bulb. He moved over to the bathroom dragging the
electrical cord through the books and papers on the floor. He
stared into the mirror, the light blazing under his chin. The
image was grotesque. With the under-lighting, his features
became exaggerated. A rabid black man, hair a tangled unruly
mess, his face covered with a scraggly beard, tight, coiled beads
on his cheeks. His eyes were swollen, and on his right temple
a septic pimple throbbed. His eye sockets, his cheeks and under
his lip were sunken holes where the shadow fell on them. He
pulled open his eye again, raised the lamp to the side and winced
as the glare pierced into his cornea. His eyes were bloodshot.
There was no foreign particle in the eye. He blinked and blinked
again. The pain was still there. The eye still hurt. He put down

the lamp and doused his eyes with water. His nose was running. His entire face ached. The irritation persisted. It got worse. He thought of rubbing the eye vigorously until the pain became so unbearable that the eye would grow completely numb. He resisted the urge. He left the bathroom and lay down on the bed in the darkness. He closed his eyes and tried not to move the eyeball. The stillness helped.

He did not hear the car drive up nor hear the two women whispering outside the door. He did hear the knocking and the calling. He didn't move. He woke up without opening his eyes. It was his sister outside. Nobody was supposed to know where he was. She continued to call. The knocking stopped. There was a long period of silence. Perhaps she feared he was ignoring her in anger. Then the knocking became more insistent. Did she think he was dying inside the room? He did not move. He wanted her to go away.

He could hear two voices. They were walking around the house. The other was Annette, his fiancée. Phyllis, his sister, did most of the talking. She kept shouting his name, was silent for a few seconds, then she sent Annette to check the back for a door or an open window. She could find no entry. Perhaps he wasn't in there and Henry was wrong about it. Was there another cottage nearby? Annette thought it better that they left. Phyllis wouldn't leave. She said he could be dying inside. Annette didn't say anything. Phyllis began to knock the door again. She kept calling his name.

He stayed still. His eyes were open now. He stared up at the ceiling. What must he look like now? His shorts would be very filthy. They had been white – and he had already worn the red ones so much that they had become painful to wear. He had grown used to the smell of his own unwashed body. He had kept a clean shirt and trousers in his bag for his return trip to town. He would have to hitch-hike home so it was important that he at least looked decent. His hair and beard hadn't been combed for days. The knots were tight and hard. He didn't want them to see him like this.

Phyllis had started to push against the door. He thought of getting up to open it. He decided to do so but his body did not respond. He just lay there smiling and wondering whether she would manage to break it down. Phyllis was a determined woman. Annette's attempts at discouraging her were futile. Phyllis said she would pay for any damage if it wasn't where he was. Annette said that perhaps somebody else lived there. It could be very dangerous if they came home and found two women trying to break in. Phyllis told her to either shut up and help or just go and sit in the car. Annette shut up and helped.

The door was rotten so after a few blows it cracked. Phyllis kicked at the boards until she could get her hand through to unlock the door. The door swung open and the room was filled with glaring white light. They had parked the car directly in front of the door and the headlights were on. He turned his head and squinted into the glare. Phyllis stood with her legs slightly apart, silhouetted by the light. She was wearing a light skirt, her legs faintly outlined through the fabric. She whispered his name. He kept staring. His eyes dripped. Annette leaned against the door looking away from the bed. He watched her. Phyllis walked into the room and moved towards the bed. When she was very close, he moved. She stopped and called his name again.

He sat up on the bed and held his chin in his hands, his elbows pressed into his thighs.

"You alright? You alright?" Phyllis peered into his face. "Your eyes are red." He closed his eyes. "This place is a mess, man. Where is the window? Annette, don't just stand there, open the windows, eh?" Annette moved quickly to the window in the bathroom. She did not look at him. She stayed in the bathroom.

"I can't believe you wouldn' tell anybody where you were. What is wrong with you? Mama is very worried about you." Phyllis was moving around the room trying to create some semblance of order. After a while she gave up. "This place is a mess. Hey? Hey? Talk to me. Are you alright?"

He stared into a corner of the room. He wanted them to

leave. His sister was staring at him. He began to smell the room properly now. The waft of air from the open windows and the cracked door stirred up the latent musk. He chuckled to himself. Phyllis must have noticed.

"Annette wants to talk to you. She didn't want to come, so don't get upset and start bawling her down, but I think this is pure foolishness, so you better talk to her. I mean, you must be gone mad, man. She deserve better. It's alright if you want to vex and confuse everybody else, but this woman hasn't done anything to be made a fool of like that…"

"Phyllis, please…" Annette said from the bathroom.

"You see? She is afraid of you. Anyway, right is right. Please, explain yourself, sir." Phyllis stood in front of him. He had to stare at her feet. "My God. You haven't even combed your hair! When last you combed this?" She placed her hand on his chin and raised his head upwards so he stared at her face. She had on make-up; pink lipstick – he hated that – she must have come straight from work. "You look bad, sah. Annette, come out of there. Come. Talk to him."

He got up and stretched. Phyllis stepped back. He then went on his knees and reached under the bed for his sneakers. He sat on the bed and slapped them one at a time on the floorboards. Then he pulled them on. He ignored the laces.

"Alright, I know you wanted to finish this thing. That is alright, but you can't just change your mind about a wedding, okay? There are other people involved and not to mention Annette. You can't be so selfish, man. People will start calling you a mad man."

He got up and moved to the bathroom. Annette moved away from him as if he *was* a madman. She sensed something disquieting about his silence. She was afraid. He turned on the tap and splashed his face.

"Look, you better say something. The cake is still there, the food is spoilt but we can work that out. Now Annette's parents will sue if this thing doesn't happen…"

"They won't…" Annette's voice trembled.

He turned to her and felt a deep pity for her. He could only

236

see a shadow for her face but he could feel her fear and despair. She looked so small and vulnerable in the dark filthy room cut through by two neat streaks of light from the parked car.

"They will," Phyllis said. "Now, you better get your act together. I don't care what creative juices moved your sorry spirit to this hole, but…" She stopped as he walked past her towards the door. He turned around and looked at both of them. He smiled slightly, shook his head and then turned around. Stuffing his hands deep into the pockets of his shorts, he trotted down the stairs onto the caked earth. He stooped for a few seconds to regain his balance, then his shadow cut through the light and vanished into the dark.

"Come, Annette. He wants to go home now," Phyllis said, walking towards the door. Annette moved behind her. They did not hear the car door open. They looked outside and saw him walking towards the edge of the wood-lot. Phyllis shouted his name. He did not turn around, and continued walking steadily until the forest swallowed him. Phyllis ran to the car and started it up. Annette stayed at the door. Phyllis manoeuvred the car towards the spot where he disappeared. She drove slowly, the car rocking on the tractor tyre marks. She blew the horn and shouted his name. She did this for about ten minutes and then she stopped the car. The din of crickets and frogs filled the silence. After another five minutes, Phyllis drove the car back to the shack. Annette stepped down to the ground and walked towards the car. She sat beside Phyllis and said nothing. They remained in silence for another few minutes until it became clear that nothing would happen.

"Let's go," Annette said. "Let's go."

The car bumped through the wood-lot towards the dirt road that led out to the brightly lit highway. Annette saw a shadow move in the forest. She turned to see him walking with his head down towards the shack.

"What? You see him?" Phyllis asked, trying to look behind her through the rear-view mirror.

"No… No," Annette said settling into the seat and looking straight ahead. "He's gone."

Vershan IV

BURNT OFFERING

Vershan IV

BURNT OFFERING

The miniature library was strewn with *National Geographics*. Small blue chairs were scattered around the room and in one corner, right in front of a large window that looked out on the asphalt playing-field, was the drummer – a man guarded by brilliant stainless steel pipes, and a barrage of drums, pads, cymbals, cowbells, chimes, tambourines rigged on stands, trays of sticks, clappers, and other noise-making contraptions – more things than he would ever need to play a simple one drop. He sat there waiting. He seemed the only one with any interest in what was happening. Everyone else seemed bored. The keyboardist sat with his too long legs touching his chest. These children's chairs were just not made for a six-foot seven big-headed, big-armed, gangly keyboard player. His two boards waited on their black firm stand. The bass player sat on a table flipping through *National Geographics*. Three women – dressed in sweat suits and looking as if somebody had dragged them there – stood to one side of the room. The only sign that they were a part of this were the microphones they held casually. The guitarist kept playing loud power-chords and then kicking at the pads on the floor. Every time a sound emanated he would scream, "Dyam, dyam. Who was fooling wid my somet'ing." The other guitarist was just getting his stuff together, plugging into an amplifier.

They were three storeys up in an elementary school. It was dark and wet outside. It was late. Weary bodies smelt palpably of stale fatigue. This moment of inertia after a desperately poor rendering of a song had depressed them all.

"Snare and bass, Las, seen?" the lead singer said.

"Just hear me out, man..."

"One drop, Las. One drop. All right?"

"Talk to de man, nuh, Pedro."

"One drop," Pedro the bass player said. "One drop, Las."

The lead singer waited. He had a music stand in front of him. His microphone was attached to a boom stand. He stared hard at the late guitarist.

"Yuh ready?"

"Yeah, yeah… One minute."

"Run it…" the lead singer said.

The first guitarist filled the room with a delicate open chord strum, each string plucked sweetly, a kind of Latin feel with a gentle pulse. For a couple of measures, this was all. He tapped the pad on the floor. The effects opened the sound until it was a wash of chimes, falsetto harmonies, insects whirring at night and shimmering cymbals.

The lead singer closed his eyes and imagined the world he wanted to enter. The music was starting to find its meaning. In flight now, far from the wet outside, far from the clutter of cars, far from the lights, far from the North American cold, he was soaring over mountains dipping and swooping and then rising suddenly. At first he saw purple and blue, then as he came closer, green, such a riotous green, lavish, startling. He was flying into the familiar and the warmth of the wind on his face was like the breath of God, the breath of revelations.

He heard in the shimmering high hat, the crackling of the dried leaves of an orange tree sucked dry by the sun. The high hat ticked and flashed in eighths, signalling the rhythm guitar to begin to define a melody. Then, almost as if in dialogue, the other guitar began to speak. This time the language was a simple dialect of circles, tight, slightly muted sounds, speaking a pulse.

The lead singer could see from far the way the sunlight glinted off the rusted shingles of the city's roofs, the sprawl of a nation before him, a place where bodies turned into faces into souls into stories into histories. The trees, the melting asphalt, the concrete, the smell of dogs burning on tyres, the offerings of early morning, souls trying to emerge from the night with a mission, to breathe, to breathe…

The bass guitar followed behind the lead guitar and now the drummer could feel the hiccup of the music, so he pressed down on the bass pedal, sharpened the tapping on the high hat, locking the cymbals together, and then snapped a cross-stick across the rim of the snare. This one drop, this steady bop, this lanky loop and stretch established the moment, and the rhythm guitar was now a bright line of cutting sound, chipping, chipping away – chekeh, un-chekeh, un-chekeh.

And the keyboard bubbled into the pot, a low drone, a sound from the belly of the music, a wookoo, wookoo, wookoo sound, the right hand hopping, barely touching, the left hand filling and then slipping away.

The lead singer was now moving, his body rocking. The music was entering him. He had alighted on a street and the bodies were flowing past with their sweat-shining faces, their laughter, their yard-recognition of the pulse of the music.

Then, as if from nowhere, the sound of horns – big horns emanating from the monitors, a patch from the keyboards – spoke an anthem twice over. The regal melancholy of a Don Drummond trombone line dragged him into a sombre place, a place of childhood, his stomach growing uneasy with the memory. Jamaica was in his head – the green, the thick heat, the voices of people. He was a child again, sprinting through the dust yard of his primary school, his hands reaching for his worn shorts to keep them up. He was alone. He was playing alone, running deeper into the forest of trees behind the school. He could see the flashing breaks in the trees' canopy. Far below him, the scar of concrete shone between the bushes. The gully. There, dead dogs rotted, broken bottles glimmered, huge boulders blocked the path of storm debris and, on the other side, in a clearing, five Rastafarian men sat in a circle beneath a blooming pouis tree. The tender yellow blossoms spilled a carpet of gold around them, and above them a surreal canopy of bright sky made them seem holy. And they beat their drums, beating out their faith, beating against the squalor of their lives, dreaming of Ethiopia. They were always there, their locks unleashed in the twilight, their

243

bodies slim, hard, bent over the drums, their toes locked into the dirt, the boom and slap of the drums mesmerising them. He stood at the edge of the circle and through the clouds of smoke, they nodded a welcome to him.

This memory was as comforting as it was sad for him. A lonely boy, seeking out love among strangers – men who welcomed him because he was African, men who listened to him, smiled at him, spoke their wisdom of Rasta to him even though he was only twelve, skinny, and uncertain of himself.

The snare called him in. His voice, thin, edgy, high, caught the opening phrase in a space, a rest – just after all ears had expected it. The pause, the slight hesitation became a sob, a hint of memory.

I still see the pouis blossom
The stagnant pools
The mosquitoes
The screaming schools
The gully bottom
Strewn with echoes
Strewn with echoes

A bu'n it a bu'n
Stray dog smokes on rubber
Burnt offering, ghetto fire
A bu'n it a bu'n
Stray dog smokes on rubber
Burnt offering holy pyre

The keyboard's looping bubble joined the sound now, and as he looked around, transported by the slow rocking of the rhythm, he saw the illumination on their faces – their bodies moving together, nonchalant, as if carried helplessly by undulating waves. He smiled at the lead guitarist who smiled back a bright riff.

Met her seven miles from the harbour
The Black Star Liner was gone

244

Couldn't find Marcus
But a dread sat forlorn in the corner
He said he lost his faith but kept the hair

The three women rose to meet the second chorus. Now he pulled back and waited for them to respond to his call. As they began in a full three part harmony, his voice lifted an octave higher, vamping on their sounds, twisting and turning his way around their words, finding the gaps, drawing attention to a phrase, pulling back, going forward, while they continued, steady, sweetly and rightly...

A bu'n it a bu'n
A bu'n it a bu'n

The faces that enter the singer's mind help him to ground himself in the art he is making. He is far from them, far from the smells that have given this song its meaning, but here, in this moment, he allows himself to be transported beyond the alien into the familiar and the beauty of it is that he can carry the rest of his people with him. He is somewhere in Half Way Tree, somewhere in the city, looking at the faces moving by him – the hustlers, the workers, the Jehovah's Witnesses and the Pentecostals with their pamphlets, the promises of truth. He was one of them. He stood at the street side and spoke the Gospel of Christ to those who came by. To the dreads, to the everyday people just trying to find their way home. This land of his was so thick with spirits, thick with the supernatural. It was the weight of these ghosts in the air, even in the middle of this Northern city, that he could feel as he sang on, coming to the bridge of the song.

Met her on Constant Spring Road
She was passing out pamphlets of salvation
And I asked her the way to heaven
She said, I believe in a myth
You see a sin in that?

I believe in the impossible
I am a magical cat
I believe in a myth
Anything wrong with that?
I believe in the impossible
I am a magical cat
I believe in a myth
You see a sin in that?
I believe in the impossible
Star burst under my hat
I'm just a magical cat
Cat
Cat
Cat

He was in a small chapel far away in the hills of St. Elizabeth, hills that turned sharply on the seaward side into a steep cliff that looked over the Southern coast of the island. A high wind blew that night. He was in the chapel standing there, thinking about the steeple, imagining the steeple to be an antenna that was sending a wave of truth and fire down into the midst of this congregation of young people who were gathered there to find God and to understand the meaning of Spirit for these times. He remembered the electric touch of fire on his skin and the explosion of words that burst from his stomach, through his mouth and spread like waves of silk through the room. It was dark, yet there was such light in the place and they knew they were touching something bigger than them. As he sang he felt the pimples rising on his skin, the dull repetition of these rehearsals forgotten. He held the microphone and squeezed it, his body twisting and gyrating, his arm moving, trying to coax the drummer to stay with the one drop, to stay with the one drop.

Odomankoma hovers above
The pattern is the same
I haven't lost my faith

I'm just feeling a little bit of shame
For looking for stray love
Among the dried leaves

He had never left that place in the hills. He took the memory everywhere, keeping secure the details of that night as one keeps miracles to bolster faith in dry times. He remembered the look on the caretaker's face when he came to the chapel to find out what was going on in the sanctuary at three in the morning – sheer panic when he saw their faces, animated, glowing with the flame of the spirit; how that poor old man had spoken about needing to know that God was not a God of confusion and madness; how he discretely tried to ask if they were smoking weed; and how they circled the man and laid hands on him and how he fell to the floor and lay there for ten minutes, not moving.

Recalling this was how he coped with his fears when faced with the future. He had seen things. He had felt things. This music was his way of finding the path back to that hillside.

Every man has a little bit of God somewhere in them, he wanted to say to everyone gathered in that schoolroom. But whereas he could have got away with that prophecy in a Kingston studio, where the spirits had been planted into the consoles and the monitors and the amplifiers and the soiled carpet and the walls, here in America, there was a dry, sterile emptiness about the place. They would not understand and Pedro (who should have known better) would have called him mad. So he said nothing. But he sang:

I believe in a myth
I believe in a myth
I believe in a myth
I believe in a myth

And just across the gully, a pouis tree shed its yellow leaves, and they swirled in the wind, turning everything tender and miraculous. The possibility of faith glowed in such a moment.

He stood in the swirl of yellow, his feet caressed by the carpet of velvet petals. He was sick for home.

He felt the pregnancy of the apocalyptic, the prophetic anticipation embedded in the character of the Kingston that raised him. It was a city that was constantly being cried woe to by prophets with microphones and a pulsing reggae beat at their backs; promised Zion by staff-wielding, dream-laden and sweet-tongued politicians; told to expect cataclysm and catastrophe by sweating, dancing, short-haired preachers. These voices had warned him to be wary of the clashing of the two sevens, to understand that these are perilous times, that these are last days. So he lived with the weight of these prophecies on him. He never consciously anticipated the end, but he saw the world in its most acute temporality and carried that sense like a mood. And as he was taken by this moment, he recognized in himself the elevated spirit of future-speakers, blessed with the gift of a word in season. He stomped, rocked, he waved and he sang, his body wet with its own healing and with the cleansing flame of memory.

And then, as if come from sleep, he opened his eyes and saw the sublimation of music had transformed the stoned boredom of the players of instruments and singers around him. In the sacrificial offering of their burning smiles, he found the language of home.

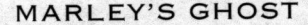

MARLEY'S GHOST

MARLEY'S GHOST

1

There is a man in a room with walls lined with old newspapers. That is the most reliable thing that can be said. A small room in a two-bedroom bungalow in a small development called Ensome City, just outside of Spanish Town. A characterless house in a neighbourhood where hardworking folk – cement and garment factory workers, policemen, soldiers, chauffeurs, low-level civil servants and enterprising street vendors – make a basic living. He has abandoned the island, the town, the district, the neighbourhood – and the rest of the house – for this room lined with newspapers. They make the place look like a gift cheaply and hastily wrapped on the inside. They are already ochred with age; the colours on the comic sections faded.

The air in this room is old. Nowhere to go, it festers into a stink, the smell of a human being undecided about living or dying and depressed enough not to care about the smell. The moisture from sweat and breath hangs in the air like a despondent fog.

The man has been lying on the single bed in the room, on the same sheets, for days. Sometimes he gets up and walks around, a tall man who carries himself like a man who has suddenly lost a great deal of weight, with the unnecessary expansiveness of someone who has been told him that he is smaller than he really is. Perhaps it is the airiness of his clothes or slowness of his movement, but something about him is in contradiction. It would not be surprising to hear him say, "I feel like I am in someone else's body." But he does not say this. What he says is, "She bound to come back… the bitch." There is no drama in the way he says this.

He scratches his unkempt hair, wincing at the tenderness of his scalp. Then he runs his hands across his face, his beard scraggly – a peppering of tight curls over his gaunt jaw. His skin has the quality of deep tanned leather stained with dark polish. Hair grows on all parts of his body – long, thick, gleaming strands on his arms, his shoulders, his toes, and his ears. His beauty is the subtlest of things. It arrives long after you have seen him and dismissed him as strange. But when it arrives, it overwhelms you with its certainty – it startles you with the brilliance of an unexpected smile.

He gets up occasionally to hunt down some stale bread from the bottom cupboard of a cracked dresser, or to sip water from a rust-stained porcelain sink in the corner of the room. Sometimes he just gets up and touches everything in the room as if trying to remind himself that he is alive. A peeling chair, the cracked dresser with a large blank wooden frame where a mirror used to be, the sink, an olive-coloured military sack, an unsteady bedside table with a massive boom-box resting on it – he touches everything. A black telephone glimmers under the bed like a wet frog about to pounce. It has not sounded in days.

The room has one high window just above the bed, a window laddered by brown louvred panels. Little light comes through this window even at the height of the day because the thick foliage of a black mango tree crowds it, its leaves sometimes poking through the open louvres.

Strips of muted light pattern the floor – which is strewn with clothes and a plague of gutted oranges. There are easily sixty or more carcasses scattered around the room, peels curling, some turning brown with decay. Their tart scent complicates the smell of human waste. Tiny fruit flies hover like moving mist over the floor and the occasional green-bottle fly darts around the scattered clothes.

This is his cell. His hiding place. He has been in this cell listening to *Exodus* on auto-replay on the tape deck since his woman left him, his African American woman who thought she could come to Jamaica and ride her way through difference, through a history that is nothing less than tortuous, through his chronic sense of failure. But she could not. She left. Now she is gone, he has been listening to *Exodus*, trying to consume himself with that inspired merger of politics and love, trying to let himself be lifted by the wisdom of the prophet. Those are the reliable facts. Beyond them nothing is certain. Beyond them hover the edges of his sanity and little is definite in that place.

He is lying on the bed, his face towards the ceiling. Forty years old – that is his age, although lately he has been losing count. These days he wants to start counting from 1945 instead of 1962. This confusion consumes hours of his day. When he can stop thinking of his woman leaving him, he starts to think of the year of his birth. Now it is February 6, 2002. He thinks he should be dead.

Sounds come from outside the room. Sounds of a city determined to pursue its Third World rituals of laughter, dubwise, gunshot, car crash, screwing, hallelujahs, praise and the telling of stories. The world goes on. A man's woman has left him. She has left him to travel back to America where she came from. He has driven her away. The world outside does not find this narrative especially remarkable. Women come and go. The world outside does not know this man, does not care about this man. The world outside does not care that this man has been in his room for six days eating oranges and trying to decide whether to take his medication or not. His woman has left. She may be pregnant. He is not sure. He wants to follow her but he doesn't know what he would say if he did catch up with her. He could sing a song, ask her if this is love he is feeling. He thinks that if he could sing that song, if he could conjure up the spirit of the man singing the song in his head – a short, skinny man with a head full of flowing natty dreads and a cocky sense of entitlement to the love of a woman; any woman, all women – if he could muster up that fiction, perhaps the people outside would care that he is locked up in a cell trying to decide whether to take his medication or not. But he has stayed in the room, eating oranges and slowly stinking up his cell with his wasting self.

He does, though, dream.

He dreams his story. He is a creature of dreams. To enter his mind would be to enter a world of muted light and dreams. The tumbling of dates – 1962, 1945, 1981, 2002 – and the narrative of borrowed histories are the swirl of uncertainties that stir up his dreams. In his mind, he has a narrative that extends beyond that which he can own or even claim as history, as truth.

So this is all that can be called reliable: a man is in a room filled with orange peel and filthy clothes; *Exodus* repeats itself on the boom box; his woman has left him and he is not sure what to do. So he sleeps and dreams and becomes. This much we know.

2

At dawn, it was always at dawn, he felt that he had died and was now waiting to understand what that meant. At dawn, a dew fresh dawn, he would walk out into the half-light and look at the world. Then the world was not so certain of its separateness from the spirit world. Indeed, on such mornings, he could see beyond the earth, beyond the trees, beyond the sky, see into the mist, see everything in spirit and in truth. At dawn, the world was unconvinced of its mere earthiness. The world seemed completely different and he felt as if he had died at least once before. It was as if, during the night, while he was lying there in his bed, his body had curled into itself as if he needed to make space. He had curled into a tight ball as if he had never left the one-room apartment on First Street where, thirty years before, he had to share the small bed with Spider, his cousin. It was as if he had to make space for another body on the bed.

After stretching, he planted his feet on the cool tiles, then walked out onto the back porch to stare into the hills, trying to remember something, still feeling as if he was sleeping, feeling as if he should be somewhere else.

This is what it had been like since his return to Jamaica. He had been away for eighteen months. It was the first time in a long while that he had been away from home for that long, in one stretch. The travelling had been hard. Cold. He missed the yard, the gathering of men in the yard to kick some ball, to sit down and chat pure foolishness. He missed that. He missed the arguments about nothing. He missed the studio filled with smoke and the echoing of music shaping itself. He missed that. He missed the taste of the air, with its dust, with its stench of dead things. He missed eating an orange, pulling on the tart sweetness, or sucking on guineps, missed the taste of their slippery seeds, the flesh bright in his mouth and the tiny cups of green skin scattered around his feet along with the carefully stripped seeds, white with only the barest hint of pink flesh on them. He missed the sun on his back. The sun on his skin. The way the heat would come on him.

He had looked in the mirror after a few months abroad and had begun to feel white, to feel as if he was losing definition, his sharp edges. He felt as if he was losing himself in the mute grey of Babylon. He hated it. He spent most of his time indoors, in the studio, pretending to be writing songs, making jokes with the musicians who were on tour from Jamaica. But he was in mourning. That is what it felt like.

When they told him that his assassins had been found and that they were to be tried and executed, he did not hesitate. He would go back.

Three men came up to Babylon from Jamaica to get him. Three men no one would have dreamed could sit on a plane together. Two were serious generals of the street who had shed much blood in their battles against each other. The other, the third, was a long time hustler, a man who had never sacrificed the independence of his criminal lifestyle for politics. He was very careful about that. He was a gunman, a robber, a t'ief and he was going rob whoever came along, and he did not give a rass whether they were Labourites or Socialist. He was a gleeful informer and the only reason he was alive was because of his firepower. But many had tried.

Few wanted to associate with him. He was a genuine mafia man. That was who he was.

The three Magi came to the house to tell him that the two men who had come to execute him had been found. Joseph sat with them around a table to talk. The whole thing was a charade. They all knew it. Joseph knew it, but it was a ritual that had to be carried out. They came to tell him that it was now safe for him to go back. Joseph did not know anything about the two men they were holding. He did not know if they had anything to do with the shooting. They asked him, they repeated the names, they described the men. He knew nothing of them. He had not seen their faces as they fired bright sparks of light from the shadows of the mango tree in the yard. He had seen nothing.

But he knew that the Magi had a lot to do with the shooting and if they came to talk peace to him, if they came to tell him that it was safe to come home, then it meant that it was safe for him to come home. If they claimed that these were the ones who did it, then it was enough for him. But the ritual of atonement had to be carried out. The ceremony. The execution. It would take place in Kingston and Joseph was to be there. And Joseph, gong as ever, said he would be there, for peace was all he cared about. Peace and justice.

He returned to Jamaica and watched them hang the two men. He stood and looked the men in the face and watched them hang. Then he left the ghetto in a BMW and drove to his house uptown. He stepped into the dusty yard and sat on a stone under his special hibiscus grotto. He sat there and no one came to say anything to him. There he filled his head with the dizzying relief of smoke that helped him reach for somewhere else. He was home.

Death was familiar.

He had watched the men hang and had seen their spirits leave their bodies. But the spirits looked thoroughly confused. They had no idea where they were supposed to go. Someone was going to bury these bodies, but would this person know to light candle and hold a nine night to tell the spirits where to go? Joseph had been comfortable with the familiar taste of death, but of death not simply as a physiological truth, but as spiritual truth – something that went beyond the body failing to breathe again. He knew, though, that something integral had died in him as he watched the stinking fear of the two men, and smelt the shit and sweat of their writhing bodies. He had chosen to stand and look. Carried by the tyranny of his reputation and the weight of his responsibility as a tough man, he had chosen to watch. But it was more than that – it was curiosity and a peculiar desire to defy death by staring at it. He watched the men die and imagined his own death. It had been an impossible decision to make, but he had made it. Now, something had expired in him.

So he smoked his pipe in his backyard and then walked into the house to sleep. He slept.

Now morning was upon him. The radio was chattering. He looked out into the slight mist and he felt that he was dead, that he was in another world. He walked onto the porch and looked at the hills. The hills looked back at him. Then he made his way across the lawn in the backyard to the cluster of ficus berry trees at the end of the yard.

The roots coiled and twisted on the ground in a network of loops and crosses. Thick roots, smoothed and worn by rain and sun like the branches of a tree. They tendrilled their way to the thick trunk of the tree. It shot up straight, chunky like the neck of a boxer, and then spread, as if to mirror the net of roots, into a canopy of thickly leafed branches. The spread of the branches was impressive, a full wide stretch making a circle of shelter. The orange berries would fall and roll under the roots, accumulate and form a carpet of orange along the ground. Some rotting, some hard with sunlight, some still freshly crisp.

He sat among the roots and felt his body going back to sleep again. The sun crawled across his skin. He was home. Around him he heard birds and insects, but he could also hear the traffic, the seepage of radios beating out a medley of reggae and the lilt and drop of radio hosts arguing with callers.

257

They say prophets, true prophets are able to prophesy their own deaths. They say that God speaks to them and assures them that their time is coming. Sometimes they argue, but always, always, true prophets know.

Joseph had seen the way those two men had died, and while he did not know of the cancer multiplying itself from his toe to his bones, to his blood, to his brain even as he lay there staring at the sky, he knew the weightlessness of being weary of the world – the hollowness of having spoken all that was burning inside his belly. He felt dry, spent. When prophets grow silent it means they have served their purpose.

He could not see the future – that he would be leaving Jamaica again in three months to go on tour, flying late at night to New York to fill Central Park with skanking white folks, to then collapse, pale and trembling, his skin pallid like dead flesh. He could not speak of the journeys from doctors to doctors to herbalists to visionaries, or of the long, bone-aching flight to that small village in Germany. He could not know that women would soon be his keepers.

He had slept out in the open for several nights and he was beginning to lose track of the days. The sun came up and went down.

He moved among the trees as if in a dream.

3

In the middle of the night he wakes up expecting to see a wide-open sky with the dusty scattering of stars framed by the dark shadow of mountains. But all he sees is a blank greyness of walls around him. No. He was in a room, but this room is so small, with walls so close to him he cannot breathe. He wonders how he has gotten here, gotten to this place with walls covered with newspapers, a room that does not smell like the disinfectant-neat room of sunlight and white sheets where he had fallen asleep. Instead the place smells of an unwashed body, the funk of rotten flesh and the heavy musk of human waste, and the peculiar tart scent of rotten oranges. He opens his eyes and begins to feel meaning crawling towards him – the hint of a narrative that he knows to be an explanation for what he is seeing and smelling.

The logic creeps nearer, the way a dream fades away and waking insinuates itself on the mind. The meaning of the smells comes in small spurts of revelation – first the pressing need to get up, to take a shower, to call his aunt to ask her for money, to ask where his woman has gone and if she will come back. And the memory of his woman – whose name he sometimes forgets because it is too painful to call her name – hits him hard. It fills him with such a terrible sense of panic that he turns away from the thought and tries and bury himself in another flight, another memory. He can tell in those brief moments that he is running. He can tell, too, that he is dying an inglorious death. He knows that if he were to simply get up, walk over to the cracked wood cabinet, open the dark brown plastic bottle and pour out three pills, if he were to take those pills and sit on the edge of the bed waiting for them to slow everything down, waiting for them to bring him back to the gloom of his reality, he would probably understand everything happening in him and around him.

But he does not want to move.

He wants to die.

But he wants to die in a narrative that is of his own making. He understands that the narrative that has been given to him is empty. In that narrative he would die for a woman. He would die because he cannot convince her to overlook his madness, overlook his cruelty, overlook his inertia, overlook his history, and simply love him. He is dying the kind of death that will warrant a brief note in the newspapers – nothing dramatic. "Forty year old man found dead in Ensome City home." He does not want that kind of death.

Stretched out on the bed, allowing the delirium of his hunger to carry his mind far from this place, letting the sound of reggae blanket him – *Exodus* playing again and again in automatic replay – he will find better meaning for himself, for his path. He will travel into his own myth. Willing himself to dream his own narrative is becoming painful but necessary. Yet he can also tell that what he is dreaming is not entirely myth. He is remembering, too. Remembering the twisted way in which his life is changing into a legend. He expects to wake up at the end of this, at the end of staying in this roomful of voices, memories, colours, textures, tastes, smells, with enough in him to make his passing a wonderfully meaningful thing. He closes his eyes.

He was born in 1962. The year the nation was born. When he was born, ska was jumping around the city. In that year, someone said that he was a child of the future. An old man touched his forehead and said, "As your fortune go, so go the nation." He would be told this so many times that he was sure he had heard the words of the old man himself – and he would live his life wondering whether he was guiding the fate of the nation or whether he was simply reflecting a nation bent on its own self-destruction.

His journey passed through the fearful, hopeful millenarian years of the 1970s, the years when everyone knew that some dread apocalypse was to come. Then he entered the chaos and sexual wildness of those 1980s, when he discovered that women loved him, when he walked from woman to woman, searching for meaning deep in their flesh. In the 1990s, he was trying to beat back the gruff voice of Capleton, chanting another apocalypse, but this time with blood in his eyes. With it came the frenzy of cars crashing, bodies mutilated, flesh exposed – the coked-up madness of a city coming of age, hungry to remind itself of its own strength. This was a country in trauma as it struggled to show that it still had possibilities, a country caught up in a mid-life crisis, looking back at the hopeful years, the years of promise and prophecy and asking, "What is left, what is left, what do I have to show for it all? Am I still sharp looking? Do women dem still go for me?"

Every narrative that enters his mind is a narrative in search of meaning. He is not sleeping when he concludes that were he to travel into the soul of Bob Marley, he would find his true self.

They were both born on February 6th. But one day, in 1981, when Bob Marley expired, one sunny day in May when he breathed out his last, something left that emaciated body and travelled across the Caribbean Sea and found its way into him in Kingston. It was the morning he stepped out of the Psychiatric Ward of the University Hospital into a brilliant day. His body, after the discarding of its fat, was a taut muscular thing, his eyes clear as day, and his mind ticking with the promise of better days ahead. He had a paper bag full of pills and, though no one was waiting for him, he was unperturbed. He was going to go up to Papine, catch a bus down to Half Way Tree and then another that would take him to Ensome City where he would clean his small house, and begin to live again. In that moment, still standing out on the concrete walkway, having shaken the hand of the doctor on duty who kept asking, "Yuh sure you alright? Yuh don' wan' me call anyone?", after smiling wryly at his favourite nurse, the one who kept saying to him, as if to convince herself that she was not mad to have had an affair with an inmate, "You are different. You so intelligent. We gwine to hear about you. Don't forget me, yuh hear?", after waving to her and smiling at the gap in her teeth, and the bigness of her muscular body that contrasted with the delicate fragility of her pale skin: after doing all this, he stood alone, breathed deeply and was about to walk when it came upon him.

It came not like wind or tongues of fire, but like a blanket. A heavy blanket that gathered around him and kept wrapping about his face, making it hard for him to breathe. He was gasping and wrestling, trying to fight it off. But the more he fought, the more the cloud spoke, the more the cloud carried into him the words of all the Bob Marley songs he knew. More than that, it carried the words of a man asking, "Oh Jah, Oh Jah, why has thou abandoned I and I to the four winds – I's Ethiopia I wan' res'. Why yuh bring me back to Babylon?"

He knew that it was the spirit of Bob Marley that was consuming him. So he breathed. As he breathed deeply, he began to feel the cloud coming into him. As it did so, he began to cry, to weep uncontrollably. He felt his body fall to the ground. Then he felt the strong hand of his nurse around him.

"I tell you him not ready yet... The man not ready yet... Jesus..."

"I's the heat, man. Jus the heat. Him discharge already. Steady him there..."

"Take him inside. Help me..."

"No, him alright. The doctor sign him out."

"Why unoo so wicked. The man need to come back inside..."

"See. See, him look better already. Hey, bossy, bossy, yuh alright?"

By then he was standing on his own again – and he felt stronger. He felt parts of him taking on new shapes. He did not have to ask any questions about what had happened. In his head two different languages spoke, two different memories. They were wrestling with each other, trying to find meaning. Then quite suddenly, sadness filled his chest again. He turned to the light-skinned nurse with her long eyelashes and her freckled face, her dark brown eyebrows wrinkled with worry, and he spoke as if to comfort her.

"Bob dead," he said.

"Who?" she asked, as she touched his wet face.

"Bob, Bob Marley dead..."

"Yes," she said. "It just come on de radio..."

He had calmed down. He was not crying. He felt his face tightening into a scowl, that familiar brooding scowl. When he spoke again it felt like his voice was coming from somewhere else.

"Bob cyaan dead, dawta. Nuh fret." He touched her hand. She seemed to know he was fine. He walked away from the clinic and as he walked by a rusty garbage drum, he tossed the bag of pills into it.

That was twenty years ago. Twenty years of dreams, of memories, of trying to chart a path that would be the one a living Bob would take. Twenty years of realizing that he is going to die without any glory or fanfare. Twenty years later, he realizes that a woman has brought him down – not some cancer, not some diabolic sickness, but a woman. It has taken twenty years for him to find out that he cannot be Bob Marley with this woman, cannot call her one of many queens, cannot adopt the tough inviolable pose, twenty years to know that he wants her to mother him. And in this interim, he is trying to dream himself to a meaningful death.

The fact is that his world is crumbling around him. Everything is falling apart. Everything is uncertain.

4

He felt the pressure in his head grow. The plane rose steeply. His head pressed hard against the back of the seat; the lumps of his locks hurt his scalp now. He could feel the slow decay of the sores in his scalp despite the ointment that smelt of mint and aloes. His eyes were closed. Nausea filled his mouth with a bitter taste. He counted in his head, then began to mouth Psalm 91, his fingers tapping the rhythm on the seat handle. The climb continued, and he felt the weight of pressure on his body. For the first time he began to think of the pleasures of death.

He leaned his head towards Rhea, who stared in front of her until she felt his eyes on her. She looked at him, her face still smooth with the dark St. Thomas soil, the brown loam of ancient volcanoes that fed the banana trees that rioted through that parish. The African wrap on her head was sky-blue. She would wrap yards of cloth around her head to give the suggestion of locks. Few people knew that Rhea did not have locks. Her hair was thick and he was always laughing at her, telling her that she would not have to do anything to have locks – serious locks. She had thick Maroon hair, black, so dense with fertility that it shone.

Each night, when they lived in the one room shack on the hills of St. Ann, she would sit there and rub sweet-smelling blue hair-oil into her scalp, and then she would yank at the hair until her comb could run through it without hindrance. She never cut it, but it never seemed to grow long, it just grew denser and denser, the curls tightening with each inch added. He teased her a lot. She was still the church girl he had met on a dusty street in Jones Town, walking to the Missionary congregation with her bible in hand, her white dress stretched tightly around her hips. Her knees knocked slightly and he could not take his eyes off the way the strange stutter of her stride made her bottom roll. She had remained serious about her God. She spoke of Jesus as a friend. No, not a friend, but like a spirit child, someone she had birthed from her own womb. There was something just so deeply intimate about their friendship. He had no reason to doubt her Jesus's existence and he accepted him in the same way that he accepted that she had brothers and sisters – they were part of who she was and he understood that. She spoke of all of them in the same way – Jesus, too – as people in her life.

Now her eyes stretched Chinese-like in her face, the black depth of her irises stark against the surrounding whiteness. She was worried about him, but tried to smile. He saw too a sense of triumph in her look and he found comfort in it. She had won. He was comfortable with that. At last, he did not have to think, he did not have to consider, to read into the motives of the people around them. He simply relaxed and let her take over. It was as simple as that. It was part of his acceptance of something larger – he knew he was going die. This was now quite clear. Jamaica was far away. He had told her that Jamaica was where he wanted to go. But she said she had other plans – they would go to Jamaica after he felt better. First they would go to Miami. There was a specialist there who would help him. Then he would go to Jamaica to recover. He would be incognito. They would stay in St. Ann, far from the madness of Kingston. It would be like those years they had spent as farmers eking a modest living from the fertile soil of those mountains.

They would then spend a year getting his strength back. He would work in the small studio that she was going to set up in the house, and they would have easy access to Miami for medical check-ups. The next tour would be to the Far East. First there would be a triumphant week performing in Jamaica – a stadium concert – then another Babylon by bus through major US cities, especially a major show in New York's Irving Plaza where he collapsed and the nightmare had begun; then the Far East, then Ethiopia, where they would settle.

That is what he wanted, she said. He nodded, but felt deep fatigue hearing it all again – the concerts, the touring, the hangers-on, the band, trying to hold it together, trying to keep the discipline, trying to deal with the weakness he felt.

But he knew what was really coming, so he relaxed, stopped fighting. She would be in charge. He would let her do what had to be done. There she was, sitting beside him as she always did eventually. Even after her face wailed with the imprint of his flat palm, she still ran her fingers through his locks, massaged his scalp until he fell asleep with her. When he had fought with one of his other women, she was always there, her room smelling of sweet hair oil, always there to comfort him. It was her duty. She accepted it. He used to feel guilty about putting her through it, but her stoic acceptance left him incapable even of that. This was what they were. Now she was rescuing him again.

Germany had been a painful time. He had never walked so much. For the first time ever, he liked the cold, the way it seemed to clear the dizziness and clamminess from the fevers. They warned him about going out, but he would walk out into the streets, limp his way through the crowds, breathe in the cold air, feel his body coming back to him, feel the sickness of an ague crawling through his system, but enjoying the pleasure of sudden freedom. He walked along the streets staring at faces. He kept his head covered, not in a tam, but with the hood of a jacket; he wore dark glasses and he walked with his head down. He could feel the heat leaving his body through his bare scalp. He started to stuff the hood with rags to keep the heat in. Sometimes he felt as if his life was seeping out of the top of his skull. He felt his songs were leaving his brain and floating uselessly in the German air.

Nobody recognized him. Not in this small town. He was just another black man, another alien coming to take people's jobs. The way he walked, the way his body seemed not to understand itself, assured them that he was just another confused, mixed-race drug addict.

He took in the town like a travel book – the quaint cobblestones, the fairy-tale facades, the snowy-topped mountains, the tidily cropped trees, everything in order, in careful symmetry. The German talk he heard bounced off him like all the other sounds – alien, strange and surreal. He knew that he was on the surface of things here, but what was below he did not want to think about. He had enough to contend with.

He walked through the town for days. In the room, he was always thinking that the next dose of medication, the next concoction he had to force down his throat would break the hold this disease had on him – and if not that, then the compresses, the incense, the diet, the crystals, the shark cartilage, the chanting of dreads in the room – or even the constant piping of "Three Little Birds" – his most positive song, the doctor said, according to karmic scrutiny. He let it all happen because he wanted to live. He could not die. Joseph cyaan dead inna Babylon. He believed this with such force, such total conviction that it made everyone around him believe, too.

The moments of clarity came in the streets. There he thought about dying, thought about the end of it all. Thirty-five years old, and he was watching time slipping by. How could it be? No. Tings not going to be alright. His skin still bloomed with sores, his blood staggered through his veins; he could feel the poison running through him. The thing was destroying him, making him weak, making him talk foolish all the time. But he also knew that he was a Dread and that in his heart he could conquer all things.

This was before Rhea came. The chaos was a buffer of faith. The order she brought killed hope.

Rhea came from Jamaica and saw what chaos he was living in. She looked at him lying in bed with a haze of incense

266

around him. She looked at him and began to cry. He had not looked in the mirror in weeks and suddenly saw in her face what he must look like. He saw in her eyes what a pathetic sight he must seem. He knew at once what she would look like at his funeral, knew what her eyes would say. Her shock and pain lasted no more than a few seconds, but it was enough. She smiled at him, and then exploded in anger at everyone else. She opened the windows, grabbed the waste-paper basket and threw candles, incense, pills, needles, crystals, concoctions and various warming cauldrons into it.

She would have picked him up and carried him down to the waiting car by herself, but she had help. She had brought with her three other women, friends of hers he instantly recognized. These three women came in distinct shades. There was Bessie, a deep and mellow woman, her black skin regal in its unequivocal purity. She always wore red and seemed always to be smiling, even when you could see flame in her eyes. Blossom was sepia coloured, her hair limpid, seemingly wanting for life. She carried herself with the aloof diffidence of light-skinned people in a dark-skinned world. Her kerchief was blue – the colour of the sea. The third, Barbara, seemed chameleon-like, matching always the mercurial patterns of her personality to the seeming changes in the shade of her skin. Everybody liked her, but no one could figure her out. They assumed it had to do with a beauty that was constructed from the contradictory qualities of symmetry and ambivalence. She was the spokesperson in times of conflict. She was able to calm things. Her colour was pale green. These women were consistent about their colours – combs, scarves, broaches, bracelets, and necklaces – always something in their colour.

They all lived in England, big-bosomed Jamaican women who thought very little of what he did, what she did, but they were old friends, her sisters, and they would be her sisters for life. They worked as nurses in London and were the only people she could depend on. They had the stern pragmatism of nurses, women who understood what it was like to help people who hated them, to clean up the shit and piss of people who could not stand them because of their skin colour. These women were the ones who came to help her to move him out. They looked disgusted as they walked through the rooms. They shook their heads and moaned deep inside their chests as if they had just witnessed the most tragic of moments.

He wanted to tell them to get the hell out of the place, wanted to call them whores of Babylon, heathens. He wanted to tell them not to look down on him and his locks and his Rasta truth. He wanted to cuss them, turn them out, bring down fire and brimstone on them. He knew their type. He knew the way they looked at him. He could feel their condemnation, the righteous feeling of triumph they felt. Not just because it was clear that his Jah was not doing much for him now, but because Rhea was the one rescuing him. She was the one they had comforted during all those years when he was showing little regard for her, she was the one who had suffered and complained to them about him, she was the one whom they had told to leave his wutliss self and move on to something better. She had left the church and turned to this Rasta foolishness because of him, over this reggae music. Now Rhea was going to rescue him.

They carried themselves with the stoic pride of women who could take anything, take everything and then be there to punish their wayward men by loving them, by feeding them in their time of weakness. For some, it was their final and only revenge, their one moment of power. Rhea was enacting this power and they were there to help her. It had nothing to do with love. They knew that Rhea loved this man. They too loved their men. They loved the men who had done them wrong, who had left them saddled with children, who had left them for other women – they loved them. That was never an issue. Their power was not in their capacity to love but in their capacity to be needed, in their capacity to forgive these men with the weight of their ancient memories, their ability to hold each detail, each betrayal, each abuse, each act of brutality, to hold it as an investment, a kind of loan to be paid back in full. This was the rite they arrived in Germany to enact with Rhea.

They paid their own fares. They did not ask her to pay even though she could. They did not argue with her. They did not like the man, but they knew what had to be done.

They cleaned him and carried him down the stairs shrouded in blankets. They laid him in the car, patting him softly like a puppy as the one in red drove them for five hours through country roads and small villages, until they reached Munich. They carried him into another hotel, with a larger suite of several rooms, a kitchenette, and a view over a lake.

They sterilized the room with steaming white towels and buckets of warm disinfectant. They dressed his sores and gave him pain-killers as Rhea made plans on the phone for all of them to travel to Miami in a few days time. They sang hymns, said nothing.

The hymns carried him back. They took him back to Jamaica, and he was too weak to fight the way they carried him to familiar places of comfort and possibility. They sang with the thick, round harmonies that could consume a room with their force, their weight. They kept guard on the door and when the doctor came the next day to see him, they blocked him from entering. They told the doctor that Joseph was already out of the country.

The doctor left, but he was followed by Joseph's disgruntled entourage who had been camped out in his room, in the hallway and all over the rooms, fucking women, smoking weed, lingering as if someone had already declared a wake. They came to the new hotel, some brandishing vulturous knives. The women stood firm. "Stab me den nuh. Stab me," the green woman said calmly. The men walked away. The women let Russell, Joseph's cook, come in. Joseph would not eat from anyone else. Not even Rhea. Russell was the only one who expressed relief at Rhea's arrival. He had felt helpless obeying the doctor's twisted instructions about food for the dread. "If 'im gwine dead, den 'im might as cheap enjoy a good livity while 'im 'ave life." Rhea agreed without agreeing. She told him to cook the food that Joseph liked. He served up mounds of mashed yams islanded in thick callaloo and okra stew, spiced with various herbs and coconut oil. Joseph ate gratefully. He trusted Russell.

Rhea told Joseph the plan. He listened. He could feel his body slipping from him. His scalp was hurting him more than ever. He knew that the sores were now all over his head. He imagined that their seepage inwards was touching his brain.

He picked up his guitar one morning and began to sing. Soon he forgot the words. He started to cry. He sat there, staring at the brown high-rise buildings and the misty skyline and his mind was blank. He could not remember the words.

Russell sat in a chair behind him. He realized what had happened to Joseph and quickly began to recite Psalm 139. As the words came out of Russell's mouth, Joseph began to sing with him. His fingers worked their way around the fret board and he found melodies to carry the psalm. The two continued like this, a song breaking out in the room, the sweet taste of holiness. Russell's face had the wooden toughness of a sun-hardened sea jetty. His locks were virtually red and clumped in disarray around his head like the heads of his fellow breddren who fished the waters of Bull Bay on the rugged South coast of the island. His face was a lumped mass of muscle and overgrown pimples. Few recognizable expressions passed through that face. But sitting there, looking at the back of Joseph's head, his face softened into strange liquid textures. He was crying as he spoke.

The song carried in the room, around and around in circles. The women did not look at each other. Their eyes were filled.

Lord you have searched I and known I
You know my sitting down and my rising up;
You understand my thoughts from a far off.
You comprehend my path and my lying down,
And are acquainted with all my ways.
For there is not a word on my tongue
But behold, O LORD, You know it altogether.
You have hedged I behind and before
And laid your hand upon I.

Such knowledge is too wonderful for I
It is high, I cannot attain it
It is high, I cannot attain it
It is high, I cannot attain it
Where can I and I go from your spirit
Or where can I and I flee from your presence?
If I and I ascend to heaven you are there;
If I and I make my bed in hell, behold, you are there.
If I and I take the wings of the morning
And dwell in the uttermost parts of the sea
Even there your hand shall lead I,
And your right hand shall hold I.

Line after line, Russell spoke, and line after line Joseph transformed into a melody. His fingers feathered the frets as his right hand brushed the strings to create a wash of harmonics. He was just barely managing to bar the chords to create clean notes. He chanted, coaxing his clumsy fingers to speak in the familiar sharp slash of the reggae chop – bright, fresh, yet always behind everything. Russell's voice was a steady bass-line making spaces and filling them, making spaces and filling them. Outside the grey of the town seemed insignificant.

"We leaving tomorrow," Rhea said quietly. "We going home."

Joseph nodded. He was ready.

5

He wakes up and knows that it is night by the sound of the crickets; their sluggish noises echo in the small room. For a moment, he is sure that a cricket is in the room with him. He panics, his heart pounding at the imposition, and then his situation comes back to him like an old sick smell – he is not trying to live. A cricket, a scorpion, a lizard, a snake, what would any of those matter to him now? The tape seems to have stopped. He reaches for it when a sudden click reminds him that it is simply turning over. Soon "Natural Mystic" grows like a web of whispers around him.

Joseph knows he has been dreaming about dying. He knows the end of the dream and yet he wants to finish the dream. He prefers to call it a dream even though he knows that he is not really sleeping. What he is doing is thinking. He is thinking so deeply that it feels like a dream. His thinking is like a prayer – a way of making some order out of his life. Or maybe it is not order he wants, perhaps he wants to recreate it.

There is a tendency to helplessness that has haunted him for years. It made him sit dumbly in the room while Melanie, his woman, virtually begged him to say, "Please stay," by prolonging her departure, by the way her body seemed to soften despite the harshness of her words, by the wetness in her eyes. He sat there helplessly saying nothing to her. So she left.

For him, to have acted then would have been utter hypocrisy. His life has been shaped by this incapacity to act.

He sees.

He sees the brutish way of this country of his. He knows personally many of the high-ranking politicians and business folk whose cynicism has led them to engage in the crude violence of the society. He knows that the stories of violent death, corruption, terror and fear are rooted in something quite simple – people taking advantage of centuries of abuse. He says nothing about any of this. He does not complain, he does not accuse; he sees. He cannot imagine a way out of this morass. He has tried to write songs about it, thinking that perhaps were he to turn away from those friends, turn from the system that birthed him, turn to the myths of reggae, he would find a way to fight, to resist. But it does not happen. He is still himself, still consumed by the rituals of his privilege and unable to speak the language of radical action. It is a failure of the imagination, he knows.

How to reconcile the two worlds he thinks are his? Melanie helped him to feel, at least for a moment, that there was a true path for him – a man who could look at his country with new eyes – her eyes, and find a music to speak to that country. Now she has gone. She has gone because he was not there to protect her when she was attacked. She has gone because he could not step away from his anger at her goading him to act, to shake off the inertia of entitlement that he wore, her way of making friends with everyone she saw regardless of their class, their colour, their age. She has gone because he told her that she was a true Jezebel – a bloodsucking women who had tricked him into bringing her to Jamaica. He told her this and never took it back. So she has gone because she was an alien in an alien world and it was hard for her to sleep at night not knowing what he would do. She left because she no longer believed his promise to be her guide, to lead her along the paths that led to the place where the berries are, the soft place of noises, sounds and sweet airs that he had described so well to her as he seduced her outside a club in a forgettable southern American town.

She left because he would not take the medication. She did not know who she would meet hovering over her late at night, and he could not tell her anything to reassure her.

Somewhere at the back of his mind he is waiting to hear her slipping the key into the lock, and then to see her peering into the room with that smile on her face. "Hey, baby," the way she would say it that would make his skin prick, his groin tickle instinctively.

He is listening over the sound of the music. All he hears are the crickets.

6

The God, tall, light-skinned, and strangely anaemic in a baggy navy-blue sweat suit, strolled through the lobby towards them, his locks bobbing behind him, his eyes flaming. He had the presence, the kind of confidence that forced people to pay attention to him. The muted sunlight from the wide windows looking out into the cluttered tarmac caught his chains, an array of crudely crafted chunky gold pendants that dangled around his neck.

Behind him hurried Bobo, a short, round man who insisted on wearing clothes that were decidedly too tight for him, who insisted, despite his copious stomach, on tucking his shirt into his tight, black leather trousers. Bobo was out of breath. He wore a pair of dark glasses that wrapped around his face. He would have looked sinister if the rest of his body had not seemed so comical. He could barely keep up with the steady, assured stride of The God.

Joseph looked down when he saw them approaching. He had hoped that they would announce the flight before this confrontation.

Rhea and the three women stood up and moved towards The God and Bobo. Bobo was pointing. The God stared hard, not at Rhea or the women, but at Joseph. Joseph caught his eye and looked down quickly. He did not want to look up. He stared at the ground, then he looked into the sky. He was trying to disappear, to throw himself as far away from this moment as possible.

He was tired. The drive to the airport had worn him out completely and he was not looking forward to the flight. It was going to be painful. The sores on his back and his bottom were weeping that morning and when one of the women had rubbed them gently with some anti-bacterial ointment, he could hear her muttering at the tragic ugliness of it all. "Why, why, why them let this happen, eh?" She was not expecting an answer. In fact for the three days they had been in the same room, these women had not spoken to Joseph except to give him simple commands like "Lean back" or "Sip" or "Lift up". They were working for Rhea, no one else. They simply worked, gave comfort as no one else could.

But that morning, one of them, Barbara, could not help herself. She wonder why anyone would allow this man to go through this, this man with sense, with money, with a name around the world, why they would let him go through this kind

274

of foolishness. She wondered aloud, as if Joseph was not there.

Now, at the airport, Barbara was standing slightly ahead of Rhea, looking at this tall lanky dread striding towards them. Joseph knew then that it was possible that he would not be on the flight out of Germany. He knew that his broken body might be taken back to another room in the city, another smoke-filled place, for someone else to rescue him, but he did not care any more. He wanted to have his guitar with him, his Bible, and the Miles Davis tape he had been playing over and over again for weeks. He would go wherever he was taken. It was already over.

The God could bring no magic with him, just the assured look of someone who was born to be in charge. The God would come and argue that they went back too far for him to let this woman come and take over his life. The God would say that he would be better off with friends, real friends, with the brethren. The God would say that he could not die. That Rasta could not die. Rhea would never say that. Rhea knew, like Joseph, that he could die. The God would say that Joseph was a bonafide dread and a bonafide dread could never die, it was impossible. The God would tell him that all he needed to do was humble himself and look to Jah and he would get a chance to travel to Ethiopia. There he would find the nice plot of land that they had both picked out those many years ago, that spot where Joseph planned to retire, put up his foot and plant, plant, plant, and watch Jah give the increase. The God would remind him of the dream. The God would tell him what to do and how to do it. The God would remind him that he has been with Joseph forever and that Joseph could not turn away from a true breddrin. The God would point out that Rhea was a *succubus*, a blood-sucking bitch who was looking for revenge on Joseph; that she was a woman and woman is never to be trusted over a breddrin. The God would say all this and convince Joseph that he should stay.

Joseph would be too feeble to say anything. Joseph would look at Russell and Russell would look back with the dazed eyes of a man in a perpetually "red" state – the look of a dog assuring its master that it would go anywhere the master desires. Russell would have no answers. Russell would feed Joseph no matter what. He would feed Joseph until Joseph could feed no more. Joseph would get no answers from Russell. Joseph would look at The God and say, "God, yuh right." But Joseph would not be able to move. It would have to be between The God and Rhea and the women.

He watched the confrontation. The God carried himself with the same sly danger that he had brought to the football field. There was nothing physically over-bearing about him. He was slight. Fit but slight. His self-assurance lay elsewhere. What he had was a quality of danger, a capacity to believe in his invincibility, in his ability to dramatically change the direction of a game. He always wanted the ball and when he got the ball things happened. His gift was simple: he was a dreamer with the capacity to dream impossible things and, more importantly, to execute them through his body's remarkable flexibility. He had found a way to respond physically to the unique rhythms that moved in his head. What onlookers saw was a man with the ability to caress a football, to toy with the intelligence of his opponents, to outthink them to the point of bafflement. This, combined with his total fearlessness, made him a dangerous man.

When he stood beside Pelé in the National Stadium, The God still felt that his title was deserved. Pelé was good, but Pelé was a man like any other. Pelé was from Brazil and he, The God, was from a tiny island with no history of football to talk of, but he was The God, and he could take on any man, any man. And he did. He took on Pelé as if Pelé was a local player, and Pelé smiled at the sheer audacity of the seventeen-year old. From the earliest days it was his way.

Now here, standing in front of Rhea, he had come to get Joseph. On the surface of things, this was a done thing.

"Bobo, tek Joseph bag and come. Russell, help me wid Joseph." He brushed past Rhea and pushed his face into Joseph's face and stared intently into his eyes.

"God," Joseph said, smiling crookedly and weakly.

"Come, breddrin." He reached round to gather Joseph up. Rhea dragged him away and he let himself be dragged from Joseph. He was not going to fight. He had come for the dread and that was the bottom line. The ritual was fine. He would play it.

Joseph closed his eyes and tried to listen to the argument. He could not follow anything. His mind was slipping away again. He was drifting beyond this airport, to Ethiopia, the brown and burnt sienna of the landscape and the rich dark green of the vegetation, to the small plot of land in St. Ann where he found himself hoeing, getting it ready to plant tomatoes and carrots – Rhea was singing hymns in the shack – to a blazing afternoon in New York, the park overflowing with people dressed in red, gold and green, prancing to the sound.

He stood there feeling the strange weight of his Gibson. His feet felt like clay, locked to the ground, while his head spun as if the weed had twisted itself on him. Everything was floating and his body felt lighter. The trees turned upside down as his voice tried to reach for a sound, a faraway sound. He wanted to shout something to that Yankee guitarist and his frantic stage antics, kneeling, lifting the head of his guitar in the air, prancing about the stage with a most un-reggae rhythm. Joseph felt both irritation and a deep fear that something was out of his control. Then he felt his body giving way. He was on the ground. The bass was rumbling. He was unconscious, but he could still hear the music in his head, could still see the light blue of the sky, could still feel the way his body was lifted and the music sounding like a reverb, going on and on.

7

The man wakes and it is still dark. He knows that something has woken him, but he is not sure what. The pain in his stomach comes on him gradually but relentlessly. It is as if he is forcing his way up from deep water, his breath held and all his thoughts focused on the strain in his lungs. He feels the strain to come up for breath – the rush of bubbles, the cool of the water and the blinding glow of the approaching light. Then he bursts through the surface, his lungs opening to take in air, his body opening to be fed by the food it desperately needs.

In the aftermath, in the calm after knowing he has survived, after finding breath again, his body begins to remind him of the brute beating it has undergone. Then comes the pain, the pain in his head, the pain in his limbs, the pain deep inside his stomach. It is the pain that has awoken him.

He lies there breathing hard, trying to work out the source of the pain and its meaning. His head is still stuck in the dream of Melanie standing there arguing with The God. The name won't leave him. The God. He knows these people. He expects to look up and see them standing in front of him, arguing in the shadows of the room.

As he lies there, the pain creeping across his ribs, filling his head with an intense pulsing, he begins to think hard about flying from everything, about going somewhere else. He is willing his mind to focus on the story he wants to take shape in his head. Two people arguing over him, over his body, over his future. Two people. One of them he knows well. It is Melanie. Yet in this incarnation she loves him, she is there for him. He wants to believe in this incarnation.

8

Joseph could see a pattern. There he was, thirty-five, and he could see a pattern. He was young, but he had been around long enough to know a pattern. He had been married for almost twenty years – they had married at seventeen. Now, nearly twenty years later, he was dying. He understood a pattern when he saw one. The pattern was always the same.

Rhea was there when things were going wrong. Rhea was the constant in his life. He did not like Rhea. He needed Rhea. He did not love Rhea. Love had fallen away too long ago. But Rhea was constant. The more things began to explode around him, the more Rhea was the constant that he depended upon. There was going to be no death without Rhea. There was going to be no crisis without Rhea. She was like his chi, a force inside him, sometimes dammed or diverted, but immovably there until he died. He would travel all over, screw all around, fall in love, let his body fall into the softness of other women, but they all understood that Rhea was the one he would go to when he was hungry, when he began to suspect that one of his women was trapping him with *obeah*. Joseph trusted Rhea because he knew that she would never harm him because she needed him. And so he needed her. He spent his life waiting for the inevitable pattern to repeat itself. Rhea was there to make sure that it happened.

Now, they were airborne, the plane heading towards Miami. He thought about how quickly The God had given up. There was that look that The God gave him, a look of deep regret. He put up a good front. He argued, he cursed Rhea, he even threatened to have her beaten up. But Joseph could tell that he was going through the motions. He was tired of Joseph now. He, too, had given up. It was clear that Joseph was sick. It was clear that the doctor's shark cartilage remedy was not going to work. Money wasted, time wasted, deprivations wasted, hope wasted. Joseph was dying. The God had looked defeated. He stared at Joseph, had assured him, "I gwine come a Miami fe you, Joseph. Don' fret. This bitch naah go control tings", but Joseph knew that he was saying goodbye when he leaned towards him and touched his head. Joseph stared back. He wanted to say something, but he felt a terrible weight on his mind, on his brain. He had nothing to say. He resorted to a stock phrase, a phrase of deep hopelessness. It made The God's face crumble. Joseph could tell that The God could not cope with him in this state. All through their time in Germany, Joseph had managed to maintain his brash, stoic front. The front of an orphan child.

The God had first met this front when they ran into each other on a bottle-strewn street in Trench Town where The God had organized a football match. Joseph watched on the side while The God toyed with the men who sweated around him. He never scored. He always passed the ball with careful precision. But passing was not his most cherished activity. The God was always intent on demonstrating that he was never alone on the field, for when you approached him, there were three spirits with him. They were the ones carrying the ball – he simply stood around while they bounced the ball around from one to the other. They were impish *duppies*, giggling at each expression of bewilderment that appeared on the faces of the men who came at The God. Joseph could see them, the three spirits. They twisted and turned and leapt up and down. Their task was never to let The God touch the ball himself. The God accepted their role and he merely followed them around. Joseph started to laugh out loud at the spectacle. He could see these things. He had always been able to see into things. He was born, his mother had told him, with an opaque *caul* over his face. The midwife declared him a dreamer and a visionary. But he understood himself to be something else, a strange boy who was never bothered by the apparitions that clotted the air in rural St. Ann where he was born and where he grew up.

The God was wearing a yellow and blue shirt with the Brazilian globe emblazoned in the middle. He wore track-suit bottoms and a pair of sandals. His arms moved as if he was trying to fly – fluid, always stretched out, his body pivoting this way and that, his eyes always looking somewhere other than at the ball. Most of the time he was staring into the faces of his opponents with an annoyingly defiant look in his eyes. They would try and look away, but they would be caught. Their eyes tried to read his eyes, tried to anticipate his next move, but they were always wrong; the spirits were always going somewhere else.

Joseph pulled the bottom of his T-shirt over his head so that it wrapped around the back of his neck, leaving his chest bare. A fat shirtless player was sitting despondently to the side, trying to get his breath back, his body dripping sweat. Joseph nodded at the fat man and then trotted onto the pavement to take his place.

The God, who did not have the ball at that point, nodded at Joseph. Joseph nodded back and scowled. The God grinned. He liked this small man, with a body like a tightly wound machine. Joseph's head was already too big for his body even without the locks. He made this even more apparent by the way he held his head up, his neck stiff, a proud strut in everything that he did. He trotted with the big-chested assurance of a star baller.

But Joseph was not a star baller, he just liked to kick ball on the streets and, as with everything else, he had learnt to do it with a street savvy and aggression that usually took him far. Someone pushed the ball towards The God. Joseph pedalled backwards to face him. He made the mistake of looking at The God's eyes. The God was smiling. Then Joseph quickly looked away – but too late. In a blur he saw one of the spirits tapping the ball over his head. As Joseph turned, another spirit had gently received the ball and was trotting beside The God towards the two stones laid a few feet apart in the middle of the road. The few people looking on were laughing and chanting, "Pile, pile."

Joseph was angry. The God was grinning. He was moving swiftly towards the goal, and Joseph was at his back, sprinting and determined to make a major statement with this tackle. He raised his left leg and threw it in front of The God, going after the ball, maybe, but definitely going after The God's shin. The God was airborne, arms now flapping like wings. He landed evenly though, the ball still in front of him. He placed a foot on the ball stopping the play. Then he turned to face Joseph who was now stretched clumsily on the ground. Then without saying anything else, The God turned and tapped the ball between the two stones. Joseph was up already. He was furious with himself. The spirits were giggling and running rings around him. The God came towards Joseph and rested an arm on Joseph's shoulder.

"Sorry, yout'. Sorry." He said. His mockery was palpable. Then he trotted back towards his end of the street, the spirits now leap-frogging and somersaulting all around him.

Joseph hurried towards a tall, leathery-skinned, grey-haired dread who was looking to make a pass out of defence. With a small gesture and a stare Joseph communicated that he wanted the ball. With it he started to trot towards The God who was looking away. Joseph could see the spirits coming before he noticed that The God was casually walking towards him, as if to tell him something insignificant like "hello". Joseph did not repeat his mistake. He kept watching the spirits, dribbling around them, avoiding their playful attempts to get the ball – though they were not restricted by the rules of the game. These spirits used their hands, tugged on garments and tripped people blatantly, making them look like total buffoons as they appeared to trip over themselves. But Joseph worked his way around them and before he realized it, he was already past The God and standing face to face with a burly man called Blacka.

Blacka made quick work of Joseph, running into him with terrible ferocity, but not before Joseph tapped the ball towards the two stones behind him. The ball rolled in. Joseph crumbled on the ground, wincing with the sharp pain of asphalt scraping the skin off his knees. He was up and moving towards Blacka, who was walking slowly back to get the ball, his shoulders shaking with his chuckling. The confrontation was too quick to draw any attention until it was over. Joseph picked up a brick from the roadside and smashed against the side of Blacka's head. Blacka went down slowly and stayed down. He was bleeding. Joseph tossed the brick aside and pulled his T-shirt back over his chest and walked down the street.

He walked quickly without looking back. He could hear footsteps behind him, but he did not turn. He calculated that if the person planned to shoot him or throw a rock at him he would have done it already. At the end of the street he turned and was able to look back without seeming to be doing so out of anxiety, though his heart was pounding. It was The God, walking towards Joseph with the three spirits sprinting around him like dervishes. Joseph slowed. The God caught up.

"Yuh eat *ital*?" he asked.

Joseph nodded. He did not eat *ital*, but he knew that eating *ital* was cool.

"Come, mek we eat some *ital* patty, seen?" The God said.

"Cool." Joseph said.

"Blacka alright," The God assured. "'Im head well tough."

"Yeah." Joseph looked down at the spirits. They were staring up at him like children.

"Dem soon go home. Is football dem come fe play, nutting else," The God said casually.

"Oh," Joseph said. It all seemed to make sense to him. And as they walked, the spirits lingered behind until they had so faded that Joseph could no longer see them.

The two walked silently for a few minutes. Then The God spoke.

"Dem call me The God." It was not a joke, but Joseph laughed. The God laughed too.

They never discussed the incident or Joseph's capacity to see the spirits running around The God. It was understood as something strange that they shared. It was enough to make their friendship happen fast. Its foundation, though, was manly trust, their shared code of manhood, the very basic notion that man-friendship was different from woman-friendship. Man-friendship was quick to forgive even if volatile. Man-friendship was uncomplicated. Man-friendship understood that women would do anything to conspire against the order of manhood. Man-friendship assumed that women did not truly know themselves. And yet, at a deep, unvoiced level, man-friendship understood that woman-friendship would win in the end. Man-friendship was a charade, really, a vain railing against the inevitability of woman power, because, at the end of the day, man could not resist the power of woman.

9

It was late afternoon in Miami. There was a wheelchair waiting from him in the jet way. They bundled him in blankets. He felt too hot but he did not know what to say. He was fatigued by his own fatigue. He knew he was in pain, but now there was nothing but pain. He was no longer able to imagine painlessness. It was becoming harder to call this condition painful. His stomach, he imagined, was a perforated bag of sores. The pain was thorough: muscular, relentless. His head throbbed.

The sun dropped slowly, created shadows on the pink and tangerine walls of the houses tucked in beneath the freeway. The city looked painted, the palm trees opened out sensually in the waning light.

When he first came to Miami years ago, he expected to find America and found, instead, the Caribbean. This was nothing like the metal and glossy brick of New York, nothing like the decay and aged order of Detroit. When things rotted in Miami, they smelt like the earth, they stunk like the sea. They did not have the restrained smell of colder places. Everything was tangible here. The heat clung to the body, made sweat, the people were alive, open, naked; they had skins and they spoke.

There were stretches of this city that reminded him of Kingston – avenues that led to overpasses with side guards that were crumbling, roadsides where stones, stretches of sand, and craggy grass infested the modernity of the place. Sometimes he would stand outside and breathe the warmth of the city and smell the stench of the ocean – not just salty, but funky with the peculiar mugginess of humid sodium. It was like Jamaica.

Once he had watched crows circling overhead. They were scattered through the open sky with its untidy puffs of clouds moving casually and independently through the blue. He could tell that something had died not too far away. Now, in Miami again, he felt for the connection to home.

The Ford van that took them through the city was comfortable enough. Rhea sat in the front. Joseph was lying across the back seats his legs propped up in Russell's lap. Russell stared out. He was thinking of his village in St. Elizabeth on the south coast of Jamaica. He wanted to return to the familiar musky smell of the sea, the dry red dirt, the smell of rotting oranges in his yard, the graves of so many generations of his family. He had the feeling that taking Joseph to that familiar place, taking him out before the sun came up so he could sit on the edge of the sea and allow the salt to heal his body, would make him better, would change him. He imagined that the sight of the hills rising untidily behind the coast would revive Joseph, take him back to a place where things were simple as a birdcall or the taste of a mango. For all its heat, Miami still seemed like an alien place, and Russell wanted to take Joseph far away. But he knew that he would have to stay with his friend, try and feed him with food that could transport him. "A man musn' dead which part the ancestors' spirit not living – a man must return to him navel string," Russell thought as the city rushed past – the wide streets, the cluttered houses and the glint of cars speeding in sharp colours across the world.

The three women were in the seat in front of them. No one spoke. Joseph looked out of the side window into the sky. He could see the way the sunset was colouring the evening. He felt nauseous. He thought about dying again. He wanted to be back in Jamaica. Back in Kingston, back in the rugged mountain village in St. Ann.

They arrived at the massive house near the sea at dusk. The streets were empty. No one had announced that the great hero Joseph was passing through. He asked the women to let him walk into the house. It had never been so empty, so orderly, so lacking in life. During the five years that he had owned it, he rarely stayed there. Rhea had stayed there for the past two years when they moved their business there after the problems in Jamaica. He came there to rest inbetween tours. The house was always full, then. It was as if a perpetual party was taking place. People were always stopping there to spend the night, to work in the studio, to just sit in his presence, to come and check out the pretty women who happened to adorn his poolside night and day. The best weed in Miami was available. It was a place of confusion, fights, gun-toting, and deep reasoning about the meaning of Babylon and the dream of returning to Ethiopia. Where the Jamaican house remained rustic, close to the roots and smelt always of poor people's dinners, this house revealed the Pimper's Paradise of Rasta success. And Joseph would come there, lament the decay of all that was righteous in the world, but be too weary to do a thing about it.

Now it was empty. The halls were silent. He walked through the wide living area, the orange glow of sunset spilling light on the hardwood floors. Everything was immaculately arranged. He felt as if he was walking into his own mausoleum. He made his way to the room he always used, a small white room in the back of the house that opened out into a bush backyard. From there he could see the sea brimming with colour. He imagined Jamaica not too far from there. Sometimes he imagined he could see Jamaica. He opened the French doors and lay on the white sheets, breathing heavily, his body weak with the exertion of this walk.

The voices of the women moving around him, preparing the room, encouraging him to put both feet on the bed, commenting on the hair he was losing, making plans for meals, all came in a wash of muted sounds. He was drifting again. Travelling.

10

In the dream was a man – an Ethiopian man. Joseph trusted the Ethiopian man. The man came backstage and asked Joseph to come with him to the mountains. It was so simple a request that Joseph had agreed. As they stepped out into a village at dawn, everything was a tender pink in the dawn light. The man led Joseph to a white car that shimmered with dew.

The man drove with Joseph in the front seat while two of Joseph's friends slept in the back for the whole journey. They drove for hours through a slash of shifting landscapes: deserts, dry pampas, lush rainforests, wide-open savannahs whose even flatness was broken by anthills. At first they seemed to drive away from the mountains, which were always in the distance, and then imperceptibly into their belly.

He saw mountains too grand, too rocky, too barren, too white and sharp-edged to be Jamaican. The aloofness of these mountains made the world below so ordinary. They entered the belly of these mountains, passing through increasingly narrow portals the further up they went.

As they climbed the air grew thinner. When the road ended, the man parked the car beside a pile of red stones. Joseph watched as he walked down the road a few yards and lifted another large stone that he placed at the top of the pile. He then nodded his head to ask Joseph to do the same. Joseph, sweating despite the cool, did the same, his feet slipping on the stones he had to scale to get to the top.

Then the man started to walk up a path into the mountain. Joseph followed. He trusted the man. Soon they arrived at a shrine built deep in the mountain. It was an elaborate thing, complete with candles that the man lit with ritual care. He then drew a crucifix on Joseph's forehead with ash and blessed him.

They sat with their backs towards the west and the man told Joseph a story about the Aztecs. It was a story about the volcano called Zencapoppoca that brought rain, that brought ash and made the land at its foothills the most fertile land in Mexico, in the world. He told of the sacrifice of animals to the mountain each year and of the need to be at one with the mountain, to keep it satisfied, to keep it calm. The story was spoken as a slow mantra and Joseph gradually became aware that the man was actually singing the story.

Joseph looked at the shrine. A blue and white sheet marked with images of tomatoes was spread on the sand. Against the metallic grey rockface was a bundle of long-stemmed flowers. Joseph could not name the flowers, he had never seen them before. They were red and yellow and attached to two raw wood crucifixes with bits of twine.

A basket made of old, dark brown reeds lay at the centre of the sheet. In it were bottles of liquor: rum, brandy, palm wine and other kinds of spirits. The bottles were at different stages of use. Some were almost empty. Joseph recognized a bottle of over-proofed white rum from Jamaica in the pile. The bottle was larger than anything he had ever seen. There were two white porcelain cups with rims painted black leaning against the basket. The cups were empty. There was a green goblet that looked as if it was carved from some precious stone. It was filled with fine grains of a red substance, the colour of the earth beneath them.

To the right of the basket was a large papaya cut into eight parts but still held together at the bottom. The black seeds gleamed in the low light and the candle flicker. In a small dish was a mound of ground, raw meat. A fly landed on the meat. The Ethiopian was not interested in clearing anything away. There were fruits everywhere else. It was clear that there was some method in the choice of fruit. Apart from the papaya, the other fruits were striking for their whiteness. All the fruits had been broken and their insides glowed with varying shades of white. There was the moist belly of sweet and sour sops, and the clean symmetry of a sliced, roasted breadfruit. The white of its flesh contrasted with the blackened and burnt outsides. There were fruits that Joseph did not recognize – white fruit against green jackets. There were several bowls of white rice and some very white-looking coco-yams. White eggs were scattered all over the sheet.

Joseph stared at the fruit without speaking.

Then the Ethiopian got up and invited him to drink some rum.

Joseph took the enamel cup of rum that was handed to him. He poured most of it into the ground, then swallowed the rest. The Ethiopian smiled.

"Sometimes a man is a mountain. Sometimes a man must be acknowledged, yes?" the Ethiopian said.

Joseph nodded without understanding what he meant.

Then the Ethiopian gave Joseph a sheet of paper folded over. He asked Joseph to keep it with him at all times. He told Joseph to bless each new abode he entered with sacrifice to the mountain in the soul. The ritual was over. They found the other men still sleeping in the car.

1 1

Now, the inevitable had happened. As Joseph's strength, his authority, his manhood had diminished, the woman had arrived to assume her rightful place. The boys had to give up the game. No amount of frolicking spirits or a field-marshall's display of the badges of male conquest could alter this inexorable march towards the ascendancy of woman-power. Joseph and The God had watched Rhea's patient planning with amusement, but with a resignation that at some point all the abuse she had taken would be rewarded. Woman is like a shadow, consuming, transforming, long-suffering; and the man is like an arrow, bright, explosive and then quickly impotent.

The God tried to fight it when he saw Joseph in the wheelchair, but he knew it was futile. He had given up on Joseph. Joseph knew this. He could not blame The God for giving up so quickly. The God was running from contamination. He saw too quickly that he could be in that position. It was not the cancer he saw. It was more insidious than that: the inevitable demise of man-power, and the rise of woman-power.

If Joseph had doubted his fate before, now he did not. The God confirmed it. It was easier now to contemplate the actual nature of dying, now that he realized that his resilience as a man had already died. He had returned to the womb already. From this cocoon he could imagine death.

His body was now speaking quite clearly to him. It is not always that one knows these things. It had to do with the incredible sense of fatigue he felt. He had never had a serious, life-threatening illness before. When he was shot, the bullet had lodged in his arm. It was still there, brought much pain, but he took it. They said that to remove it would be to end his guitar playing. He suffered the pain just as he had suffered the pain in his foot. To remove the toe would have diminished his stage presence – he could not accept that. But death, since he imagined it as something that happened violently and dramatically, was something he had not contemplated much. To do so would have been to engage in the kind of debilitating fatalism that, as a dread, he could not accept. His own death was alien to him.

Joseph had seen death. He had seen people killed. He was always startled by the simplicity of death. Not that it was easy to kill people. Killing was painful and it took a great deal of effort. The body wanted to live. The body fought to live all the time. Like chickens beheaded. They run sprinting around the yard, gurgling blood, spilling blood, their muscles flexing, their whole posture erect and almost dainty. People described it as a maddened run, but it was no madder than the average live and head-intact chicken's wide-eyed sprint. The circling movements, the lifting of the knees and every muscular action were the same, despite the brain being taken away.

The body did not like to die. The body fought death. He had seen it. On films, people took bullets and collapsed, as if accepting death calmly and according to a script. In life he had seen people take bullets and curse about the most insignificant things. Death did not bring profound wisdom. He had watched a friend moan and groan about the pain of a bullet lodged in his head, about the headache he was feeling. He watched his friend grow very angry, saw him get up, about to hit out at somebody who was trying to help him by staunching the blood with a towel. He was not out of his mind. This was how he normally behaved. He was angry and he wanted to do something about it. Just as suddenly, he lost consciousness, fell silent and never woke up. No last statements, no thoughts about a loved one, nothing like that. All Joseph could remember was his friend's annoyance at the guy who was trying to help him.

The death of others was the most normal thing in the world. It was the afterdeath that was extraordinary. He found the missing of people exceptionally difficult. Missing the person, looking out for the person, hoping to see the person in the street, then realizing that the person would not be around again. Gone forever. Thinking that, after five years, the person would not suddenly return. That after thirty years, the person would be thirty years gone. Thirty years out of circulation. Thirty years out of memory. Thirty years faded into something tiny, something insignificant – a moment, a look, a gesture. That would be thirty years of absence. He found that extraordinary.

He had stopped going to funerals after he became a serious Rasta. For a while he even believed that the dead could not be true Rastas. This was a strain of doctrine that had crept through the fundamentalist dreads and he accepted it with the brashness that had come to characterize his new faith. "Mek de dead bury de dead," he would declare boldly. "Jah cyaan dead." It was against the vows of the priest to touch "deaders". For a Rastaman to touch the body of a dead man would be for that man to desecrate himself. It was written.

So he stopped going to funerals. He stopped lingering around the places of the dead. He never carried a coffin, never drove behind a hearse, never went into a church to give last rites to the dead.

12

A sick man is in a studio playing his guitar. This narrative is more than a fiction, it is a dream that Joseph has had for years. It is a dream that has consumed him ever since he felt he could fly. When he felt the pressure of his sickness coming on him, he found comfort in the willingness of his mind to dream. And with each dream he would add to the story. The plot of the story was familiar to him. It was a legend. The legend came to be his own narrative. It was a narrative that usurped his history every time.

He would allow his mind to travel on airplanes, to drive through quaint German villages, to mingle with the ganja smoke and roots talk of great Rasta singers and players of instruments. He would sit on his porch and look out into the open sky and find himself dreaming about what dying would mean. In his dreams, death slipped into his body.

The story was the same every time. He would make that great song, that stunning song, and the whole gathering would weep as he played the song, and as they did, his hair would start to fall out in clumps. His locks would start to fall to the ground. And all the characters that had crowded his head would come crawling out to see the tragedy of his passing. They would hold his body, lift him, carry him to a bed, and he would rest his head on the lap of Rhea and he would say to her, "I am going" and she would sing "Fly Away Home". And in that moment, his arms would fall away, and the three women would come and hover over him and pray for him and plant more dreams of home in his head, and slowly, ever so slowly, he would fade away. It was heroic, in full colour, and gloriously holy.

13

He has lived in this state long enough to know that he has been away too long. For years, the thoughts of home have been a physical thing to him. They had a smell, a taste, the feel of a landscape, the scent of a moment. In the mornings he would feel that strange nausea of excitement and unease that he used to feel before facing the day. But now it was a comforting feeling – the feeling of home with all its strange anxieties.

His mother had been absent. He had not understood this then, for he had never stopped regarding her as a victim of his father's strange silences, his father's capacity to withdraw into the inscrutable density of his books or his cigarettes, sucked on with a sweet passion that was hard to describe. His mother would walk through the house singing of how much she had lost. And she had lost much. His mother had one day come into the living room with the stoic, dull quality of a woman unfamiliar with the ritual histrionics of self-pity, she had come into the living room and said with such sincerity, such pained honesty: "You don't even touch me. It has been months since you have touched me."

This is the same face he saw when Melanie came to ask him, "Why don't you talk to me, tell me what is going on?" The same pitiful look. "You don't even touch me. Why has it been months since you have touched me?"

He had found this American woman, loved her and lost her. She connected always in his mind with home. He missed home. He missed the rituals of being a hero. He did not think he could give it up so easily. Yet he was sure that after the withdrawal of his illness, after the falling away of his locks in clumps, after the anti-climax of his survival and after his plans for exile to Ethiopia had ended with the defeat of that land, the death of utopia, even after coming to settle in this simple town, a place completely unsuited to his own sense of reality; he was sure that, after all this, he would find peace, find some quiet and learn resignation to his new existence.

But it has not worked.

Here, lying in this room, the tape player repeating *Exodus* until the lyrics become one song, he is still alive and she is still gone. He is washing himself with music that will purge the memory of blues and country music that the woman had brought into his house, the music she heard all her childhood. Lying there, he wonders how he will get to touch her again, how he will get her to come back, where he will find her – if he can find her before everything falls apart. He feels as if he is going to have to make decisions.

He is tasting, again, the metaphor of home. Jamaica was what he needed, he knows that. He knows he had to come home to live, just as many travellers know they have to come home to die, even though he feared it, feared the violence, the madness on the streets. In the months since he has been back he has felt the fear fading. He can feel his body shaping itself around the comforts of the familiar.

He had wanted to find a woman in Jamaica, someone who would understand him after his years away, someone whom he could be with, someone who would want to be with him, want to make love with him, to make certain that if it was anyone, he would be the one to say no. It would be the woman, a Jamaican woman, who would be saying to him, as his mother had said to his father, "You don't touch me – you have not touched me in months. I want you to touch me." Such a woman would feed him, would wait for him, would make him feel like a man – a woman who understood the way a man's body needed to be touched. A woman who spoke his language. A woman who seemed to understand that in his silences there was some dignity –some quest for dignity. That is what he missed.

He had planned to come back to Jamaica to find this, but what he did was bring an American woman home with him, a woman who made each morning seem like an unknown space. She made his tongue feel heavy with its inability to make sense, to make her understand.

Now she has left him, walked away from him, and here he is, trying to think of whether he should go and find her, or whether he should stay in this room and let his dreams consume him.

The country is as old as he is. He has grown up with the country, and now he knows just how that island feels. He feels like the island. He had promise, but now he feels old. He feels used up. When he contemplates the forty years that he will have lived, when he contemplates what he will do at the stroke of midnight on the fortieth year of his life, he has a sense of what people in Jamaica must be feeling right now. They are waiting to see if something, someone will come and rescue the country, but are wondering if it is not possible that death will come before that rescue comes. He looks at the forty years of his life with sadness, a strange weariness. It depresses him.

14

Coming out of sleep, it takes a while for Joseph to understand that his weakness may have had something to do with his hunger. The tape is still going. The world outside is defined by the radio. Voices chattering, images of faces looming over him. Then they disappear. He keeps returning to his dream that is no longer a dream but a narrative with sequence and meaning. He has to return to it because it gives him a sense of grounding. But the narrative is being interrupted by voices, by the sound of the telephone that has been ringing for a while now, after a long silence.

Joseph is hungry. He feels the hollow inside him. It no longer hurts. It is a dull pain. He is not dry. He has been drinking water from the tap, walking to the toilet, cupping his hand under the tap and drinking until his stomach hurts with the pain. Then he goes back and lies down and waits.

He is dreaming of Melanie. Melanie is lying on a table, her legs apart, and a man in a mask, a man with tendril hands that look uncannily like the hands of The God, is leaning down between her open legs and doing something to her. Joseph can tell that the man is feeling deep inside her for something, and when he seems to have it in hand, he is grimacing with the effort of moving it, pulling at it. Melanie is in pain, howling, twisting. There is blood underneath her, spreading. The light in the room is blue.

Joseph opens his eyes. An abortion. Perhaps she has had an abortion. He struggles to grasp the idea. He closes his eyes again.

Like the fragmented samplings of a surreal dub track, the voices of the world, the sounds of the radio, enter Joseph's mind and slip out again, bubbling behind his dreams and over them. The distant sounds of an argument down the street between a man and a woman, the yell of the *kisko* and ice cream seller on his scooter, the tinkle of the postman's bell, the dogs' sharp bark, the twisted paths of his dreams, all gather in his head.

"This country gwine to hell, Mr. Brown. It going to hell…"

Movement of Jah People!

"Why yuh say that sir?"

Rest on your conscience, oh yeah, oh yeah!

"We selling the land, selling the land to tourist, to white people."

And move your window curtain…

"It's a old habit, my friend, but what to do?"

Good, good, good loving…

"Revolution, Mr. Brown…"

This could be the first trumpet, might as well be the last…

"You mean political revolution?"

'Cause every lickle ting…

"Yes, Mr. Brown."

"My God, my good man. I think somebody should get your address and put you in a museum. You're a relic, man. Don't tell me, sir, but are you a Marxist?"

Open your eyes…

"Yes, Mr. Brown. Revolution is what we need. We want to nationalize everything, Mr. Brown. And we execute all corrupt officials… and t'iefs and robbers must be whipped in public. "

Woe to the downpressors…

"My friend, I am afraid you're mad. You must have fallen asleep twenty years ago, man. Manley is not Prime Minister again, you know, fellow? The Berlin Wall is history."

Let's get together and feel alright!

"Yes, an damn fool people like you will burn too. Yes. You t'ink I don't know how much coffee land you own up in dem hills. You t'ink the people don't know what a capitalist exploiter…"

Exodus!

"Sorry, got to go. Next. *People's Voice*, what's on your mind."

Exodus!

"Mr. Brown?"

Yeah, yeah, yeah!

296

"Yes, m'am, you are on the air."

Rule equality...

"Mr. Brown, I believe is oral sex killing our nation today..."

Set, set, set, set, set!

The voices come in and out. His mind catches a phrase and follows its meandering way into chaos, then everything slips away. The music blankets him, and then he wakes to the sound of voices, the litany of blood, the litany of corruption, the litany of scandal, the litany of fear.

When he opens his eyes he is on the stage, sees the silver glare of the lights above him. He sees the fluttering of the canvas cover that is stretched over the stage, sees the labyrinth of scaffolding, sees two white boys dangling from the scaffolding, staring down at him in shock, then he sees Melanie's face. He sees the fear in her eyes. Then he closes his eyes again as he feels them lifting him.

Someone was arguing with his woman, Melanie, the American woman, the one who left him. She used to be Rhea. But Rhea does not have her swampy, low-country, Southern accent. This is Melanie. This is the woman who wrapped herself around him in their small bed, the woman he screamed at, told her she was so typically Yankee, so bloody self-righteous and no different from the pigs from that country. The woman whose faced had crumbled with sadness at the flash of his words, at the fact there was no way that he could take them back. This is the woman who left him. Packed her bags and left him. The one who, when he asked her, "Are you going to leave me here to die," had said, "You would be happier dead. You know that." And she had left with that. Left and gone on a plane and gone far away.

She laughs and throws herself against him, embraces him, touches him like she has not touched him in a long time. All around them, people are leaving. They are going away from them – going away from the dream. She is laughing and asking him if he wants something to drink, some iced tea, or lemonade; offers him rum in a white and blue enamel cup. She asks him if he has taken his medication. She asks him if he needs a bath – a warm bath to cleanse his soul. He has dreamt this before. He can tell that he's going to keep dreaming this for as long as no one comes for him, comes to rescue him.

15

He wakes to find himself where he has always been, in his apartment in Ensome City, sweating and frightened by the dream. Yet the dream is not complete. It is never complete. These vivid snippets are all he can remember – the laughter, the feel of her body against his, the sense that she is some-where waiting, the heavy ganja-smelling presence of the roots man in his skin, and these hurtling departures of all the people he knows.

16

No one comes to rescue him. Time is no longer clear. Perhaps days have passed. Perhaps some hours, but long enough for the room to smell like a tomb – a tomb with a freshly buried body. The rot is thick in his nostrils. He wants to fly. He wants to fly so much. But he is anchored. The anchor holds him in the room, in the heat, in the smell of his body decaying.

But he does manage to climb through the thick citrus grove, long neglected and cluttered with intense brush and the tangle of twigs and limbs from the prickly trees. As he walks he makes a song for the names of home in his head. The heat is steady, though a soft breeze dances around him. He breathes. He keeps wiping the sweat from his hand, switching the brown paper bag from one hand to the other. He tastes the salt dripping from his moustache into his mouth.

He finds her sitting beneath a flowering pouis tree at the far end of the pimento barbecue. The wash of orange light from the fading sun and the spread of petals on the floor around her make her white dress golden, tender and graceful. Her face is lined with the markings of her years – her cheeks sharp, her lips still full but wrinkled. Her head is bandannaed and her white scarf moves with the leaves' shadows. Her feet are bare, resting on the soft petals.

But he knows it is she. Years later, beyond forty, beyond fifty. He has lived to see her and he recognizes her.

He catches her eyes. They brighten. He waves and lifts the bag up to her. The brown bag weighted with his offering.

The last fifty yards fill his head with the pounding of blood, the wheeze of his chest, the grunt of each effort to move, to reach her.

He feels love seeing her there, feels tenderness for the woman who smiles at him. When she speaks, the rich earthiness of piedmont soil falls from her lips. Her voice carries him to swamps that seem to belong to another country – somewhere hot and dense, somewhere gummy with its humidity. The trees there are alien things, grotesque, bearded, dark green trees that give off smells as intoxicating as liquor.

He lays the bag in her lap and she opens it while looking at him.

"Are you taking medication?" she asks, or seems to ask, but it is like wind. The voice does not stay long. It leaves her face and her mouth does not move. She is smiling a simple closed-lip smile as the voice fades.

"You sure you all right?" the voice says.

He can see a tangerine-coloured face looking back at him, but that too fades. Then it is Melanie sitting there patiently, her stomach distended, her dark mahogany arms roped with muscles, her hair dangling in long tight braids down her face, and her eyes glowing with recognition – those black eyes, those deep black eyes.

She bends over the bag and opens it slowly. Her hand reaches in and extracts the damp balls of rolled tamarind flesh spotted with the sparkle of brown sugar. She nibbles the fruit with her lips and holds her body as the flare shivers through her. She holds the sticky fruit out to him and he bites into the gummy flesh, the crunch of sugar against his teeth.

Joseph dreams her. He dreams her as part of him so many years ahead of them. He imagines them together like that and this frightens him. It frightens him, because he is afraid both that it may never happen and that it may happen. After all, he is dying now. He is dreaming the death of a hero.

The music keeps coming back to him through the haze of memory and dream. What he wants is the woman who has left him. And maybe this is what love means: the capacity to imagine love far into the future. An impossible place where the paths are not charted and are cluttered with prickly bramble.

"It is my birthday," he says to her.

"How old are you, baby?" she asks.

"Forty," he says.

"Forty? But you died at thirty-six," she says. She is sucking the tamarind balls.

"No, I didn't," he says. "I…"

He cannot speak any more. The music fills the room and then suddenly the music stops.

He wakes to hear the tape player clicking. The tape has stuck. He is forty. He is not thirty-six. This seems to make sense.

He reaches to touch her. She is not there. She has gone.

He sits up and stares at the walls – the newspapers. He feels the dust under his feet. He is not dead. He is forty. It occurs to him that were he to stand, were he to walk to the door, were he to step into the streets, were he to travel the miles, he would come to this swampland and find something like love. And he will find a new name, and perhaps he will work out another dream, another legend of love. It comes to him quietly like a memory.

He stands.

The room spins slowly. He takes a step forward and feels the lurching of his insides. The tape clicks on, the sound growing louder until it fills the room with its echoing.

Vershan V:

SCRATCH MADNESS

Vershan V

SCRATCH MADNESS

The chord was an E-Minor, a fat, simple chord. And the chord continued there, never veering away, never changing. That simple slash of chord, and the other instruments danced around it. The dub of the moment was haunting. He came to the club with a dream in his head and the edge of his fear upon him. He spoke to no one, he simply sat and waited until the band began and then he walked onto the stage and as he walked onto the stage he imagined himself trying to drag meaning from his memory. But meaning would not come. He knew the song he was supposed to sing, he knew the words, he knew that everyone was waiting for him to sing the words. The drummer rolled him in once, and he stood still staring into the flaming white lights that heated his face. The drum rolled him in again after going around the block one more time. He remained silent. The audience was moving with a sense of anticipation, a strange faith that allowed them to take this moment of uncertainty and make of it an epiphany.

He should have taken his medication that day. He had been praying a lot that morning. It had been months since he had prayed at all and that morning he knew he could hear the voice of God. He wanted to call Aunt Josephine or his father – to find his father and tell him that he was seeing into the past and making sense of it. He wanted to run outside into the stormy Kingston morning and tell someone that he had come to truth. But he knew that they would take him and lock him up. Instead he sat there and felt drunk with the images in his head. He was like that for the whole day, and now, in the aftermath of the storm, he was standing in the club. Outside the city was humid with the vapors that rose from the puddles, from the mud, from the plants. They were waiting for him to sing. Their faces, the tourists, the local people, the familiar and the unfamiliar – they were all there and he could feel the wave of the music taking him into the words. He heard the drum roll again, as if from a distance and then he heard Pedro start to sing the chorus. It woke him up. Woke him to what he would do. Speak, it said, speak. And he spoke.

Catch my eye, the way it sharp like a razor. I carry a transistor in my head. It was planted there by angels. I am not a mad man. John was not a mad man. Not John Blow. Not John Public. Don't take me simple. I know Patmos. Patmos is a stone in the sea. Patmos is a flimshow. Patmos is a acetate dub plate, lock into the needle of my antennae. John is not a mad man. John is a Baptist incarnate. John look and see a pig and say blood and fire to the pig. John see flesh and speak of flesh incarnate. Don't take me simple. I am not a mad man. Catch my eye. I live in a dream to catch the wind. I catch the taste of the wind, like a tongue on my skin. The dub of memory. The dub of momentum. Every lawn is a Patmos. Every dance is a Patmos. Every revelation come from the wind.

The band seemed to trust the strange madness of this talk. And they stayed with him, riding that one rhythm. Maybe they too saw the city he was seeing, the smell of the streets, the smell of the lives of those around, the look of sheer fatigue in the faces, the smell of poor people's dinners. They rode with him through his revelation. The bass and the drum walked in lock-step agreement and he stood still talking into the night air.

I see tings. I stand an' look into the eastward brink where the mountain blue and everlasting like Mount Zion. Short pants and my backside expose. Knotty, knotty head. Mango in my finger smelling like a wet 'oman, a wet womb. A queen majesty. But I vision what I vision. I vision I as a bird flying. Bird sailing through the masterful sky, the maverick sky, the mellifluentic sky, the Macabbee version sky. So I feel like David and the sky is Goliath and the bird is the eye of the giant. And I sling back I shot and the

bird swoop, for the bird is the Holy Ghost wid, ahhhh bright wings!
And the bird turn and come to me and I becomes the bird for I is a
bird and I have the spirit of the hawk in my skin, the spirit of the
falcon not the falconer, for the falconer is Babylon... I possess the
spirit of the winged beast – fly me to the moon, fly me to the moon.
And the bird swing low, and the bird come among the living, and
the bird reveal itself in this shitty, this ghetto, this Ocean Eleven
where duppy still trod; and the bird come across the image of himself
in the sky, and the bird fly like madness to reveal himself to himself,
and the bird get vex wid him image, and the bird decide fe rush the
bird and bird connect on bird. Blood. Piece of blood in the beak and
the bird dead. Fall dead like so. And David still a pull back the
slingshot.

Now the drummer whipped him into a dance. Like David
naked before the Lord. Like David carrying all his mess with
him before the Lord. And in that dance he found himself
again. But he could not stop. He could not stop the whiplash
of his body to the sharp accents of the drum and cymbal, to the
roll of the bass going to strange circles about him. He turned,
he opened his arms, he held back his head, and then he
shouted with such force that his voice caught up with its own
echo in the room.

"VERSHAN!!!"

And they all knew. Everything was now left up to the drum
and the bass. They filled the room with a clean, pared down
dreadness. The music was at its most basic, and the lights
flashed red. The audience was now transformed by the light
and the sound into worshippers who could suddenly speak in
tongues. They danced inside themselves, caught in the sound.
They too came with their own madness and were finding a
path out of it.

He sang now, the song he should have started, the drum
and bass carrying him along, and the man on the board, the
sound guy on the board, tweaked and turned the sound of his
voice into something bigger – something with the capacity to
repeat itself and to change itself in one singular moment.

305

This is a dub version,
This is the mellow of a dub plate,
Come down Mr. Bassy
Fat me up wid a muscular sound,
For I journey into memory,
Come to sing a revelation.

And the church sang:

Roots man know the gospel way.
Roots man know the gospel way.
Roots man know the gospel way.

I am the storyteller.
I am Anancy.
I am the architect of mystification.
I come before the Arawak.
I sailed I yacht into dis harbour,
Bearing the seeds of the fruit of life
I plant Eden in dis land
Wood and water.
Wood and water.

These words came to him as he stood in this place, his head
an antenna to the mystery. They all imagined he was red with
marijuana, but he was not. He was in that place of incredible
euphoria where prophecies are made. He wanted to be there
forever but he could tell that the crash would come and the
drugs would have to be called in to calm him. But in this
moment, he would not stop. He stood on the spinning stage
and spoke into the night while the singers sang behind him.
Harmonies from everyone – the drummer, the bassy, the
keyboard player – the world was singing and he was the
preacher, the prophet, calling them to walk with him.
When they said:

Roots man know the gospel way
He said:
Let me hear yuh down there

When they said:
Roots man know the gospel way
He said:
Ah can't hear yuh!
So they said:
Roots man know the gospel way.

In this country even the mad person has a place. He walks the streets and he sees things. They stone him, they will beat him, they will laugh at him, but he lives amongst them and there is a strange way in which his madness is seen as a sighting of something bigger than himself. Not that they thought he was mad as he sang this song, but he was. Such a performance, such a moment of sheer release would stay with him like the memory of another life. He was a man alone and this would haunt him sometimes. He woke in the morning and wished he could call his origin and find it with him, comforting him. But he had no one to call. So he had to speak his way into this truth. The E-Minor chord was now a simple wash of sound. The guitar's bright casket of light was now walking beside him and he fell into step, skanking on the spot even as he spoke.

A man live with Jezebel and learn the mystery of a bird what fly into its own image and dead. I make dub. A man mek music and touch a one, and a one is healed. I see dat with my own two eye. Gospel way. For long before Jah vision I, before the Egyptian mummy collude wid the ice hunter of Switzerland, the Peruvian virgin, long before the cataclysmic… I know big word. Cataclys-mically sound… Ahhhhh. Long before the conspiracy of the digital as oppose to the analogue, which analogolous to a finger versus a stick, so lick me with a prick and I will speak a revelation without no tricks. Hatrick in your systematic! Wheel… Wheel.

The music stopped. The snare and bass drum came together in a lashing, sharp barrage of reports that said, "Stop! Stop! Stop! Stop!"

The silence is full. The crowd pulses for a moment like an after orgasmic groan and then grows still. They know they are watching a man on the edge of his hopelessness and they stare,

307

wondering if he will fall or if he will, somehow, be miraculously saved by his music before their eyes. He speaks a dream that he is having as he speaks. It is a story. It is what he would tell his father or his mother or someone whom he could love. He tells the story…

One day I bring a bird in my hand to man, the music man and the healer. And I say, "Man, heal the bird." And man say, "The bird dead", and I say, "Why?" And man say, "The bird see itself in the glass and the bird don't know what to do." And I weep. And man say, "Why weepest dou yout?" And I say, "For the bird." And man say, "Heart of flesh, heart of flesh. I hope you will weep for eye when I fall." So I say to the man, I say, "But you can't fall." And he say, "Heart of flesh, heart of flesh."

This ghetto smell stink. Every ghetto want a messiah. Every ghetto want a prophet. Man show the gospel way. So I tek the bird in a piece of Gleaner and I walk wid the bird and find a soft place under a mango tree and I bury the bird. Yeah. I bury the bird.

Then he turned his back on the audience. He looked at Pedro and Pedro nodded. The drummer cracked the snare and the drum and bass kicked into gear. The music was upon them again and the Pedro and the crew began to sing. He stood there, feeling some sense of release, but drained.

He knew then that he needed to be on the stage to live. It was not that he was happiest on stage – he had had happier times – but on stage he could believe in the illusion of a gathering of arms to hold him up. The microphone was loud – it amplified his truth, and he could show himself to be what he was on the stage. The music was a covering over him and the magic of performance was a wall to keep him from himself and to keep them from him. When he tried to talk to others about the things in his head, he stumbled; here on stage he did not. And yet no one said he was doing anything out of the ordinary. The rigid order of the drum and the bass, the flight of the dubwise kept him in a spaceship that was going somewhere. He liked the security.

He turned and saw the people dancing again. And he began

to skank. To let the chord consume him again. He felt lighter. He would go home tonight, take his pills, lie in bed and try and slow his mind down. They said that one day he would not even have to do that. They said that he had seen something once, some cataclysmic thing that shattered him and scarred him. But the healing would come. He hoped that it would come, though with this music growing out of his fevered brain, part of him wondered if he wanted to stop having the madness.

He walked back to the microphone and started to declare himself again:

The island of Patmos is a movie screen and John never go mad to see it. Come follow me, crowd a people. Come follow me, crowd a people. I shall carry thee unto the arch triumphant. Every trick I shall commit shall reveal itself unto thee. Fly me to the moon, fly me to the moon. Fly me to the moon.

So I build I ark of the true covenant. Build I temple of wisdom, and I gather around that temple the very instruments of praise and celebration and confusion to stunt the unbeliever's growth. All heathen will tremble. And I say to the heathen them, I say whosoever shall come into this ark must be pure of mind, not as the world see purity but as the heavenly see purity. For thy feet shall be bare, and thou shalt come with psychological purity, seen? An' whomsoever enter the ark and stay within the ark shall live. But whosoever shall flee and vank from the ark shall not prosper. I am a ranking survivor, I am the original dub organizer, I have lived out I ways and times and outlive the heathen. For I have seen the glory of brutality. This city flow with the blood of sacrifice. This nation build on the blood of sacrifice for the sea is red, the sea is red like the moon and we know why the machete is sharp, why Don D slaughter the queen, the rhumba queen, for is a madness in this nation, blood red. Babylon system can't prosper in this place. Aaahhh. But whomsoever shall rest in the embrace of the ark shall prosper. Look at the moon. See how the moon red. Whomsoever shall rest in the embrace of the ark shall prosper. Verily, verily. Alright operator, wheel it in now. Come again.

The music continued while he closed his eyes and transported himself into the familiar places of comfort. The world he created with this music was a world different from his own. But he liked this world and believed this world and soon this world was real. Maybe it was the disjoint between the two worlds that would slowly frustrate him, that would slowly eat away at him. It was the fact that sometimes these two worlds did not know what to say to each other that made him grow weary, fatigued by the travelling. He wanted to save the world, but he could not carry it for so long. His mind could not handle the weight of the challenge. He wanted to be Marley, carrying the weight of his world on his shoulders and handling it; but he felt like something more tragic, something more vulnerable, like a dread Don Drummond solo; this is how he felt and this left him weary. He felt tired already. Twenty minutes of one song and a set to go. He turned to the microphone, nodded at Pedro who wound the band down. Then, still looking at Pedro, he mouthed, "Three Little Birds". The band stepped into the unusual request easily. He sang, soothing himself as he did.

Rise up this morning
Smiled with the rising sun

And for a moment, everything shimmered.